# Raising Demons For Fun And Profit

## by Mark McLaughlin

**with Special Guests
Michael McCarty, Michael Kaufmann
& Kyra M. Schon**

## RAISING DEMONS FOR FUN AND PROFIT
## BY MARK MCLAUGHLIN

*Raising Demons for Fun and Profit* is a work of fiction. Names, characters, places, and incidents are products of the author's imagination. Any resemblance to actual events or persons, living or dead, is entirely coincidental.

First Printing, October 2009

Sam's Dot Publishing
P.O. Box 782
Cedar Rapids, Iowa, 52406-0782 USA
e-mail: sdpshowcase@yahoo.com

Visit www.samsdotpublishing.com for online science fiction, fantasy, horror, scifaiku, and more. While you are there, visit the Sam's Dot Publishing Purchase Center at http://www.samsdotpublishing.com/purchasecenter.htm for paperbacks, magazines, and chapbooks. **Support the small, independent press...**

# DEDICATIONS

To sitcom witches: Because there's a laugh track, people don't seem to mind that you worship Mephistopheles.

To cartoon talking dogs: Because you're animated, no one notices that you're obviously possessed by Satan.

To deviled eggs: What a pity people eat you before you can hatch into monster-chickens.

To booze: Everyday, you turn millions of perfectly nice Jekylls into insidious Hydes.

To snakes: Why do people associate you with evil? You don't have any hands, so you can't do anything too incredibly wicked.

And to thirteen very nice devils in my life: Greg, Pamela, Michael McC., Michael K., Dan W., Kyra, Tyree, Jerrod, Nancy, Michele, Steve L., Dan B. and the most devilish of all with his pointed ears and orange fur – Tang.

# CONTENTS:

# I. THE RICH ARE DIFFERENT

## She's Got The Look

"Something new...something *fresh*..." Hopelessly adrift in a sea of fashion magazines, Pretzel flipped nervously through high-gloss stacks of *Mademoiselle*, *Glamour*, *Harper's Bazaar*, French *Vogue*, *Miss Vogue* for teens, *Marie Claire*, *Sky*, and a half-dozen foreign editions of *Elle*. She glanced at Jasmine, who was still trying to squeeze her way into a brown velvet Vivienne Westwood catsuit. "It's not going to happen, you know."

"Pee pills." Jasmine began rolling the leggings down. "Just a few pee pills away."

"And an extra kidney. Where's my Japanese *Elle*? The one with Magda on the cover."

"She looks like a whore." Jasmine brushed a long curly lock of magenta hair off her round face. "An enormous whore. *Massive*. Her left tit is bigger than my head."

Pretzel found the magazine and held it at arm's length. "My God, you're absolutely right. Gaultier must have discovered her – he's adores big freak girls. The woman is a *horse*. A horse on its hindlegs."

"With gigantic tits."

Pretzel was not to be outdone. "A *Clydesdale* with obscene mutant *cow* tits. Somebody should fly her to one of those needy countries and have her nurse all those skinny little babies."

"Not much nourishment in silicone, darling." Jasmine laughed as she threw the catsuit back onto the pile of clothes on the couch. She poured herself her fourth glass of Dom Perignon that morning. "But seriously. Are you making any progress at all?"

"None. I can't believe I got roped into all this." Pretzel tossed an armful of magazines into the air. "Stupidest fucking idea in the world. Starving models raising money to feed starving children? Who could possibly tell them apart?" Her eyes widened. "Definitely *no* Kate Moss. She can't be more than – what? 85 pounds? The press would tear the whole thing to shreds. Maybe I should get that Magda cow after all."

"Good God, no – she's *too* big. You might as well throw Liz Taylor or a Russian tractor up on the catwalk."

Pretzel crossed to her work table, shooting a look at her reflection in the mirror above it. She still looked fantastic — to-die-for cheekbones, silver pageboy cut, Acapulco tan. A fashion journalist had to look her best to be taken seriously. And she was hot now: all eyes were upon her. Her first novel, *Strapless*, was No. 3 on the *New York Times* bestseller list, and publishers were still bidding on her next book, *Catwalk Days, Doggy-Style Nights*.

But she had to face it: she was picking up weight from stress-eating and too damn many hors d'oeuvres. In another month she'd be as big as Jasmine, if she didn't do something about it. She opened her purse and found her Gucci pillbox. She picked out two yellows, then debated between blue and green before finally selecting a yummy pink one. Jasmine brought her a glass of champagne to wash them down.

"Darling, what's this?" Jasmine slid a maroon faux-leather valise out from under some catalogues. "This would go with that jacket I bought last week."

"Another stupid idea. I'm supposed to be judging the Miss Fresh Face contest for *Sizzle*. These are the finalists. Snotty little rich girls from all over America."

Jasmine gave her a small smile. "I was once a Miss Fresh Face, you know."

Pretzel studied her friend's plump, still pretty face. "We could get you up on that catwalk again, you know. I know this darling French doctor – liposuction, a little nip and tuck, injections of monkey gland extract –"

Jasmine shook her head. "I shouldn't even *think* of losing weight. It's impossible around Farouk. Every time I lose an ounce he buys a dozen cheesecakes. He's into big hips. Literally."

The women refreshed their champagne glasses and found some smoked salmon in the mini-fridge. During their snack, Jasmine handed Pretzel the maroon valise. "You said you were looking for fresh. Maybe you should use some of these girls. Just a thought."

"You might have something there." Pretzel opened the valise over the work table and scattered the pictures, to see which ones popped out at her. "Bimbo," she said, tossing one off the table. "Bimbo. Bimbo. Slut." Three more pictures hit the floor. Suddenly she gasped.

"What are you looking at?" Jasmine said, examining the seven pictures left. "Which – "

Then she, too, saw the photo. Saw ... *her*.

A pale, luminous face. Thin, but not too thin, with full, pouting lips and an elfin chin. The cheekbones were wide, generously sculpted. Her forehead was high and narrow. And those <u>eyes</u> – huge, soulful, a little sad, extremely wise. Haunting, timeless eyes.

"Who is she?" Jasmine whispered.

Pretzel picked up the photo and looked at the information written on the back. "Veronica Gilman. From a place called Innsmouth."

\* \* \*

The next week, Pretzel had Veronica Gilman flown in.

She met the girl at the airport and was instantly charmed. Veronica was tall and willowy, with a throaty purr of a voice. She wore a black dress trimmed with white lace and carried a white umbrella trimmed with black lace. She also wore black silk gloves with the fingertips cut off. They had lunch in a sushi bar, where the girl ordered double portions of tuna, shrimp and octopus.

"You certainly have a healthy appetite," Pretzel said cautiously.

Veronica smiled, revealing a bright expanse of small, even teeth. "I simply *adore* seafood. Don't you? It's low-fat and *extreeemely* nutritious. A person hardly needs to eat anything else."

Pretzel watched the girl nibble daintily at her fishbits. "Those gloves are fabulous." She looked closer. "Oooh, they're studded with little pearls. I love the whole black-and-white look. Very Audrey Hepburn, with a touch of Goth-grrrrl. Tell me about this town you're from. This Innsmouth."

"There's not much *to* tell. New England. Old money. A lazy, crazy seaside town: lots of eccentrics. Punks and hermits and maiden aunts. Everybody knows everybody, for better or worse. *Steeped* in tradition, like a soggy old teabag!" Veronica laughed – a high, jubilantly warbling giggle. Pretzel was vaguely reminded of a show on dolphins she'd once seen on public TV.

A short blond waiter stopped by their table. "Can I bring you anything else?"

Veronica flashed her huge eyes at him. "Mmmmm. More octopus, please." She turned back to Pretzel. "So. I can hardly *wait* to hear about this fundraiser. It sounds *tremendously* exciting, It's a terrible thing, world hunger and what-not. I'm flattered you think I'd be able to help."

Pretzel reached out and squeezed the girl's hand. She was surprised by how muscular it felt. "This event needs a fresh face, Ronny – can I call you Ronny? A fresh face and a new look. That new look is *you*, my dear. A classic look with a modern edge: Old World meets New Wave. The Ronny Look. The Innsmouth Look."

9

Again, Veronica let loose with that high, warbling laugh.

* * *

That evening, Pretzel, Jasmine and Veronica converged at the HotBox, a dance club that Jasmine suggested. The club was lucky for the former model – it was where she'd met her meal-ticket/millionaire/chubby-chaser Farouk.

Pretzel wore a black leather mini and bustier from the Gaultier collection. Jasmine wore her old figure-shrouding favorite: slightly baggy, red-velvet hip-hop bib overalls with matching pumps. Veronica wore black lipstick, her gloves, a black lace evening gown with fishnet shawl, and black stiletto heels.

"You be looking so fine," Jasmine said to Veronica in what was possibly the world's worse possible approximation of homegirl lingo. Her wits weren't entirely about her: she had just done a line of coke in the ladies' room with a Hispanic transvestite named Caliente.

"You're *too* kind," the Innsmouth girl purred, absent-mindedly running the fingertips of one hand over the pearls of the other's glove. She turned to Pretzel. "Any celebrities here tonight? I thought I saw Cher a moment ago."

Jasmine shook her head. "That was Caliente."

Pretzel popped a pink pill and a couple baby-blues. "There's Rod Plunge over by the flamingo ice-sculpture. Gay porn star. Should I ask him to do the hunger thing? Get him on the catwalk? I mean, just because he's a porn star doesn't mean he's not worrying about starving babies. The press would absolutely eat it up." She looked around, slightly dazed. The pills were beginning to kick in. "Where did Ronny go?"

Jasmine nodded toward the dance floor. "Over there. Doing the Petit Mal with Johnnie Depp."

Pretzel watched as the Innsmouth girl twitched and jerked ecstatically among all the giddy clubhoppers. Green and blue flashes from the swirling disco ball overhead gave the dance floor a sort of manic underwater effect, and for one freakish moment Pretzel felt that she was watching some sort of nightmare nature documentary. Behold the slinky, murder-mouthed moray eel: see how it gracefully weaves among all the mindless little prettyfish, sizing them up, biding its time, flexing its jagged jaws, waiting to *bite bite bite –*

Hot pain in the side of her face brought her to her senses. It took her a moment to realize that Jasmine had slapped her.

"What is *wrong* with you?" Jasmine was looking at her with utter incredulity. "You were whimpering like a scared puppy. Right in front

10

of Barbra Streisand's personal shopper. I told him you had asthma."
The plump woman handed her a gin & tonic.

Pretzel sipped at the drink, savoring its faint tang of pine. "I'm fine now. A little anxiety attack, that's all." She looked back at Veronica, still dancing, this time with some pretty-boy male model. A lovely girl. Fabulous. A superstar in the making. Nothing to fear, nothing at all.

And yet ... It suddenly dawned on her that there was something vaguely disturbing about the girl. Those pouting lips ... those huge eyes, haunting and more than a little wideset ...

She turned to Jasmine. "Is it my imagination, or does Veronica look like ... in this light, mind you ... " She cocked her head to one side. "A carp?"

The plump woman considered this for a moment. "Yes, but a gorgeous carp. Like one of those darling two-color Koi. Farouk has a whole pond full of them." She tapped her chin thoughtfully as she watched Veronica bump bottoms with Ashton Kutcher. "We should play it up! Sea-green eyshadow. Big flaming orchids in her hair. Silver lamé and a seaweed boa. An island look. Primitive. Exotic. Powerful."

"And *very* Third World." Pretzel raised an eyebrow. "*I love it.*"

* * *

The next month flew by in a mad blur. After considering dozens of designers, Pretzel and Jasmine commissioned Cosmo Sarkazien, a Versace protégé, to whip together some superslinky variations on the tropical theme: sharkskin micro-minis, kicky cyberpunk/hula girl couture, black fishnet body stockings, and more, more, more. They asked Naomi Campbell and Linda Evangelista to tutor Veronica on catwalk poise. But it turned out she needed very little instruction; the girl was an absolute natural.

At first Pretzel and Jasmine had wanted to hold the fundraiser at a New York homeless shelter, but at Veronica's suggestion, they moved it to an abandoned church on Easter Island. The girl's family owned a beachhouse there – that was where they went when winter hit Innsmouth hard. The tag on Veronica's keychain was an actual chunk from one of those enormous heads.

A week before the big event, Jasmine, Pretzel, and Veronica flew down to the island with Cosmo and his boyfriend, a Las Vegas magician with an impossibly golden tan named Johnny LaRock. Pretzel was hugely impressed with the beachhouse — it had the biggest hot tub she'd ever seen in her life. For the most part, the place

11

was decorated with pirate goodies, nautical oddities, and quirky little statues of what looked like scrawny dogs with scales and batwings.

She told Veronica to fire up the hot tub and then headed for the bar in the living room. The Gilmans kept an enormous supply of liquor on hand, including some odd green bottles shaped like conch shells and sea-horses. She opened one of the conch shell bottles and took a sip: some sort of dark beer, it seemed. Rather sweet, with no bitterness at all. She drank half of the glass sea-horse's contents in three swallows. Bottle in hand, she went to see how the tub was coming along.

Veronica was already lounging in the bubbling water. "I see you found the Essence of Anemone," she said. "Come on in. The water is *perfectly* lovely. Just strip down and jump in."

Pretzel was beginning to feel lightheaded. "Essence of what? Anne who?" She finished the bottle and slipped it into the water to let it swim. As she removed her top, a button came off in her hand and she realized, with a giggle, that she didn't care. She couldn't even remember who the designer was, or why it even mattered. Before she knew it, she was as naked as a coffee bean and brewing in the big yummy cup with Veronica.

Jasmine entered the room leading a handsome, dark-complected middle-aged man. "Pretz! Ronny! Look who showed up!"

Pretzel smiled at him. "Ali Baba?"

"Veronica," Jasmine said, "I'd like you to meet my gentleman friend, Farouk Alhazred. Farouk, this is my friend Veronica Gilman, from Innsmouth. It's in New England somewhere —"

"I am familiar with Innsmouth." Farouk's upper lip curled into a sneer. "And with the Gilman name."

Veronica's huge eyes narrowed to slits. "Hello, Mr. Alhazred. Read any good books lately?"

Jasmine put her hands on her hips. "Do you two know each other?"

Farouk turned to her. "Do you recall, my precious lamb, my telling you of an extraordinary book written many centuries ago by one of my kinsmen? The *Necronomicon*?"

"Vaguely. Has it come out in paperback yet?"

The Arab simply stared at her.

"When it does," she said, "tell them to put Fabio on the cover."

"The *Necronomicon* is a book of ancient wisdom, of secrets from beyond the stars and beneath the sea. It tells of evil beings who long to degrade, to torment, to ultimately destroy all of humanity." Farouk

12

turned his stare toward the Innsmouth girl. "I am leaving now, but I shall return. And I expect you to be gone, Daughter of Dagon. Return to the black mud of the ocean floor. That is the only home this world can offer for you and your filthy kin."

Pretzel laughed nervously. "Farouk *darling*, please, ease up on the girl. Veronica is going to be very big. She's having lunch with Giorgio Armani next week. That's one of his suits you're wearing."

He placed his firm, tanned hand along the blonde woman's jaw, cradling her face. "Pretzel, you are a child, a lovely spoiled child, and you are playing with a serpent that has crawled out of the depths." He brought his lips close to her ear. "She wears those gloves all the time, yes?"

Pretzel thought for a moment. She still felt extremely groggy from her sea-horse cocktail – it was difficult to gather her thoughts. But yes, Veronica *always* wore those gloves, those black gloves with the fingers cut out. She looked up and realized with a jolt that the girl was *still* wearing them. In the hot tub.

Farouk bowed toward Jasmine. "When I return, you can expect a gift of jewelry. A traditional necklace of soapstone stars. It has powers to protect the wearer from evil."

The Arab left the room. Jasmine waited to be sure he was out of earshot before she turned toward Veronica. "You'll have to excuse Farouk. I've never known him to be superstitious or – well, so *B-movie*. He must have had you mixed up with somebody else. I'll go have a talk with him." She smiled apologetically and then followed her boyfriend.

Veronica moved with an eel's grace to Pretzel's side. "And what do you think, my salty, twisted friend? Do *you* think I am some sort of naughty sea serpent?"

"That's depends." Pretzel took the girl by the hand. Then she quickly grabbed her glove by the cuff and pulled it off.

Between each finger stretched a half-inch of translucent, lightly veined webbing.

"I think I'm going to be sick," Pretzel whispered.

Veronica edged closer, smiling. "Not feeling well? Nurse Ronny knows what to do. You'll love it – better than a B-12 shot." She opened her mouth wide. Two thin, flexible pink spines lanced out from under her tongue, embedding themselves in the soft flesh above Pretzel's left breast. The blonde woman passed out a moment after the hot fluid began to pulse into her body.

13

* * *

Pretzel spent the next two days in bed with a high fever. Every now and then she stumbled to the bathroom to throw up, or gulp down glass after glass of cold water. She found it impossible to rest. Whenever she did manage to fall asleep, she would soon find herself having nightmares about horrible, nauseating things – worm-riddled sailor corpses, babies with tentacles, giant yapping clams with eyeball-covered tongues. She also dreamed of a super-old stone building that seemed somehow to be inside-out and backwards. Frogfaced fishpeople swarmed in and out of the place, laughing and plotting and singing froggy songs. Somewhere inside slept a giant snot-covered bat-lizard-monkey-devil, a snake-bearded boogeyman that called out to her in a voice like poisonous syrup. It told her that it loved her, and that she would soon be more beautiful than she could ever imagine, and that she would have luxury and pleasure and power forever and ever. Then it told her to find Dagon. Yes, Dagon would know what to do...

At one point, Jasmine came to her room to check on her. Pretzel noticed that she was wearing a necklace of stone stars. She found it unspeakably repulsive and screamed that it was tacky, hideous, a piece of trash. Furious, Jasmine stormed out of the room.

At last the fever passed, and Pretzel felt better. Better than ever, really. Jasmine went out of her way to avoid her, but that was fine, perfectly fine, so long as the plump woman wore that ghastly necklace.

* * *

"There you are." Carrying a sketch pad and several notebooks, Cosmo Sarkazein crossed to the kitchen counter next to Pretzel. He was a slim, elfin man with short red hair and seven small gold hoops in each ear. "I've been looking all over for you. I had to get away from Johnny. He's driving me crazy, bitching and moaning just because we left his conditioner behind. Anyway, do we have a final line-up – a *definitive* line-up – for the big event? I hope we've got Yasmin Le Bon. She's super-nice, she really is. Why'd she ever marry that huge prick Simon?"

"I think you answered your own question, darling." Pretzel opened a drawer and after a moment's searching, pulled out a melon baller. "Jasmine used to look like Yasmin, you know. People thought they were sisters. But then Jasmine discovered food. As for the line-up: big names. All the big names, except big fat Magda and tiny little Kate. Oh, and no Yasmin — she's got a sick kid. I told her to give the

14

brat an aspirin and she hung up. We've got Naomi. Niki. Brandi. Cindy. Eva. Linda. Claudia. Nadja. Irina. Tatjana. Saffron. Shalom. And of course, Veronica, lovely Veronica at the center of it all."

Cosmo examined her face. "You know, I never noticed before, but you kind of look like Veronica. Around the eyes, I think." He then looked down at what she was doing. "Oh. My. This is interesting. Are you making sushi? Are those even fish?"

"Veronica had these delivered. A pretty island boy brought them by. You'd have loved him." Pretzel dug her fingers into the mass of chopped sea-life on the marble countertop. "There's something about all this fresh salt air that makes me feel so alive. And so hungry." She dug out a few green and red strands and thrust them into her mouth. Then she began to gnaw on a large, juicy, dark-orange egg sac. "Want some?"

Johhny LaRock popped his golden-maned head into the room. "I thought I heard voices in here. What are we having for dinner?"

Cosmo turned toward him, his hand over his mouth. "I'm never eating again," he muttered from between his fingers. He rushed past Johnny, away from Pretzel and her sea-feast.

The tall, tanned magician moved toward the blonde woman, studying the array of minced goodies before her. "That's quite a spread you've got there. Are those local delicacies?"

Her slime-streaked lips stretched into a smile. "I take it you're not as squeamish as our Mr. Sarkazien."

The magician checked his reflection in a silver soup ladle he'd found in the sink. "Cosmo's a very sheltered person. He hasn't seen that much of the world." He wiped her mouth with his thumb and forefinger, then licked the juice from his hand. "I've seen a lot more of it. I get around." He gave her a wink and pointed his finger like a gun-barrel at her. "I'm Johnny LaRock. The name says it all."

"We haven't known each other very long," Pretzel said, "but I think it's safe to say that you're a complete bastard. A vain simpleton with more hair than brains. More tan than tact. And by the way, Mr. Magic: I predict that you're going to say 'ouch' in the very near future."

The magician smoothed his eyebrow with his left pinky, which sported a ruby ring that once belonged to Liberace. "That's ridiculous. Why would I say —"

Pretzel grabbed his elbow in a grip of iron and pulled down, so their faces were at about the same level. She opened her mouth, aiming for the base of his throat.

15

\* \* \*

"I'm worried," Jasmine said.

Pretzel looked up. She was sunning herself on a huge beach towel – the fundraiser was only two days away, and she wanted to be rested so that the event wouldn't tire her out. Not that she was feeling the least bit tired since her recovery from the fever. "Is that a fact? Well, I'm worried, too. Worried that your sense of style has completely evaporated." She pointed to the necklace. "What next: earth shoes?"

"Farouk made me promise to keep it on. Humor me." Jasmine sat down in the sand and sighed. "Everything's going wrong. First Farouk went weird on me. Then you were sick, then Johnny and Cosmo got sick...then you and Veronica started treating me like utter crap. The models arrived a few days ago and now most of *them* are throwing up – at least, more than they usually do. I hired a private nurse and sent her to their hotel to look after them. I'm beginning to think this whole Easter Island idea was a complete mistake."

"Well, of course you think that." Pretzel stood up and gathered her beach towel. "Because it was Veronica's idea. A fabulous idea. This stomach-flu thing is *nothing*. A bug that's going around, that's all. Face it, sweetie: you're as jealous as hell. Jealous because she's thin and in, and you are stout and *out*."

"I can't believe you're saying all this. I've always been nice to Veronica, and I've been working my ass off for this fundraiser. You haven't even noticed. All you can talk about is Ronny, Ronny, Ronny. Good God, you're even starting to look like her." She got to her feet. "We *are* friends, no matter what you say. We've known each other for *years*. You're just mad at my silly old Farouk and taking it out on me. Talk to him when he comes back." She stepped forward to give Pretzel a hug, but the blonde woman moved away from her.

"Farouk? I'd thought he'd left for good after he dropped off that – " Pretzel waved her hand at the necklace. "– that rubbish."

"He wants to be here for the fundraiser. He thinks something is going to happen because it's on May first. Beltane."

"What's that? Some quaint Middle-Eastern holiday? The day they pray to Allah to send more fat chicks?"

"Now you're being cruel. Beltane is an ancient fertility holiday. He told me all about it. Sacrifices. Orgies. Fucking in the fields."

Pretzel walked away from Jasmine. "Your precious Farouk has gone insane. Just keep him away from me."

Once she'd returned to the house, Pretzel chopped up some sea urchins and jellyfish and had lunch. Then she went straight to

16

Veronica's room.

She found the Innsmouth girl and Cosmo sitting on the edge of her bed, drinking Essence of Anemone and studying a chart drawn in his sketch pad. "Progress report?" she said, lounging on the bed behind them.

"Things are coming along *swimmingly*," Veronica said. "I've taken care of Naomi and Linda, and I'll be seeing Claudia this afternoon. Cosmo has worked his magic on Nadja, Niki and Saffron." She consulted the chart. "You handled Eva and Irina, yes? Johnny is making himself useful – he's already tended to Tatjana, Shalom and Brandi, and he'll finish up with Cindy later today. All with time to spare. I love it when a plan comes together." She poured a glass of the liqueur and handed it to the blonde woman.

"I'm really learning to like this stuff," Pretzel said. "By the way, I talked to Jasmine before lunch."

"Life would be so much easier if she would just take off that necklace," Veronica said.

"Can't we just kill her and be done with it?" Cosmo said. "We could shoot her, or poison her."

Veronica nodded. "Yes, and then chop her up and throw the bits into the sea. She'd be quite a chum then! Wouldn't take more than a minute."

"Well, if you think that would –" The blonde woman stopped and shook her head. A frantic little voice – *what are you THINKing?* – echoed through the oily black abyss of her mind. "No, no, no. Of course not. She's no danger to us. She doesn't know a thing. Besides, I can make her change. I *know* it. I've done it before. She used to be bulemic, and I fixed *that*. Too well! The real problem is Farouk. Jasmine said he'll be returning for the fundraiser. Should we be alarmed?"

The Innsmouth girl crossed to the window and looked out over the ocean. "Forewarned is forearmed. I am not worried about this mad Arab." A slow smile crept over her full lips. "He is a big man, and his complexion is like rich coffee with a dollop of cream. I shall have his skin made into a bolero jacket and some kicky capri pants."

\* \* \*

On the day of the fundraiser, the skies over Easter Island were filled with private jets and helicopters. Everybody who was anybody was at the church, along with swarms of pop stars, paparazzi, high-class pushers, callgirls, partyboys, hangers-on, has-beens and wannabes. The pews had been removed from the nave, replaced by director's chairs sprayed gold metallic.

Johnny LaRock studied the crowd over the edge of his glass as he sucked down his Manhattan. Like Veronica, he now wore black gloves without fingertips. He turned toward Pretzel and smiled. "I can't believe this crowd. Wall to wall stars. There's Yoko Ono...Eartha Kitt...Rex Reed...Is that Liz Taylor?"

"An army of aging rich-bitches," she said. After much deliberation, she had finally decided on Chanel couture for herself: something tailored and powerful. To suit the theme of the event, she'd pinned a gold sea-horse on the jacket. She watched as the magician moved through the crowd and sidled up to a chubby old salt-and-pepper brunette dripping with emeralds.

Pretzel tried to find Jasmine in the room, but she was nowhere to be seen. Where was she? And more to the point, where was that troublesome bastard Farouk? A waiter with a food tray passed by, and she snatched up some morsels of sushi with a gloved hand.

In the ladies room, she watched as a world-famous newswoman, a lesbian tennis star and an upscale hooker from Brazil snorted up lines of coke as they gossiped. She joined the group and invited them to try a sea-green powder that Veronica had given her the day before. Before long, the three women were writhing happily on the floor. Pretzel locked the door and gave each a dose of her venom – the Kiss of Dagon, as Veronica called it.

When she returned to the nave, the fashion show was already underway, and Veronica and Naomi Campbell were sauntering down the catwalk in fishnet and black lace evening gowns. Waitresses in gold metallic bikinis offered the guests fluted glasses of Essence of Anemone. Some bouncy Euro-disco dance mix was blasting over the sound system. Suspended from the ceiling by gold chains were video monitors, continuously running underwater scenes of sharks feeding, lobsters fighting, octopi lazily gliding over the ocean floor.

Pretzel slipped backstage, where Cosmo was frantically primping the girls preparing to go on. "Have you seen Jasmine?" she said.

"I don't have time to worry about your fat friend." He sighed hugely. "This church is a nightmare. It's too damp! Claudia's hair is all frizzy! The whole place smells like cheese!"

One of the girls tapped Pretzel's shoulder. "Jasmine's on the phone in one of the dressing rooms."

Pretzel found her planted in front of a tray of hors d'oeuvres, alternately shouting into the phone and cramming her face with calamari. She noticed with exasperation that her friend was still wearing the starstone necklace.

"Please, just *stay away*. I mean it!" Jasmine cried. "It's only a fashion show, for Christ's sake, not some crazy cult conspiracy! If you and your– Farouk? *Farouk?*" She hung up and flung the tray to the floor. "Stupid bastard! He's going to ruin *everything!*"

Pretzel could feel a jumbo-migraine coming on. *Calm down*, she told herself, *nothing's as bad as it seems*. "What's he going to do?"

Jasmine rolled her eyes. "He's on his way here with some stupid freaked-out holy soldiers and they're going to take the place by storm."

Pretzel shook her head. *I stand corrected*. "We've got to tell Veronica. And the bouncers. But first we've got to get you out of here."

"*Me?*" Jasmine put her hand to her chest. "I'm the only one Farouk will listen to. Why in the world would you want me to leave?"

The blonde woman sighed. "Because Farouk is right. There *is* a cult conspiracy. You're the only one who's not in on it. And if you're not one of us, you're fish-food."

"Oh my God! *You're all–*" Jasmine stared into space for a moment. "I guess I don't know. What *are* all of you?"

Pretzel took a deep breath. "We worship the power of the sea and its Dark Lords."

"But that sounds fun! Why didn't you invite me?" Jasmine pouted. "Is it because of my weight?"

"You want to join us? Oh, Jasmine, that's fabulous! I guess we thought – well, what with Farouk being our enemy and your boyfriend, too–"

"But darling, he's just a man! A really, really <u>rich</u> man, but still, just a man. If the Dark Lords of the sea are good enough for you, they're good enough for me. Where do I sign?"

"Well first, throw away that awful necklace! It's like garlic to Dracula."

Jasmine took off the necklace, and in her excitement, accidentally snapped the cord, scattering the star-shaped stones. She kicked away the ones that had fallen at her feet. "Do we get to be vampires?"

Pretzel drew closer to her. "Something even better."

She was about to give Jasmine the Kiss of Dagon when a colossal explosion shook the building. "That can't be Farouk already!" she screamed.

Jasmine winced. "He was calling from his car phone. They were on their way here."

Pretzel took her friend's hand and together they raced to the fashion show. There, they found that the front doors had been blown to bits, along with much of the surrounding walls. Farouk marched through the rubble. He wore a khaki jumpsuit with various black holsters containing a mini-arsenal of weaponry. Several other similarly dressed soldiers marched behind him.

"Really, Farouk!" Jasmine said. "Those doors weren't even locked."

The Arab stopped and stared at her. "I am here to save the world."

She nodded. "I'm sure you are. But while this is all very macho and it has me terribly excited, you must understand that it upsets me when you interfere with my career. I'm a working girl, and unless you're ready to put a ring on my finger or at least set me up in a Park Avenue penthouse, I'm going to have to keep on working."

Farouk blinked, speechless. Finally he said, "My darling, you are dealing with a virulent evil from beyond the boundaries of time and space. This isn't a relationship issue."

"Oh, so *you* get to say what is or isn't a relationship issue? I should be allowed to do my work, pick my own friends and have a good time without you blowing the doors off a church on Easter Island during a fashion show." Jasmine put her hands on her hips. "That isn't too much to ask."

One of the soldiers tapped Farouk on the shoulder. "Sir, are we still going to destroy the ancient evil today? If now's not a good time..."

"Now is a *very* good time!" Farouk turned back to Jasmine. "You're just going to have to trust me on this." He then fired a pistol into the air. "*Attack!*"

Jasmine and Pretzel crept along the wall to the bar, where each grabbed a champagne bottle. They then hid behind some ferns, drinking straight from the bottles as they watched the battle. For fifteen minutes, Farouk and the soldiers fought the venomous models and various other glitterati. Johnny LaRock was the first to go, disemboweled by a soldier's bayonet. As he writhed on the floor, bleeding to death, he took a moment to check his reflection in his attacker's shiny black boots.

Some of the models sprouted barbed tentacles, which they used to whip at the eyes and groins of the soliders.

"Can you do that?" Jasmine said.

Pretzel shrugged. "Probably. I'd rather not." She looked around

20

the church. "I don't see Ronny. This whole thing was her idea. The first scuffle in our war to take over the world, and she's nowhere to be seen. That *is* disappointing."

Naomi's severed head rolled to their feet, venom dripping from her dead lips.

"Well, that tears it," Pretzel said. "If Ronny can't be bothered to fight alongside her own army of evil super-models, then I'm leaving. Come on, let's get out of here."

"I'm with you. I am completely feed up with Farouk." So saying, Jasmine zipped back to the bar and grabbed a couple fresh bottles. Then the girls slipped out of the church.

Farouk's limousine was parked right outside. "They left the motor running!" Pretzel said. "Cocky bastards. They must have thought this whole thing would take two minutes. I need a drink. Hand me one of those bottles, darling."

Jasmine took the wheel and they headed down the road. A few minutes later, Pretzel said, "Say, there's someone naked on the beach over there. Isn't that Ronny? Stop the car."

They got out of the car and sat on the hood. Yes, the nude figure was indeed Ronny. She appeared to be chanting and dancing around one of those enormous stone heads. This one had gill-like grooves carved into its cheeks. The eyes seemed buggier, too.

Jasmine pointed out to sea. "Look at all those bubbles. What's the deal there?" A huge frothing patch of turbulence churned violently. "Maybe we should just drive on."

Pretzel shook her head. "I know what that is, and driving away won't do any good. The world isn't big enough to escape – that."

Suddenly Ronny spotted them and began walking their way. As she approached, it soon became obvious that Veronica Gilman was not like other women. She was still extraordinarily beautiful, yes, but in the short time since they'd last seen her, Ronny had grown iridescent scales all over her body. And she had another addition: flapping gill-slits on her cheeks, neck and under her breasts.

"You're just in time, ladies," Ronny said. "I have only to recite one more incantation to awaken Dagon from his timeless slumber beneath the waves. Even now the Deep Ones are throwing open the doors of his sunken temple. Dagon will in turn awaken Cthulhu, Master of the Ocean Depths, and that will spell the beginning of the end for humanity."

Jasmine raised an eyebrow. "All this work just to wake up some old fish? Somebody should buy him an alarm clock for his birthday."

21

She ran her hands through her hair. "What's this –?" she said, but then stopped.

Ronny advanced on Pretzel and put her webbed hands on her shoulders. Poisonous claws shot out of her fingertips. This new dose of venom brought up patches of scales on Pretzel's slender arms.

"Join me in the final chant, sister," Ronny hissed. "Then we will sacrifice this fat land-hog –" She nodded toward Jasmine. "– to our new masters."

"Don't do it!" Jasmine said.

"Dagon k'hra! Cthulhu ph'galla m'nak!" Ronny and Pretzel intoned together. "M'hraa gl'gra ph'thaka! M'baga Dagon blaggog! Cthulhu blaggog!"

As they intoned, a fresh surge of furious bubbles rose up from the ocean floor. Then a claw, mud-streaked and as huge as a house, broke the surface, followed by a muscular, scaled arm. Deep-sea fish and octopi flopped and tumbled in the ooze that slithered down its length.

As Ronny and Pretzel continued to chant, Jasmine brought forth the item she had found tangled in her hair – a star stone from the broken necklace.

I believe it's time," Jasmine said, "for you to get stoned, Ronny." She bounced up to the Innsmouth girl and popped the stone into a gill-slit beneath her left breast.

With a shrill cry of hellish pain, Ronny fell writhing to the sand. Black blood poured from her lips and gills, followed by gouts of thick, greenish slime. This outpouring, thankfully, did not wash out the offending stone. Her flesh began to blister around her scales, until she looked like a huge trout that had been attacked by a swarm of bees. Her eyes – so big, so lovely – popped like two huge pimples, spraying yellowish goo across the sand. She continued to bubble and seethe until all that remained was a pile of bones mired in a multi-colored paste of ruined flesh and ruptured organs.

Pretzel and Jasmine looked out to sea.

The claw clenched into a fist as it sank back down beneath the roiling water.

Pretzel, however, still had her new scales.

"Oh, dear," Jasmine said. "I was hoping that little skin condition would clear up after I finished off Ronny. Well, we've saved the earth."

Her friend nodded. "Actually you did, but at least I didn't stop you. So what now? Should I turn you into a sea-creature, like we talked about earlier? That might be fun. Swimming around with the dolphins all day. They're supposed to be very smart."

Jasmine thought for a moment. "I think we're forgetting something. The only thing we'd be able to drink underwater – is water."

Pretzel gasped. "Nightmare! Yes, let's stay up here on land. I can always wear long sleeves. Speaking of drinks, let's go to the beach house."

They returned to Farouk's limousine and headed down the road.

"Next week," Pretzel said, "I was supposed to go with Ronny to a big to-do in New England. A birthday party for some Miskatonic University girl named Wilma Whateley. From some place called Dunwich. Her family is fairly established – old money and all that. Since Ronny's out of the picture, do you want to go with me? I'd hate to go alone."

Jasmine shook her head. "Tell little Miss Whateley you can't make it. We'll go shopping in London instead. Forget about smalltown girls. They're nothing but trouble."

"Yes, of course you're right. What was I thinking?" The blonde said. "She's probably some slutty coed who'd give us just as much grief as Ronny. We certainly don't have time for the Dunwich Whore!"

23

# Silky, Slinky, Fabulous – To Die For

Tawny Nicole, creamy Damon, café au lait Giselle. All three had lovely skin and wild, golden hair. All three wore fabulous new outfits of shot silk. And all three were gazing upon Theophile Comte with sparkling green eyes.

"You are a genius, Theo darling," Nicole said, stroking the sleeve of her bolero jacket. "A mad genius. The Oscar Wilde of fashion."

"Oh, *please.*" Damon sighed with exasperation and rolled his eyes. "He is a modern-day Baudelaire." He patted his scarf into place and sighed again, this time with contentment.

Giselle laughed her tiny laugh. "Try Aleister Crowley." A golden bell on her ankle bracelet jangled as she walked to the full-length mirror next to Theophile's work table. Ordinarily, harem pants did nothing for her... These, however, were marvelous. Absolutely to die for.

Theophile grinned hugely. Moonlight streamed through the skylight of his loft apartment, illuminating his bald pate. "You look lovely, my dear ones. Absolutely lovely." He handed each of the models a petite black cup. "Now let us see how my pretty rags *work.*"

The three drank the amber liqueur within the cups. Nicole purred as her jacket merged with her flesh. Wavy golden fur cascaded from her arms, her back. "Haute couture from Hell," she whispered. "You have outdone yourself, Theo."

Damon licked his lips. "Delicious. A touch of mint." He set down his cup and flexed his long, curved claws.

"Yes, there is mint in the brew," Theophile said. He adjusted his turtleneck to hide his double chin. "And catnip and valerian and satyr's blood."

Giselle dropped to all fours. She noticed an errant curl on her right flank and licked it into place. "However will you change us back?"

The bald man raised an iron-gray eyebrow. "Change you back? Surely not! This is my greatest triumph, my dear ones. You shall stay this way forever...and in a moment, I shall join you. But I must confess: you were my guinea pigs, after a fashion."

Nicole looked to Damon, who in turn looked to Giselle.

"Speaking of fashion," Theophile continued, "I certainly like what I see. The season definitely calls for fur. Excuse me while I slip into my own silk suit." He moved toward a large, flat box lying beside the full-length mirror.

Giselle jumped on top of the box; the gold bell jangled one last time as the ankle bracelet fell from her back paw. She growled at the bald man. Damon and Nicole drew closer, claws tapping on the hardwood floor.

"My dear ones!" Theophile bit his thick lower lip. "I gather that the three of you are upset... Because you can no longer model? Is that it?"

"Of course not." Damon sighed deeply and rolled his slit-pupiled eyes. "Don't you see? We can't let you have that suit. We simply can't. This sort of look requires– Panache. Style. Flair."

"Too true," Nicole murmured. She tickled Theophile's potbelly with the tip of a claw, drawing blood. Rich, fatty blood.

Giselle's laugh now sounded more like a hiss. "You may be the designer, old man," she said, "but the catwalk is ours."

Theophile opened his mouth to protest. And at that moment, his dear ones pounced.

-

# Finesse

"I need something special for my show tonight." Zannika tap-tapped her nail-thin heels down the aisle, past monkey-fur miniskirts and sequined bustiers. The artist bit at the tip of a black-lacquered fingernail. "Something deliciously nasty."

Her manager adjusted the lavender rose in the lapel of his lemon-yellow blazer. "Ernst told me they've got some new fishnets in every neon imaginable."

"Earth to Yoyo: neon is out, out, out." Zannika sighed hugely. "This place is full of whore clothes. Let's try somewhere else."

"In a minute. Ernst went to get us some Dust Bunnies." Yoyo glanced over a display of pins and selected a jade spider in a silver web. "We ought to buy some little thing. This is nice."

"I should dye my hair red. Flame red. I'm so tired of platinum-blonde. Aren't you?" The artist glanced in a three-way mirror and wrinkled her nose. "It's so severe. I'm surprised you haven't said anything by now."

Yoyo brushed the bangs of Zannika's pageboy cut with his fingertips. "Your hair is gorgeous. You're the only woman I know who could get away with brown hair. An *earth tone*, for Christ's sake."

"That was years ago. Back then I'd try *anything* once."

A pencil-thin boy carrying a silver tray entered the shop from a back room. On the tray were two small glasses filled with blue liqueur; the rim of each glass was coated with white powder. Yoyo and Zannika downed their drinks and licked the rims clean.

"Buy your little spider so we can go," the artist whispered in her manager's ear. "It's time for some serious shopping."

\* \* \*

It was a vile, ripe, impossible day. Heatwaves writhed up from the sidewalk like translucent tentacles. The heat stifled most of the shoppers but curiously, vitalized the streetpeople. Bag-ladies and hard-eyed funboys held sway on such a day, second only to the likes of Zannika. She did not perspire or even glow. Her pale skin was always dry and cool.

Zannika was a graceful, elongated creature: her hands and arms and legs were long yet elegantly, perfectly curved. She loved to look at herself in the mirror. Sometimes she wondered what she would look like with a penis. Penises were usually lumpy, ghastly-yet-comic things. If, through some unlikely miracle, she should ever sprout a fleshy spout, she knew it would be the absolute best: a sculpted alabaster masterpiece.

Their next stop was The Long Look. Within the next half-hour, Zannika spent more than eight hundred dollars on gloves, hats, perfumes, and hair toys.

"Oh, Yoyo." She brushed her fingertips lazily over her manager's rump as he bent over a display of brooches. "I would ask what Mr. Soap Opera's got that I haven't, but I'm afraid I already know."

"That's the one thing I hate about being on the road with you. I can't keep an eye on Andros." Yoyo pouted. "I was on the phone with him and he kept going on about that cow Pauline. He says they're only friends, but I've been watching the show and he's always got his hands all over her. I know it's just acting, but *still*..."

"Andros is a common sort of man. That sort is notoriously indiscriminate. Why do you even put up with him?" Zannika poked her manager in the side with a pinky finger. "It's a miracle you can be so urbane with all those awful male hormones brewing inside of you."

Yoyo smiled. "It's the cross I must bear."

A young black-haired woman in a leather jacket came up to Zannika. "I know you! You're playing at The Black Box. I just love your show."

"That doesn't mean you know me." The artist crossed to the makeup counter and began to examine the mascaras, the lipsticks — anything so she wouldn't have to make eye contact with a fan.

The woman followed close behind. "I've been telling my friends, 'Go see *Meat for Daddy*. It's so unreal!'" The fan glanced at the lipsticks. "Try the deep purple."

At last Yoyo came to Zannika's rescue. "Ms. Taint does not feel comfortable talking with her fans," he said, taking the woman by the arm and turning her in another direction. "Her act is so very personal. You understand."

"Oh, I'm sorry. I didn't mean any harm." The woman turned toward Zannika. "Really, I didn't."

"That's fine, dear," Yoyo said. "Ms. Taint understands. Deep down she loves all of her fans." He gently pushed her away. "Bye bye, now. And thank you."

\* \* \*

"Why in the world am I carrying these?" Outside of The Long Look, Zannika handed her shopping bags to Yoyo. "A day of lugging

27

these around and I'll turn into one of those awful muscle-women. Where now?"

Yoyo squinted down the street, past storefronts of faux marble and metal. "There. The Snake Pit." He pointed to a small boutique a block and a half away. The display case was filled with what appeared to be mannequins twined in telephone cord.

"It's not too Goth, is it?" Zannika's heels shot sparks as they hit the sidewalk. "I don't do retro." As they drew closer to the shop, she realized that the dummies were in fact wrapped in barbed wire.

Inside, the store was in fashionable disarray. Jewelry and scarves and boots were strewn on the steps of silver stepladders and hung from thin silver chains. Scattered on small tables were glowing spheres of blue glass. The walls were splashed with thick, shiny clots of black and red paint. The high ceiling seemed to be covered with dark lace or netting. No clerks or customers were in sight. Beside a bell on the counter stood a small engraved sign — WE LIVE TO SERVE.

Zannika tried on blue metal earrings shaped like fingers. "These are darling. I could wear them during my act. And look at this belt." She removed a long strip of shiny pinkness from a chain. "What do you think it's made of?"

An obese, perfumed shopboy appeared so quickly at her side that she gasped in surprise. "That belt," he breathed in a hollow tone, "is made from the sun-dried small intestine of a crocodile." His silver contacts rode his bulging orbs uneasily, occasionally flashing slivers of his dark brown irises. "Isn't it extraordinary?"

Yoyo picked up a small stone statue from one of the tables. "This little fellow. Is that a tail, or is a snake crawling up his ass?"

"A snake: but look closer. It's on the way out, not in." The shopboy grinned, revealing very small, very yellow teeth. "That figurine depicts the Egyptian god of insanity. He arrived this morning — isn't he delightful? The syllables of his name happen to create a riotously obscene phrase in English. Since I do not wish to offend, I shall call him 'He-Who-Devours-Wounded-Moths.' More than anything else, ancient Egypt is an attitude, don't you think?"

Zannika noticed the woman in the leather jacket talking with a group of young people outside of the display window. She watched them out of the corner of her eye, hoping they wouldn't enter the store. Thankfully, they moved on.

"I happened to overhear mention of an act." The shopboy lowered his eyes. "Are you performers?"

28

"Ms. Taint is." Yoyo took Zannika by the hand. "She is a performance artist. There's a show tonight at The Black Box. Her act is the most — "

She dug her nails into his palm. "We mustn't take up the nice young man's time. He must have a trillion things to do."

A phone shrilled at the counter and the shopboy went to answer it.

"You know I hate to talk about my act," the artist said. "Why, why, *why* did you even bring it up?"

"I just answered his question." Yoyo rubbed his sore hand. "Besides, he might tell some of the other store patrons. A little word of mouth goes a long way in this set."

"This set? The place is as empty as a tomb."

"You might try being just a hair *friendlier* with fans and fans-to-be," Yoyo said. "They're your livelihood. At least give them a little smile."

"I'd rather give them lobotomies." Zannika rubbed her temples. "I'm not feeling very well. I'm getting a headache."

"Dr. Yoyo has just the thing." He reached into his breast pocket and pulled out a small cigarette case, but before he could open it, the shopboy returned. He held a long grey pipe which appeared to be carved from some sort of animal bone.

"You are not feeling well? Beautiful people should feel beautiful." The boy cocked his head to one side. "Might I suggest a headache remedy dating back to the days of our little friend, the eater of moths?"

Zannika looked into the pipe's bowl. It appeared to be filled with dried flower petals and bits of crystal. The shopboy lit the mixture with a silver cigarette lighter and took a puff himself. "Very pleasant," he said. "Very soothing."

The artist began to suck at the pipe. The mixture was spicy – like clove cigarettes, except sharper. She detected a faint blue glow around the shopboy; perhaps the petals were mildly hallucinogenic. Yoyo had a green aura that clashed with his suit.

A soft, sweet humming filled her head. She held up her hand and marveled at the coils of coral and deepest purple that swirled between her fingers. She felt so much better now. Perhaps someday she would come back to this shop and– What? Have sex with the shopboy? No, he was kind, but an awful eyesore. At any rate, he probably favored some oblique, antediluvian predilection. Get more of the pipe mixture? She could probably ask for a shopping-bagful. The Snake

Pit, she discerned, was an obliging establishment.

"I think Ms. Taint has had enough, Minty," Yoyo said as he took the pipe from Zannika and returned it to the shopboy. "We still have a few more stops to make." The shopboy merged with the shadows of the boutique.

"How did you know his name?" Zannika said. "He didn't tell us. He wasn't wearing one of those tacky name tags."

"I've been here before. Do you think I would take you to a completely unfamiliar shop?" Yoyo shook his head. "I prepare for these outings. I want our time together to be perfect. Because you are perfect. No, I take that back: perfection does not allow for potential, and you have worlds and worlds of potential."

* * *

It seemed a mistake to return to the street, Zannika thought, and yet what could she do? She couldn't stay in The Snake Pit forever. She had to prepare for her show. The humming in her head, at first so comforting, was beginning to bother her, and the sharp red and orange auras of the pedestrians hurt her eyes.

She looked down at herself. Her entire body crawled with glowing coral and
purple snakes. Pythons. People always told her she was special, but she never really believed them. She assumed (often rightly) that they merely wanted something. Now, here was visual proof that she was different. Others wore their auras like tacky raincoats. Hers was vibrantly alive.

She plucked at Yoyo's blazer, begging for him to walk slowly. He recommended a few more boutiques, but she was no longer in the mood for shopping. She felt a little better by the time they reached the hotel. "I'm going to take a nap," she said. "Would you be a dear and piece together some sort of outfit for the show? I wish I could do it myself but I'm dead to the world. Dead, dead, dead."

Zannika stumbled into the bedroom, slipped out of her dress and threw herself on the bed. Though her body came to rest on the sheets, her mind did not. That part of her floated down through the fabric and springs of the mattress. In the distance she heard Yoyo on the phone: "Meet you there, lover." Poor Andros, the cuckolded soap stud. Her mind sank through metal and concrete, floor after floor, faster and faster, down through stone, stone, stone. She felt squeezed by the stone, the way Daddy used to squeeze her.

She had erased Daddy's face from her memory. All she remembered of him was his horrible desire. He had been an awful man, and she was living her revenge – telling the whole world about wicked Daddy through her art. She lived to communicate her feelings: not to any one person, but to the masses. Yoyo was the only exception. His shallowness made him a treasured confidant.

At last she passed through the stone into a fiery river of magma. And in this fierce fluid state she felt strangely aroused. The earth's hot blood washed lasciviously over her presence, searing away all of her cares, all of her limitations, leaving only passion and insatiable hunger.

Aeons passed, liquid stone boiled and churned, roiled and burned, and still Zannika flowed with the heat, even after the creature in yellow roused her and covered her with a second skin of shining rags.

She allowed the creature in yellow to lead her through the foolishly angled structure until they emerged into a great space of towering slabs dotted with brightness and a great looming void beyond. Chattering creatures pushed at her as they hurried along. The creature in yellow pushed her into the open belly of a large beast of metal.

She wished to drink the hot living fluids of the creature in yellow, to drain him utterly dry, to reduce him and all the chattering creatures to dust. Inside the metal beast, the creature in yellow poured a clear liquid into her throat that helped to ease her thirst. The creature made her consume tiny roundnesses of white and pink.

Zannika turned her eyes toward the creature's face and suddenly found herself wondering if they were going to be late for The Black Box and if they had enough cash on hand for the taxi.

Yoyo put the flask of vodka and pill case back in Zannika's purse. "I hope you like that outfit. I thought a metallic look would be just the thing."

"I'm hungry," she said. "When can we eat?"

"Miss One-Meal-a-Day? Miss Salad-Bar-and-Mineral-Water? The club can scrounge up something for you." Yoyo patted her hand. "At least you're talking. Do you need another pill? We have a special audience tonight, you know."

"No, I don't know. Some little art league?" She looked out at the stars. How could fire look so cold? "I'm still hungry. The stars are confusing me. Are we there yet?"

* * *

At The Black Box, Yoyo went off to talk to the stage manager. In her dressing room, Zannika wolfed down a steak, two baked potatoes,

31

and a slice of chocolate cake. She decided never to return to The Snake Pit. The mixture in the pipe had reduced her comprehension of the world to a primal state. True, the effect had worn off, but it still frightened her. She was an artist: communication was essential to her.

She was deafened by applause as she strolled onstage. The club was choked with swirling smoke. She picked up a remote control from on top of a large metal box in the center of the stage. With the press of a button, she activated the wall of televisions that served as the background for her performance.

Scenes from obscure, fetish-oriented porno movies sprang up on the screens. Zannika set down the remote control and opened the metal box.

"Meat for Daddy!" she cried, pulling out a raw chunk of beef brisket. She slapped it on the floor and against the wall of televisions. On one screen, a tall blonde with wrinkled lips sneered as she picked up a handful of clothespins.

"Daddy loves meat!" Zannika screamed. "Daddy, Daddy, Daddy! Feed me meat, Daddy! Show me that you care!"

The smoke coiling up from the audience had a spicy, familiar smell. Zannika pulled a raw chicken out of the box, selected a screen, and smeared the carcass against an especially exuberant close-up. She glanced out over the audience and blinked with surprise: she could detect auras of red and orange among the audience members. Offstage, she saw Yoyo laughing with a short, fat figure with a blue aura.

"Meat! Meat! Meat! Daddy's meat is so complete!" The artist reached again into the box and began to toss chunks of ground chuck against the screens. "Daddy likes cow meat! Pig meat! Woman meat!" As she screamed her litany, she suddenly realized that the audience was chanting along with her. "Red meat! White meat! Daddy wants all the meat!"

In the front row, the woman with the leather jacket stood on her seat, screaming, "I love you, Zannika!" Angered, the artist threw a heavy slab of meat in her face. The woman sank her teeth into the prize.

The glistening flesh on the screens also took on auras. Red, orange, magenta. Zannika suddenly began to feel hot. As hot as magma, as hot as the earth's core. And she was hungry again.

The black-haired woman removed her jacket, her tank top, her pants. Several other members of the audience also began to disrobe. Zannika felt drool streaming down her chin. She glanced back at the televisions and saw they had all been turned off.

Holding hands, Yoyo and the fat shopboy walked onto the stage. "Adore Her," they cried out in unison. Then her manager shouted, "She-Who-Hungers shall feast tonight. Worship Her, for She-Who-Hungers shall lead us into the Beyond. She-Who-Hungers desires all. Knows all. Reveals all."

"I'm not–" As the heat within her rose, Zannika found it difficult to speak. "Don't ... don't..." Don't what? She stared at the audience. What were they doing to her?

This time, the heat did not stop with her mind. Her body turned feverish and began to expand. The metallic dress ripped and fell away as she billowed into an enormous, spongy mass, dripping with hot digestive acids. Purple and coral pythons of living power squirmed across her bulk.

Several members of her frenzied audience climbed on stage, and she writhed with pain and delight as they thrust themselves into her: first little parts, then limbs, then entire bodies. She engulfed them with tingling ecstasy. For a moment, she considered sparing Yoyo... Then a pang of ravenous *need* coursed through her. She thrust out a fat ribbon of tissue and wrapped it around her manager's throat. Another length of pink fiber shot forth to embrace the shopboy.

*Why*, she wondered, had they turned off her videos? Her act wasn't done yet! She stared sadly, longingly at the wall of televisions. Then she caught sight of a reflected image, segmented across all the dark, shiny rectangles of glass. An image of–

Herself.

She stared and stared, dumbfounded. She was now one big *face* ... but not just any face. Big black ovals for eyes and a wide, curved slash of a mouth, set in an expression of banal idiocy.

An enormous, luridly enflamed, have-a-nice-day Smiley Face.

People from the audience were still climbing onstage and thrusting themselves into her, allowing themselves to be instantly consumed. She wanted to tell the people about desire, about meat, and as always, about Daddy. But her mind refused to focus on the task. She could feel her red-hot appetite sizzling away her intellect.

Zannika tried desperately to cling to her power of speech. The struggle, however, was futile. Every time she opened her mouth to say something, a cluster of fans crawled inside.

# II. LITTLE WEIRDOS

## The Pint-Sized Revenge of Baby Caligula (with Michael McCarty)

"I have some good news and some bad news and some great news," said Dr. Emil Matapathamos, the world's most talented and resourceful fertility specialist. He also had many other talents, but those were on various backburners these days, for fertility was his current obsession. The tagline under his name on his business card said it all: *If You Are Alive, You Can Be A Parent. Guaranteed.*

Amber and Desmond Belmont sat in front of the good doctor's mahogany desk, facing a stack of those cards in a silver tray shaped like an outstretched hand. They both nodded at the doctor, waiting for him to share the good/bad/great news.

But he said nothing.

Dr. Matapathamos simply sat behind his desk, languidly tapping his lips with a pencil. He was a fiftyish fellow, dark-haired and bearded. His handsomeness was marred, but only slightly, by numerous small scars on his face and hands. He was a man of adventure, and adventures always leave their marks.

"Well?" Amber said at last. "What's the news?" Mrs. Belmont was slender and beautiful, with green eyes, wavy red hair, and the best breast implants money could buy.

"Yeah, what's the news?" echoed her chubby, balding husband. "What's up? Tell us the bad news first! Get it out of the way."

"I have reviewed the test results, as well as my notes from the examinations I've performed," the doctor said. "What I have to tell you is so strange, and yet so fabulous, I fear it may alarm you. So please, listen to me with an open mind. I shall tell you what I have to offer, and let you decide from there. Fair enough?"

Amber pointed at the doctor's business cards. "I'm alive. I want to be a parent."

"Yeah, me too!" Desmond put a plump arm around his wife's shoulders. "We both want to be parents. Make with the baby! We'll do whatever it takes. We've got loads of money."

"Yes, I suppose so," the physician said. "I'm sure there's plenty of money to be made in the porn industry."

"Adult entertainment!" Desmond said. "My dirty movies are

34

artistic expressions of human emotions and stuff!" He smiled warmly at his wife. "When I first met Amber, she was just a filthy whore, letting guys bang her for ten lousy bucks a pop. Now she's an international film sensation."

"But ... guys still bang her, right?" the physician asked.

"Yeah! But the movies make a Hell of a lot more than ten bucks!" Desmond pounded the desk with a meaty fist. "Now let's talk babies!"

Dr. Matapathamos sighed with irritation. "Please try not to damage my furniture. That enormous gold pinky ring of yours could have left an awful scratch. Now, about that baby..." He sighed again. "I want you to know, I have helped women in their late seventies to become mothers. I have helped men with raisin-sized testicles to become fathers. But you two..." He shook his head and tapped his lips with his pencil a few more times. "You two... Desmond, your sperm has no mobility whatsoever. It's asleep. I've never seen anything like it. Amber, you had a few abortions when you were a teenager. They weren't performed by professionals, were they? And, your reproductive tract has been somewhat of a high-traffic area for many years. The inner scarring and stretch-marks ... not good. Plus, your hormone levels are completely askew. Basically, you have what one would call a 'hostile womb.' All that, by the way, is the bad news."

"My God!" Amber said. "I wasn't expecting to hear that!"

"Yeah," Desmond added, "her snatch ain't hostile! It's real friendly!"

"Now, don't despair – for here is the good news!" Dr. Matapathamos said. "I have figured out a way for you two to actually bring forth life, as impossible as that may seem. And because it is an experimental treatment, I am willing to give you a substantial discount. I have devised a method whereby I am able to enhance the strength and mobility of a man's sperm cells by subjecting his testicles to concentrated waves of theta energy."

"Hey! He wants to do stuff to my nuts!" Desmond whined as his hands moved to shield his privates.

"Oh, for Christ's sake!" Amber hissed. "He's a man of science. If he says your nuts need stuff done to them, then stuff is going to get done to them!" She turned to the doctor. "So what does this theta energy stuff do? And how big a discount do we get?"

"Yeah, how big a discount?" Desmond asked. "And what's going to happen to my nuts?"

"No need to fear for the safety of your 'nuts,' as you call them, sir," the doctor said with a gentle smile. "Your testicles will be gently bathed in theta energy, also known as time particles. This miraculous scientific breakthrough is the great news to which I referred earlier. Theta energy will cause your male glands to regress through past generations, to a time when your family tree was at its reproductive peak."

Amber and Desmond blinked in unison.

"In other words," Dr. Matapathamos said, "I'm going to send your nuts back through time."

Amber thought about this for a moment. "Will it give him caveman nuts?"

Desmond grinned. "I wouldn't mind having caveman nuts! Really big, hairy ones!"

"No," the doctor replied, "it probably won't give him caveman nuts. But with livelier, zestier semen, it should be no problem for you two to create a fetus with the strength necessary to survive in that ungodly, war-torn cavern you call a womb, Mrs. Belmont."

"If my inside parts are so bad," Amber said, "maybe they should get a dose of that theta stuff, too."

The doctor's dark, sculpted eyebrows both arched in surprise. "That thought had occurred to me – how delightful that it should occur to you, too. I've never given *both* potential parents the theta energy treatment before! I was only hesitant to suggest it because we'd be venturing into uncharted territory–"

"Yeah, yeah!" Desmond shook both fists in the air, as though threatening to punch God. "Let's do it! Uncharted territory! We'll make the best baby ever!"

"He'll be great! Or she!" Amber said. "Like Einstein with muscles! Or Betsy Ross with big hooters!"

Dr. Matapathamos chuckled. "Betsy Ross? Madame Curie would be more accurate! Actually, if I recall correctly, Madame Curie did indeed have big hooters... But I digress. Since you are both being so agreeable about the experimental nature of these procedures, I think a twenty-five percent discount is in order. We shall begin the theta energy therapy tomorrow morning, eight a.m. sharp!"

\* \* \*

Fast forward, two years.

On one side of the desk sat the doctor, tapping his lips with a pen his insurance agent had left behind. On the other side sat Amber and Desmond Belmont – but now Amber was at least one-hundred pounds overweight and her husband was sickly-thin, with twitching hands, eyes and lips. On his bony lap rested a fat, dark-haired baby wrapped

36

in a torn blanket.

"Baby Stevie has been acting strange lately," Amber said.

"Yeah, creepy even," Desmond declared.

"Odd baby behavior?" the doctor said. "Is that what you wanted to see me about? I'm a fertility specialist, not a pediatrician. I'm sure all babies exhibit odd behavior from time to time. But since Baby Stevie is the result of an experimental procedure, I certainly would like to see how he's coming along."

Suddenly the baby jumped out of his father's lap and onto the desk. He adjusted the blanket so that it draped his body toga-style, then pointed a plump, accusing finger at the physician.

"Cut the crap, doc," the baby said in a high, nasal yet commanding tone. "First of all, my name is not Baby Stevie. It is Caligula. You may call me Baby Caligula, if you wish. When you exposed my father's tired testicles to theta energy, you sent them back to the fall of the Roman Empire, thus channeling my own splendid nutsack from that time-period. Apparently this moronic clod is a descendant of mine! You only wanted to bring forth the sperm of that glorious era, but something went wrong. You also brought forth my memories, my intellect, my personality – my very soul!"

"So I see," the doctor said. "Probably because Amber received the treatment as well... That must have something to do with it."

"Yes indeed, you insipid quack!" the baby scolded. "Just look at that fat whore who, I am sad to say, is now my mother. You turned her cervix into a gaping time-tunnel! And I, Baby Caligula, am its hapless, helpless victim! It sucked me in and then spat me out as the wretched creature you see before you. Look at me: a puny drool-bucket with a wet noodle stuck in a soggy diaper! How can I be a decadent, ruthless leader when my willy is as soft as a sock? How can I have endless orgies with loyal servants when my penis is the size of a midget's smallest toe?"

"Last week," Amber said, "he made all the babies at the Happy-Time Day-Care Center disappear. The supervisor there said she turned her back on the kids for just a minute – when she turned around, they were all gone! Baby Stevie was the only one left. I don't know how he did it, and he won't tell us! Now, no day-care center will take him. He's driving us crazy! I'm eating like a pig and Desmond has no appetite at all."

"Amazing," the doctor said, writing down Amber's comments in his notepad. "Simply amazing."

"You'll think it is amazing when I'm through with you!" Baby

Caligula walked over to the corner of the doctor's desk and started tearing apart a small, potted fern. He quickly knit the leaves together and set them on top of his head. Sadly, his crown of laurels looked more like a Caesar salad. "I've been planning my revenge since my rebirth, when I realized that my new father was not my beloved Tiberius, but merely some ignorant bum who makes porno movies. And my new mother! A slut, a hooker, a common whore!"

"Hey!" Amber cried. "Who are you calling common?"

Baby Caligula jumped off the desk and quickly scaled the nearest file cabinet. "It is time to seize control!" he shouted. He made an elaborate series of gestures with his wee, pudgy hands. "I learned a few tricks when I was struck in that fat slut's gynecological time machine."

With that, a swirling vortex of sea-green mist opened up in the floor at the base of the file cabinet. Out of the mist marched two-dozen infants, each carrying a shiny miniature spear or sword.

"What the Hell...?" the doctor whispered.

"Say hello to my infant infantry!" the baby babbled. "Since I can't rule Rome – I'll rule your office! It shall be my new base of operations. I've had a few opportunities to visit the Internet in recent weeks – father always has his computer on, to see how many perverts are visiting his many porn websites. I first read up on the Roman Empire – they should never have installed those lead pipes to carry their drinking water. A tragic mistake. Then I looked up some military websites, and I now realize, today's armies would be powerless against a battalion of babies. No soldier would ever dream of shooting a poor, innocent infant – even one with a spear!"

"When your soul made the leap through time, it would appear that your megalomania hopped on for the ride, too," stated the doctor, writing down more notes.

"You call me mad?" The tiny tyrant stomped his adorable left foot. "Perhaps I am mad! Yes, you have to be crazy to be a baby. All you do is eat and crap, day after weary day. What kind of an existence is that? I used to have fun sucking mother's boobies, but she switched me over to a hideous, rubber-nippled bottle after only three weeks."

"I'm sorry," Amber said, "but you kept nipping me with that little tooth in the front." She turned to Dr. Matapathamos. "He was born with teeth! He's a monster!"

"No, *she's* the monster! An unfit mother!" Baby Caligula stared at Amber, his wide blue eyes gleaming with rage. "She doesn't even sing 'Three Blind Mice' to me any more. I love that song! It's so deliciously violent – especially the part where the evil woman with the kitchen knife mutilates those terrified, sightless little animals. She chops off their tails! Are you familiar with the song, doc?"

The physician nodded. "Certainly, yes. If you want to hear it again, why don't you just sing it yourself?"

"Good idea! I shall have to do that," said the diminutive despot. "But now, my first order of business is to appoint my rocking horse as leader of the New Roman Council! Guards, fetch my horsey!"

Several of the babies marched back into the vortex, and came out a moment later dragging a baby-blue rocking horse with yellow ribbons in its purple mane.

Baby Caligula climbed down the file cabinet. He then knocked over a side-table which held a box of cigars and a lighter. He picked out an especially fat cigar, bit off the end, and lit the stogie – apparently the designers of the childproof lighter hadn't considered the cleverness of a time-travel baby. He climbed onto the wooden horse, put his leafy crown of laurels on its head, and started rocking back and forth.

"Blecch!" The infant took another puff of the cigar and said, "Doc, what are you supposed to do with these? Smoke 'em or flush 'em? They taste like poopy diapers." He tossed the burning cigar into a metal wastebasket by the side of the desk.

"What–? There are papers in there! You're going to burn the place down!" Dr. Matapathamos came out from behind his desk and grabbed the wastebasket, which was now filled with fire. He dropped the hot metal container and flaming papers scattered across the room. Soon the curtains, sections of the rug, and a table covered with books and research papers were all ablaze.

The doctor, Amber, and Desmond all hurried out of the smoke-filled office. The troop of terrified tots all rushed back into the misty time-vortex. Baby Caligula rushed in, too – but a moment later, he came back out, clutching a pink plastic ukulele. He made a sweeping gesture to close the vortex behind him, and then cried out, "Alas, soon my empire shall be no more! And so I must follow the glorious example of Nero, who played the lyre while Rome burned..."

Minutes later, a fireman named Clarence Tate tried to enter the office, but he couldn't get through the door. It was later revealed that a chair had been pushed against it on the other side. A tiny, charred corpse was found in the center of the room, next to a puddle of molten plastic.

Mr. Tate swore he heard a tiny, nasal voice singing "Three Blind Mice" as he chopped at the door of the burning office with his fireaxe.

# Mr. Sticky-Lips

If you're ever traveling by bus across the country and you see a smiling, grubby, thirtyish man in a purple baseball cap ... a filthy, jaundiced little weirdo who really enjoys his chocolate, bar after sticky bar ...

Don't make eye contact.

I did – and from Chicago to Cleveland, he decided I was his best friend ever, so he shared his life story with me.

He didn't know I had a tape recorder in my duffel bag, because I was going to be taping an interview at the literary convention where I was going.

He didn't hear the soft click as I hit RECORD.

I don't really know why I taped his ramblings. I suppose it was because he had such a sad look in his eyes. Ever see that painting, "The Last Supper"?

He had eyes like the guy in the middle.

He also had a big plastic bag of chocolate bars on his lap, and his lips glistened with thick brown goo as he chewed and spoke, chewed and spoke. I got off the bus about five minutes after he finished speaking.

His current whereabouts are anybody's guess.

This is what Mr. Sticky-Lips had to say:

My dad was a mechanic and my mom was just mom. But being mom was really a full-time job because there were nine of us kids. I was the youngest. My dad didn't help out much around the house. He just sat on the swing on the back porch, drinking beer and looking at the sky. We didn't bother him none, because if we did, he'd whip off his belt and snap us with it. Mom was deaf in her right ear because he once snapped her on that side of her head and I guess he did it too hard. I always stood on her left side when I talked to her.

Mom disappeared when I was eight. She didn't take any clothes or make-up or nothing. She still had the TV on, and a pot roast in the oven. I think the aliens came and got her. I mean, what other explanation could there be? It wasn't like her to miss her favorite soap opera.

I ran away when I was fourteen. My dad probably didn't even notice. I did leave a goodbye note, though. That's just what it said. "Goodbye. Signed, Bart." That's my name. Bart.

I bummed around from city to city. I hitchhiked a lot. I was big for my age. A guy on the road can make a few bucks here and there, if he's not too picky. You know, doing people favors, stuff like that. Sometimes I even got a chocolate bar.

My mom and dad never bought us candy because they said it would rot our teeth out and we couldn't afford a dentist. I haven't been to a dentist in my whole life, but that's okay. My teeth are really strong. I always carry a toothbrush, too. I've got one on me right now, tucked in my sock.

For a few months there, I belonged to what I thought was a church. They were nice to me at first. Even gave me my own room. There were a lot of us in that house. We had to pick sweet corn in work-shifts and we weren't allowed to smoke or read newspapers or ever leave. It took me a while, but I figured it out. That was what folks call a cult.

They kept adding new rules, like, "don't call your relatives" and "don't wear anything with purple in it" and "don't eat any of the sweet corn you pick." One day they said, "don't eat anything with sugar in it."

That's when I figured out they were evil.

One night I set fire to the community room and in all the confusion, I escaped. Half the cult got burned up, and some jumped out of windows to get out of there and busted some bones, but like my dad used to say, you can't make an omelet without breaking a few legs. I think maybe he meant eggs.

Eventually I found a nice mall with really crappy security and I was able to live off that place for a whole summer. One of the stores had crummy air-conditioning, and they'd wedge the employee entrance open to let in a breeze. I'd sneak in and out that way, and hide stuff under the stairs by that entrance. It was pretty slick. Sometimes I'd sleep under those stairs. It was really dark under there. Nobody could see me. I felt like some kind of movie-star cat-burglar-type secret spy.

I got my hands on some new clothes, some suitcases, and some money from a couple different cash registers. I got me a driver's license from a lost-and-found box – the guy even looked a little bit like me. So for a while I was able to travel in style.

You'd be surprised by some of the jobs I've had. Of course, they weren't exactly what you'd call nine-to-five jobs. They all paid in cash. A little nude modeling, though we weren't the kind of models who just stood around. Some videos, too. Never had a desk job, though on one of those videos, they've got me strapped to a desk with duct tape.

Like I said, I never got to have any candy when I was little, so whenever I had a few extra bucks, I always bought myself some chocolate bars. Chocolate tastes so good, so yummy – so much better than anything else on this planet. Eventually I figured out that aliens must have brought it to Earth. I mean, what other explanation could there be?

So some nights, I'd stand outside and cry out to outer space, "Aliens, take me to your chocolate world so I can be with my mom you stole! You owe me that much!"

But even though aliens are usually chomping at the bit to steal humans, they never came for me. I think my advanced intellect must have scared them off.

*Then!* Then I figured out a way I could trick the aliens. A way to join them through the back door. A person's got to be really clever whenever they're dealing with aliens. They have those giant brains, you know. They think really big thoughts. The biggest.

I discovered that if I ate enough chocolate, I mean a lot, really a lot, I could elevate my mind to a higher plane of existence. I figured, if I got my mind high enough, I'd be able to reach the plane of the aliens. I could actually feel my mind rising up, up, up – soaring up to the chocolate door of the alien's secret dimension. Way past Mars, and that's pretty far off. A few times, I think I pushed my mind past Uranus. It helped if I drank a lot of coffee.

I wanted to see what else I could add to the mix, to get to that door faster, but the police caught me trying to break into a pharmacy, and that ended that. For a few months, anyway.

Since then I've been in and out of funny farms. They're not really very funny, though. I once got out of one by setting a fire, because really, those places are no better than cults. These days, I just cooperate with the doctors, since I've found out my meds sometimes work with the chocolate. Especially if I wash them down with coffee. And vodka. Or whiskey. Or tequila. Any old booze, really. Booze is made out of fermented plant juice, you know. They say folks should eat three or four vegetables a day, right? Plants, vegetables ... same thing. In fact, they go down better if they're liquid. They taste better, too.

Every time some doctor sees me, he'll say my liver is going to hell and I'll probably be dead in three months. Ha! They've been saying that for five years now. What do they know? Maybe whatever

I'm doing to my liver is good for me. Making me live longer. Or, maybe it's going to make me live in a *different* way. After all, once I get past the chocolate door, everything will change. Maybe I'll leave my body behind, all dead and everything, but the real soul-ghost of me will still be alive, having been prepared for any future lack of a body by my amazing liver!

I bet that's why it's called a liver. Makes sense to me.

You know what I think? I think the doctors don't want me to know the truth about how things really are. Each day, I feel myself getting a little bit closer to the chocolate door, and soon, I'll find out what's behind it. I'll be able to join the aliens and my mom. I'll even let the aliens probe my soul-ghost, since I know how much they need information on us humans.

It's the least I can do for them. They've been taking care of my mom all this time, letting her watch alien soap operas and make pot roasts out of yummy alien animals.

When we get back together again, I'll always stand on my mom's left side, just like when I was little, so she can hear everything I have to say. Unless the aliens have fixed her bad ear. Yeah, I bet they have. Why, I bet they can fix anything. Maybe they'll make a new body for my soul-ghost. Stuff like that is probably really easy for them.

Me and mom, we'll walk through fields of chocolate flowers and laugh under a chocolate sky. I know that probably doesn't sound pretty. All that brown. Kind of sounds like poop, doesn't it? Like a big stinky poop-world. But that chocolate won't be stinky at all. We'll get so used to all the different shades of brown, they'll start looking like a whole rainbow of colors, sweet magical colors. Oh, I know it will be beautiful. I can hardly wait to get there.

Wow, look at me, what a big pig I am – eating all this yummy chocolate in front of you without offering to share.

Have some. It's really good.

Not hungry? Oh, okay. Suit yourself.

I think I'm going to take a little nap now. Don't be sad or anything if I never wake up.

That's just means I'm with mom.

# Your Turn

She sweeps toward you, laughing, her lace-swathed arms outstretched. She is the Red Nurse and she is about to put her large hot hands on you.

So you run, because you know no one survives her brand of care. You see a small blue house with all the lights on and toys scattered in the front yard. The Red Nurse abhors children so you hurry up to the door and start knock-knock-knocking. Oh please, let all the horrible children be home.

The door glides open and a beautiful young Asian man with platinum hair takes you by the hand and wordlessly leads you inside. You slam the door behind you and command the young man to lock it. He shrugs and does as he is told.

In the kitchen, he makes you a peanut butter and jelly sandwich. "*Say* something," you insist. "I'm being chased by the Red Nurse and I want you to take my mind off her."

"Well, let me think," he says. "How about this? My name is Peter. My mother is French and my father is Japanese but I never knew him. I'm making you a P, B & J because it has a lot of fat and sugar and protein in it and those are all good things to eat when you're scared. So here, eat this. Want some milk?"

You nod and take the sandwich. You watch as Peter picks up an empty glass from the counter and turns around. Time passes. He's just standing there *doing* something, but you can't see what. So you watch and eat and watch. Finally he turns around and hands you a full glass.

The glass is fridge-cold and filled with a white liquid.

"What is this stuff?" you ask, eighty-five percent disgusted, ten percent amused, five percent intrigued.

"It's milk," Peter says.

"No it's not. It came out of you."

"Well, yeah. It's my milk."

You look him up and down. "What did it come out of?"

He brushes his fingers along your jawline. "If the Red Nurse catches you, you'll never have any milk ever again."

Something jumps up on the counter, startling you – you almost drop the milk. At first you think it's a cat, but it's too big, and it's a biped, and it's wearing a gold mask and a black rubber suit crisscrossed with zippers, and you suddenly realize it's the Cat Man, and you KNOW that the Cat Man is a very good friend of the Red

Nurse, and you turn toward Peter and shout, "Is this a trap?"

He cradles your face in his hands and says, "No, no, no, calm down, the Cat Man is mad at the Red Nurse and he's staying with me. He's the one who put all the toys in the front yard. Pretty smart, huh?"

You face the Cat Man. "How do I know this isn't a double-cross? Why are you mad at the Red Nurse?"

"She lied to me." His soft little voice sounds like a big tree growing. "She promised me Australia and India and most of Africa and all I got was Hawaii. I mean, Hawaii is pretty and all, but I was expecting a lot more. We had a deal. Hey, if you're not going to finish that, can I have it?"

You let the little guy have the rest of your sandwich. He removes his mask to eat and you almost pass out because his face is so ugly (pale damp flesh, protruding blue-green veins, watery golden eyes). He eats like a frenzied boar-hog, grunting and heaving and gurgling as he chews.

Peter taps his chin thoughtfully. "So Cat Man. What's the plan? How you gonna get back at her? What sort of nasty trick do you have up your black rubber sleeve?"

The little guy flashes a slick grin. "Tell ya what. You two help me and I'll cut you in. Petey, you can have France and Japan and any ten of the fifty states of America. And you, Scaredy Pants: you can have Germany and Argentina and any ten states, too – but Petey gets first pick. Is it a deal?"

You wonder why your mouth tastes like oranges. Then you realize that while the Cat Man was talking, you drank the whole glass of Peter-milk.

* * *

It takes days of cool persuasion and heated negotiation, but finally the Cat Man and Peter convince you to join in on the scheme. It takes so long because they won't tell you what the scheme actually *is*.

Peter leads the way down into the murky basement. At the Cat Man's command, he fills a laundry bag with things from a big wooden crate under the stairs. You aren't quite sure what the things are, but they look like black books or boxes.

The Cat Man hangs the Seal Of Wounds That Won't Heal on the handle of the old furnace's heavy metal door. He swings the door open and you find yourself looking into one of the ultra-white corridors of the House of the Ankh. In you all crawl, one, two, three.

"That was easy," you say.

The Cat Man waves a blacknailed hand dismissively. "Getting into trouble is always easy." He reaches back into the opening and pulls out the Seal, closing the way behind him.

"Why did you do that?" you whisper hotly into his damp triangular ear. "That was our escape hatch!"

Suddenly an Iguana Man guard rounds the corner of the hall. The Cat Man pulls a wee gun out of one of his many pockets and shoots the reptile between the eyes. The silencer is almost as big as the gun, so the shot only makes a tiny *pfffft!*

"Hatch schmatch," the Cat Man hisses. "What a big wetsy baby you are. Let's get moving."

You help Peter carry the sack as you follow the little guy through the winding halls. On both sides of you: walls dotted with framed certificates (there's one signed by Hitler) and doors, doors, doors, hundreds of them, all white, some slightly ajar. Every now and then you peek into one of the rooms. In the various rooms you see: locusts feasting on exposed brains; looping, living guts stuck with glowing pins; orifices crammed with gardening implements; and you keep saying to yourself, *Italy, they promised me Italy.*

In all these rooms, set high up on the walls, are video monitors, all playing exotic, brightly-lit torture scenes. For ambiance, perhaps, like music in elevators.

At last you come to a door guarded by two Iguana Men. The Cat Man plugs them both with his tiny gun before they even have a chance to reach for their weapons. Dying, one of the guards shits his pants, filling the hall with an eye-watering ammonia stench.

The room you now enter is huge, and filled with computer stations. Each station features a bluish-gray zombie, staring at a monitor and typing. A cable runs from the side of each monitor to the base of the spine of its zombie-typist.

"Here we are," the Cat Man says. "Took a little longer than I thought to find it. She changes the location of this room constantly."

"Is this the nerve-center of operations?" you ask. The little guy shakes his damp head. "Nah, this is just where they play the torture videos."

Each zombie is wearing a black burlap shirt. The Cat Man rips the shirt off the nearest zombie, revealing a square slot in the middle of its back. He presses a button by the slot and a video cassette pops out.

Peter opens the sack and takes out a video labeled SWEDISH HOT-TUB DUDES, which he slides into the zombie-slot. One by

46

one, he replaces the torture videos in all the zombies with selections from his porn library.

"Is *this* the big plan?" you say, exasperated. "Why did you two even bother to get me involved? You didn't need me at all!"

The Cat Man takes your hand and tugs gently downward. You kneel to look him in the eye. "You, my friend," he says, "play a vital role in this curious enterprise. A starring role. Starting *now*."

He unzips one of his many zippers, reaches in and pulls out a sort of collar, studded with small gems and computer chips. You want to look at it more closely, but before you can, he snaps it around your neck.

From another of his pockets he pulls an oval device covered with buttons. He points the thing at you and presses a big red button.

* * *

And now you are a woman, or at least, female: the Green Nun.

Of course, the name is all part of the joke. After all, the Red Nurse isn't really a nurse. Most nurses like to cure people, not chop them into bits. And while nuns aren't supposed to like sex, <u>you</u> certainly don't have a problem with it.

Like the Cat Man, you wear a skintight, many-zippered rubber suit – yours is lime-green, with a yellow and blue swirly pattern over the breasts. You don't wear a mask, but you do cover your face with a bridal veil.

The revolution was a success: the energy from the torture rooms – the secret source of the Red Nurse's power – has been channeled away from her and into you. And you feel *fantastic*.

Your first order of business was to give the Cat Man a kiss and a big hug. Then you twisted off his smelly head. You confiscated the remote (as if he could ever control *you*), that tiny little gun, and of course, the Seal of Wounds That Won't Heal, along with the other goodies in those deceptively deep pockets of his. You commanded your new guards, the Tarantula Men, to seize and detain Peter. Then you shifted the location of the zombie room to a transdimensional bunker in Q Sector. There's no air in Q Sector, but the zombies won't mind.

In the Imperial Boudoir, you watch as the Tarantula Men strip off Peter's clothes. You raise an eyebrow at the sight of his convoluted genitalia.

"You were supposed to save us!" Peter cries.

"I *am* saving you. For myself."

You press a green button on the nightstand and a silver

communications monitor rises out of the floor. The screen lights up to reveal the bristly face of the Head Tarantula Man.

"Any word on the Red Nurse?" you roar.

His mandibles tremble. "She has escaped the grounds. Six-dozen death-squads are out searching. We think she has found her way into the Swamplands."

"The Swamplands! But – that's where the Resistance is headquartered!"

You grab a crystal dildo out of your curio cabinet and fling in at the screen. The monitor explodes in a shower of shards and sparks.

Out of the corner of your eye, you see Peter yawn. *Yawn?* How enraging! "Am I *boring* you?"

He smiles apologetically, then nods to the left and right at the Tarantula Men holding him. "Maybe we should talk. But first, get rid of your goons. You wouldn't want them to hear what I have to say."

You command the guards to chain him to the bed. They do as they are told and depart.

Peter stretches out on the mattress. For a prisoner, he seems awfully unconcerned. "I really envy you," he says. "You get so far *into* it, you can actually forget what's going on."

His words disturb you, and yet you say, "Continue."

"You. Me. Her. The three of us." He taps his chin. "I used to be the Purple Queen. You were the Brown Hunter. She was the Yellow Bishop. Then I was the White Dollmaker. You were the Blue Shaman. She–"

You turn away. "*Enough!* I don't have time for these games."

"No," he says, "that's the problem. We have too much time, and only for games."

You think about this for a moment. Then you sigh. "Say whatever else you've got to say."

"I love you. But I love her, too. Even though she doesn't care about me." He laughs softly. "She's still wild about you. And we're *never* sure how you feel about either of us! It's sad, really, and so very tedious. But at least we have our games! Tricks and terrors, puzzles and perversions. They make it all seem so glamorous."

You turn back to him, wiping at your eyes with the veil. "I think I liked it better when we were–" Were what? What? "–playing."

"Well, then," he says, "let's keep playing. But bring back the Cat Man. I made him the last time I was evil, and ... well, the game's more *interesting* when he's around. He's so deliciously treacherous."

You give him a small nod. Then you push another button on the nightstand and a new communications monitor rises out of the floor.

You square your shoulders. "Reanimate the Cat Man's corpse," you thunder, "and bring him to my antechamber."

Peter's reflection beams at you from the rounded silver edge of the monitor. How happy he looks. You open a door on the nightstand and bring out a corkscrew and a magnum of passionflower wine. Before long, you and your handsome prisoner are laughing and taking swigs from the big bottle.

There is a knock on the door. You purr, "Be back in a second," and then glide away from the bed. At one point, you glance back and give Peter a wink.

You enter your antechamber, where a Tarantula Man waits, holding the Cat Man in his arms. The little guy's head has been reattached, but he is still extremely groggy.

You open one of your zippers and take out a gold pill case and a shiny greenish-blue sliver of metal. The case holds a single hyperstrength super-energy pill, which you slip under the Cat Man's tongue. Then you slide the metal sliver – a cerebral implant – deep into his damp triangular ear.

These words you whisper into that ear: "Go into the next room, straight to the bed. There you will find a chained man and a stainless steel corkscrew. Use the corkscrew to remove the man's brain, a little bit at a time."

You smile to yourself. Pretty, silly Peter. You still can't believe that your false tears fooled him. Bored? Soon he will be *bored* out of his skull! Serves him right for acting so damnably sincere, so *real*. Ordinarily you like that sort of thing, but not when it's your turn to be the evil one.

# III. OUR CREATURE PRESENTATION

# Toadface

John Masters was always hungry. Hungry enough to eat a whale. That's all there was to it. He was on a high-protein, low-carbohydrate diet and so far, he'd lost fourteen pounds. At work, he found himself constantly looking up at the clock, wishing those sluggish mechanical hands would spin him closer, always closer to his next meal, so he could leave his computer monitor and hurry to the company cafeteria and wolf down a plate of meat – any kind of meat – and some green vegetables.

Every evening after work, he would stop at the Pantheon Coffeehouse to enjoy a sugar-free caramel mocha latte. It was hot, rich, creamy and altogether wonderful, and it didn't break any of the rules of his diet. The coffeehouse was also a great place to hang out because some of his friends and coworkers went there, so there was usually someone to chat with while he enjoyed his drink. The walls were covered with loaded bookshelves, so if none of his friends were there, he could at least find something to read.

One night, he stopped by the coffeehouse and saw Meg, a project manager from work. She was very pretty, with green eyes, black hair and a friendly smile, and Masters often thought about asking her out for dinner. He hadn't done so yet because he had a couple worries holding him back: he was still about twenty pounds overweight, and he was ten years older than her. Maybe she didn't consider him attractive.

Masters walked up to her table. "Hi! How's life been treatin' ya?" He waved a hand toward the other chair at her table. "Are you here with somebody?"

"No, go ahead and sit down," she said. "Well, we have a new director in our department. She works from eight a.m. to eight p.m., so of course she expects the rest of us to work around the clock, too. She must have the words 'salary' and 'slavery' mixed up – she thinks they mean the same thing."

"Tell me about it. My director is the same way. I think he just sleeps under his desk at night." Master took a sip of his drink and then continued. "He's always asking me to do things outside of my regular

50

duties. Last week he asked me to fix his computer – as if I knew how. I just called one of the guys in technical support."

"Makes sense. So what was wrong with it?"

Master smiled. "Loose nut near the keyboard."

Meg shook her head slightly toward the other side of the room. "Speaking of loose nuts," she whispered, "look over there. The booth near the men's room."

Masters lifted his mug to sip from it, and also to hide his face as he glanced in that direction.

The man in the booth had gray-white hair and a greasy, heavily wrinkled face, with huge, startled black eyes, a thick-lipped mouth and a puffy double-chin.

"He looks like the frog prince," Masters whispered.

"More like the toad king," Meg replied softly. "Maybe he's on the same diet as you. Earlier, he was eating a tuna salad sandwich, but he just ate the tuna salad and didn't touch the bread. No, I take that back – he did touch it, he just didn't eat it. He licked off all the salad gunk. So how's your diet coming along?"

They began to talk about his meal plans. Masters told her what foods he was allowed to eat and which ones were strictly out-of-bounds. He told her about some of the ways he prepared different foods to make them more interesting, since boredom was the usual reason for people straying from diets.

"So would your diet help me with my thighs?" Meg asked.

"Your thighs are fine," he replied. He then lowered his voice. "If you want a second opinion, ask old Toadface. He's coming this way."

A moment later, the thick-lipped man was standing over them. Masters noticed that he had a flabby, pear-shaped physique, probably from licking up too much salad gunk. The man's shirt was wet and stained around the armpits.

"I wasn't eavesdropping," Toadface said in a high, nasal voice, "but I happened to overhear you two talking about some diet. May I join you?" Without waiting for a reply, he grabbed a chair from a nearby table, pulled it over and sat down. "I'd like to hear more about this diet. It sounds extremely interesting."

"Basically, it's all about eating protein." Master didn't want to explain the whole complex matter to this bizarre man, so he decided to give him the condensed version. "You just eat a lot of meat and some vegetables, and no sugar or complex carbohydrates. Drink plenty of water and the weight just melts off."

"The water wouldn't be a problem. Can it be any sort of meat?"

Toadface blinked his wide eyes with rapt curiosity.

"Yes, I think so," Masters said. "After all, meat is meat."

The man cocked his head to one side. "But do some meats have more protein in them than others?"

"I suppose so." Masters had never thought about it before. "I guess lean meat would have more protein in it, since there's less fat content."

The man smiled, revealing an abundance of yellowed, oddly narrow teeth. "But if the animal – the source of the meat – ate a lot of protein itself... Then it would probably contain even more protein. Yes?"

Masters couldn't bear to look at that hideously eager, hungry smile a second longer, so he glanced at his watch, pretended to be surprised at the time, and stood up. "Wow, I almost forgot. There's a movie on TV tonight I'd really like to see. I'd better get going."

"Yeah, I'm running later myself," Meg said. "See you at work, John." She gave him a big hug – something she'd never done before. He wondered if it would be okay to give her a little kiss, a peck on the cheek. But no, not with Toadface standing by.

Masters watched her leave, lost in thought. Toadface said, "What's the name of the movie?"

"What movie?" he replied without thinking. Then he remembered his impromptu lie, but it was too late.

Toadface was clearly upset. His mouth stretched wide in an ugly grimace. Then the grimace turned into a vicious smile as the man looked down from Master's face. "You just came from work, didn't you?"

With a rush of panic, Masters realized he was still wearing his name tag. JOHN MASTERS, ACCOUNTING. INNSMOUTH QUALITY CONSTRUCTION.

There was nothing for him to say, so he just turned and walked away from the table, dismayed that the clammy creep now knew his name and where he worked.

* * *

Later that night, Masters fried some chicken and made himself a salad. He wondered if Toadface would give him any trouble. Would the flabby freak suddenly show up at his office?

Masters worried about visiting the coffeehouse again. He'd never seen Toadface before, but perhaps the weirdo would start hanging out there, ready to make trouble.

He decided the best thing to do would be to start visiting a new coffeehouse for a little while. Surely another place would be able to make him a sugar-free caramel mocha latte. How hard could it be?

Later, with bedtime drawing near, he made sure all the doors and windows of his rented house were locked. After all, anybody who knew his name could look up his address in the phone book. As he double-checked the last window, which happened to be in the kitchen, he looked out to admire the ocean.

He was relatively new to Innsmouth. He'd moved to the city for the job a year ago, and he rather liked this quaint seaport community. His new place was on a hill with a nice view of the Atlantic from the rooms on the east side.

As he looked down at the rolling waters, he noticed a couple walking on the moonlit beach. The fact that they were down there at eleven-thirty didn't surprise him. People always seemed to be walking down there, no matter what the hour.

Did Toadface ever walk the beach? As he though about it, it occurred to him that he'd noticed other funny-looking folks around town. Some of them even had that same bulgy-eyed, puffy face – though most were not as extreme as Toadface's. Maybe it was some sort of disease or hereditary condition.

He went to bed and drifted off to sleep. He dreamed about following a cat through the mall – for some reason it was very important for him to catch that cat. Then the cat was gone, and he found himself speeding through murky ocean depths, teeming with purple and black eels.

He ended up in the corner of an underwater coffeehouse, where instead of mugs filled with java, the bulbous-eyed clerks gave their customers large shells filled with squirming chunks of freshly minced sea-worms. And really, the business wasn't set in a house – it was in a cave, lit by ropy growths of luminous seaweed festooned upon the walls.

Everyone there was humanoid, and that was the most normal adjective anyone could apply to them. They were all naked, and covered with a variety of aquatic adornments – warts, gills, fleshy fringes, even tentacles. Some had hair, but most were bald, and a few heads were topped with finlike crests.

From out of a side corridor drifted Toadface, grinning hugely. He too was naked, revealing flapping gills in his armpits. The space between his legs held a bizarre cluster of pulsing, elongated lumps.

"Okay," Masters said. "I'm ready to wake up. I'm willing myself to wake up right now. Right now. Right now. So how come I'm not waking up?" His words sounded impossibly clear – but then, this was a dream, wasn't it?

Toadface laughed. "You'll never wake up. Your soul is down in Innsmouth's most prestigious suburb. Lucky you!" The creature's mouth didn't move as he talked. The words seemed to be sounding in Master's mind.

"What are you telling me?" Masters said.

"I'm telling you that this is no dream." Toadface drifted closer. "The body loosens its grip on the soul during sleep. It was quite easy for me to draw your soul down to our lovely little grotto. It is a special talent of mine." His bulging eyes grew even wider with insane glee. "And you shall remain forever in this sunken realm, where the Silent Ones rest in eternal slumber."

"Hell, no!" Masters said. "I'm not staying down here! I'll just go back into my body."

"Not likely!" Toadface cried. "Your body is dead now. It has no soul. You are a ghost, a phantom, a spectre! I shall go and eat that delightful high-protein body of yours. I've decided to try out your diet." The creature winked at him. "How do you like this little adventure? Much more exciting than any movie. Of course, you made up that whole movie excuse, didn't you?" He waggled his fingers at Masters. "Time to go – dinner time!" Cackling uproariously, he turned and drifted down another corridor.

"Wait!" Masters shouted. Suddenly an eel swam near him, and he raised his hand to shield his face. He screamed with shock when he saw that his hand was composed of shimmering blue motes. He looked down – his body was now a man-shaped cluster of tiny lights.

He suddenly realized that Toadface was getting away. He flung himself forward through the water, and found that he could move quite fast. He zipped down the corridor and saw the flabby weirdo a short distance ahead of him. He followed him out onto the ocean floor. "Get your fat toad-ass back here!" he cried. "You think you can just drag me to this underwater freakshow, laugh in my face, tell me you're going to eat my body, and then just leave me stranded at the bottom of the sea? Is that the deal, Toadface?"

The bug-eyed man stared back over his plump shoulder. "Don't call me that! Go away! I don't want you following me!"

"Oh, that's rich!" Masters said. "So now *I'm* bothering *you?* You sure didn't think this thing through!" He surged forward and leaped onto Toadface. But as soon as he touched the freak's skin, a curious sensation rippled through him. It felt like a sort of cold tingle – and it seemed to convey a message. It was like jiggling the handle of a locked restroom door: the message clearly indicated that the space in question was OCCUPIED.

"Give it up!" Toadface crowed. "I'm awake, so you can't get into me!" He flapped his arms and swam away.

"Oh, is that the deal?" Master said, right behind him. "So I can get into somebody who's sleeping, right? You really are stupid, Toadface – you told me too much!"

"Maybe I did – but I'm still going to eat your body! And it's dead, so even if you follow me to it, you can't get back in!"

"Then I'll haunt you forever, you ugly bastard!" He continued to pursue Toadface, past slime-covered rocks and huge, pinkish-gray stone pillars etched with images of fish-headed people with tentacles for arms.

"Hey, what is this place?" Masters said.

Toadface didn't say anything, but he turned his head to shoot a frantic glance to the left. Masters followed his gaze, and saw that the freak had looked toward a ruined building made from pillars and cracked slabs of that pinkish-gray stone. It looked like some sort of temple from an old gladiator movie. Except the temples in those movies weren't covered with carvings of fish-people.

Then he remembered Toadface's words from that bizarre underwater coffeehouse: *this sunken realm where the Silent Ones rest in eternal slumber.*

He turned to the left and rushed toward the temple.

"Where are you going?" Toadface screamed. "Get away from there!"

"Not a chance!" Masters said. He entered the seaweed-shrouded maw that was the temple's entrance. He rushed through the curving halls of a strange stone maze, and was surprised to find that he could tell where he was going, even though he had to be in utter darkness. Apparently this new form of his didn't need light to see. It seemed to sense the contours of the world around him.

And he was able to sense something else: some being was indeed sleeping in this deep-sea maze. If what Toadface had said was correct, he could slip into a sleeping body. There might be someone or something else in that body, but so what? He wouldn't bother waking it up.

Toadface had said these Silent Ones were slumbering for eternity. Maybe he'd be able to borrow one of their bodies. It would be like driving a car with the owner sleeping in the backseat.

Suddenly he heard Toadface, not too far behind him. "You don't know what you're doing! Get out of here *now!* I'll find you a different body, I promise!"

Masters laughed. "Oh, yeah – like I'm going to make a deal with you!" He rounded a corner and suddenly found himself within a large chamber with a high vaulted ceiling. In the center of the chamber stood an enormous altar, upon which rested –

Hell, what *were* those things? There were three of them, each about eighty feet long, with flat-topped, snakelike heads, fishy faces, blubbery lips, lacy gills, bloated bodies, sinewy tentacles for arms, and legs like those of a giant iguana on super-steroids.

Masters felt dizzy with an emotion that was hard to place. Exhilaration? Horror? A little of both? He used to think his old human body was too fat and unattractive. Now he was about to climb into something definitely worse – and yet infinitely better, because it was clearly powerful and quite *alive*. He could feel the life-force pulsing forth from it, like heatwaves from a glorious summer sun.

He looked over the selection of bodies, picked the biggest one, and slipped in with a tingle of delight.

Almost instantly he could sense the presence of another soul – the body's true inhabitant. But that soul was asleep, and as he studied that strange, cold entity, gently prodding it, he realized that it was lost in dreams, embedded in some sort of cosmic coma, far deeper than any ocean.

"Get out of there!" Toadface shouted. "That is the hallowed body of G'hlaballa – you are perpetrating an unforgivable blasphemy!"

Masters willed the tentacles of his new body to move – he pictured them rising from the slab, swirling and flexing.

And they did. Some force or spell was compelling the body's true soul to sleep, but apparently that power only held sway over the soul – not the body. The driver was indeed asleep in the backseat. But the motor was still running.

He wrapped one of the tentacles tightly around Toadface.

"No! Stop!" the flabby pest squealed. "What are you going to do?"

Masters rose off of the slab. He battered at the wall with his free tentacle, pounding until he'd created a hole large enough to serve as an exit. He stepped out of the temple and began to walk across the ocean floor.

He walked aimlessly, carrying Toadface like a child toting a filthy old doll. He lost track of time as he admired the beautiful plants and interesting creatures of this strange realm. He felt remarkably at peace now that he had such a strong body. There was nothing in the world that could hurt him.

Eventually he found himself near the shore. He could discern the full moon through the water. He surfaced and saw that he was near an empty stretch of beach.

He looked at Toadface. The soggy, ugly thing wasn't moving. The little man still had a heartbeat, though, so he was simply unconscious. Perhaps Masters had been squeezing too tightly.

He thought about what to do with Toadface. The vicious freak had some kind of strange power over souls, and knew how to separate them from the flesh.

Masters could easily kill Toadface, but he didn't want that rotten bastard's soul to part from its corpse and start following him around like a rabid puppy.

He looked around and saw, in the distance, the lights of Innsmouth. He knew of a location on the outskirts of the city where he'd find the answer to his problem. He began walking.

Thirty minutes later, he stood at the edge of a warehouse construction site. He stuck Toadface's body into the thick, wet concrete of the building's foundation. He pushed the flabby form down deep, until it could go no further.

And there he left it – body and soul.

Suddenly he felt extremely hungry.

From where he stood, he could see both Innsmouth and the open sea. Both contained plenty of protein. But what sort of meat did he want?

Finally he began to trek back toward the sea. He didn't want to bother with little bites. That would only frustrate him. He needed real food and plenty of it. He felt utterly starved. Ravenous.

Hungry enough to eat a whale.

# The Loiterer In The Lobby
# (with Michael Kaufmann)

In my maddened ears still echoes the clickety-clack of frenzied digits pounding away at off-brand keyboards, and the drone of vile voices muttering strange litanies over static-ridden intercoms. When I close my eyes, I can see the furtive greenish glow of uncouth computer screens, and surely I can still smell the brain-blasting bitterness of simmering coffee-pots, whose contents were fresh back when the Earth was young. Strange are the ways of the Ancient Gods, but stranger still are the memos of hell-spawned office managers.

But let me start my story at the point most advantageous to the telling of all tales of extra-dimensional horror: the beginning. My name is Nathaniel Whereabouts, and in the Summer of 200–, I moved to the city of Arkham to attend Miskatonic University, to pursue a double major in Quasi-Religious Sociology and Quantum Metaphysics. But mine was not a rich family, and my scholarship funds began to dwindle at any astonishing rate.

One especially chill October morning, while reading the *Arkham Coupon-Clipper*, I happened to notice an ad that promised to augment my precarious finances:

NEED CASH? Available most evenings? Well-groomed? Professional manner? Quick typist? Computer skills? Interested in extra-dimensional devil-gods? Steady work is just a phone call away!

This was followed by a local number. Yes, I needed cash – desperately. And I was a quick typist, available most evenings, well-groomed, professional, and well-versed in all matters computer-oriented. And I thought extra-dimensional devil-gods were pretty darned interesting, too. In short, I felt I was a surefire candidate for the opportunity at hand.

My call was answered before the first ring had time to finish.

"Forbidden Works. Miss Ghoorish speaking. How may I help you?" The low murmur of her voice was like the silken burble of a moonlit stream.

I introduced myself and added, "I am currently in search of employment, for my current monetary situation is worrisome to the extreme."

"Broke, eh?" There was a faint rustling of papers. "Well, there's plenty of work out there. I run a temp agency for a rather specific line-up of clients. Come on down to the office, we'll hitch you up."

"And how might I find your fine establishment?" I enquired.

"Directions... Well, let's see..." She cleared her throat. "North of Arkham, the rolling hills echo at sunset with the languid cries of mournful whippoorwills. Follow the Snothman Turnpike through those hills, past the barren heath of which no one likes to speak. Turn left when you espy the red gleam of Mars and the mad twinkle of Antares over a forbidden barn in which an unspeakable act was committed over two-hundred and twelve years ago. Then go about a quarter of a mile, turn left at the bait shop, and look for a blue station wagon. Park next to it. Ring the melancholy doorbell of the strange dark house looming before you like an unhallowed monolith from some twisted dimension of dread."

"I'll be there in twenty minutes," I whispered.

* * *

I followed her directions to the letter, and it wasn't long before I was standing before that strange dark house, ringing that melancholy doorbell. I trembled when I read the message spelled out in a disturbing curlicue typestyle on the green plastic doormat – WELCOME, YOU FOOL.

Slowly the door opened.

I found it difficult to look directly at the woman who welcomed me into the vestibule. I suspected, based on my knowledge of Quantum Metaphysics, that the personage in question was skilled in obscure form of stealth technology. I knew that such scientific premises have been applied to supersonic aircraft – but people? Who knew? It was as though her very presence warped the infrastructure of time and space, so that a glance in her direction only resulted in a glimpse of a little cherrywood table to her immediate left. I found it impossible to determine *where* I had to look to actually see *her.*

"Come into my office," she said, and so I followed the slight creak of her footsteps into the depths of the house, past oak-framed portraits of people who must have been her family members, because I could not see them anywhere.

We entered a room filled with bizarre curios from ungodly dollar-stores. "You look like a good kid," she said. "Clean-cut. Trim. Reserved. Love the velvet waistcoat. You should do well with my clientele."

For the next half-hour, we discussed the terms of my employment. Her visual elusiveness began to grow on me, and I soon

59

found it rather charming – coy, almost flirtatious.

"Let's start you out with Piranha Health Foods," she purred. "Piranha – yes, a good place for you to stick your toe in the water."

\* \* \*

Piranha Health Foods was located in an ill-famed strip mall off the Shoggoth Express. The store was part of an international chain that sold all-natural foods, homeopathic remedies, and hand-carved fetish dolls.

I began work there the next night, to help them to catch up with clerical duties after-hours. Basically, my duties included typing, bookkeeping, and preparing reports on a series of experiments being conducted in the Amazon rainforest.

My supervisor, Miss Blubb, was an obese woman with three chins, deepset green eyes, and short blonde hair highlighted a gentle sky-blue. She had an enormous belly and tree-trunk legs, yet her chubby arms and petite hands were far too small for her body, and she kept them folded tidily atop her mountainous bosom.

I had a black metal desk in a back storage room that doubled as a work area, filled with filing cabinets, bins of dried goods, and shelves of jars, bottles and boxes. Every few days, a branch office in South America would e-mail me the results of their rainforest experiments, and I would download the information, correlate various statistics, and present the results to Miss Blubb.

"These statistics related to the tikkuni vine experiments are fascinating," I said to Miss Blubb one evening. "But I am not quite sure what they are hoping to achieve in applying the toxic juice of the berries to cell samples. One would think they were trying to encourage genetic mutation..."

Miss Blubb gave me a small smile. "The ways of research are complex. One must calibrate a far-flung assortment of theorems to arrive, ultimately, at the truth."

"And what is the truth?" I whispered with nameless dread.

"How does one define truth?" she replied. "It is like trying to define 'air.'"

"But 'air' is very easy to def–"

Unfortunately, 'def–' merely provided a misspelled reference to the sort of ears my comments fell upon, for Miss Blubb had already slammed the door on her way out.

\* \* \*

"Miss Blubb speaks very highly of you," said Miss Ghoorish, the next time I didn't see my temp service supervisor. "If you like, I can also get you a few evening hours every now and then at Medusa Cosmetics."

"But I don't know anything about cosmetics," I said. "Cosmology, yes. But not cosmetics."

"You won't be handling any of the make-up," she said. "Just paperwork. Too bad you have such a good complexion – they also make flesh-tinted acne medication, and I could have arranged a discount for you. You'll be working for Miss Vreck, a dear friend of mine. Who knows, it might lead to a permanent position. Yes, if you are interested in a solid career, you should take a look at Medusa."

\* \* \*

The corporate offices of Medusa Cosmetics were located on the thirteenth floor of a legend-shrouded bank building. They didn't sell any of their beautifying wares in those offices – there they simply stored, updated and tabulated paperwork from salons worldwide.

Miss Vreck was a bone-thin woman with large, yellow eyes and cheekbones so sharply sculpted, I feared they might break through her skin if she smiled too quickly. She wore her thick black hair piled high, and her long nails were always painted bright neon-green.

One of my duties was to assist in monitoring messages sent by e-mail regarding customer complaints. I compiled and referenced the information by several categories, including the nature of the complaint and the possible side-effects of various products.

The majority of complaints were from customers who had misused their purchases, resulting in temporary irritation. Others were obviously allergic reactions that would pass with time. But some of the complaints were of a more insidious nature. For example, what could be done for the woman whose wrinkle concealer had caused gill-flaps to open up along her jawline? And were there any pat answers for the young Goth gentleman whose use of Midnight Mystery No. 7 eyeliner had resulted in transparent eyelids that actually served as optical filters, allowing him to see people's auras?

I was worried that those cases might result in lawsuits, but Miss Vreck did not seem concerned. "Can these folks really claim damages?" she said. "Why, to my notion, both individuals were actually enhanced. Certainly neither has any cause for complaint."

\* \* \*

And so the days and weeks passed, well into winter. Some evenings, I put in my hours at Piranha Health Foods, and others, I tended to my duties at Medusa Cosmetics. During the day, I absorbed precious knowledge as I pursued my studies in Quasi-Religious

Sociology and Quantum Metaphysics.

But during that long winter of busywork and scholarly endeavor, I began to notice subtle yet disturbing parallels between my various interests and occupations.

For example, well is it known among students of Quasi-Religious Sociology that the now-extinct K'tunga people of the Amazon used to worship a sloth-limbed, potbellied, praying-mantis-headed, web-spinning deity named C'zog-Kamog. Indeed, no meeting of any group of Quasi-Religious Sociologists is complete without an in-depth discussion of the serrated stone knives used by the high-priests of C'zog-Kamog to relieve their sacrificial victims of the burden of skin, their god's favorite comestible.

Plus, rows of ancient symbols carved into the walls of a certain guano-streaked cave on the Yucatan peninsula clearly indicate that the god preferred to eat flesh that – to roughly translate an especially cryptic phrase – "grew like the beetle-swarms of the k'bongah tree." Many Quasi-Religious Sociologists believe the phrase in fact refers to skin that is experiencing rampant genetic mutation.

In the course of my studies, I also chanced upon a shocking reference in a textbook by the esteemed Dr. Emil Matapathamos, suggesting that the K'tunga people, before regular sacrifices, used to smear their imprisoned victims with the juice of tikkuni berries.

I mentioned these matters to Miss Ghoorish at one of our regular meetings.

"Well, that's all very interesting," she said, "but what does all that have to do with the cost of sprouts in Brussels?"

"Don't you see?" I said. "C'zog-Kamog enjoys eating the flesh of victims smeared with the juice of tikkuni berries. Piranha Health Foods is currently studying the chemical properties of that juice, which is roseate in color. In fact, the visual effect of that juice smeared on human flesh *would not be unlike that of make-up.*"

"'Would not be unlike'?" she repeated. "Why didn't you just say it 'would be like'?"

"You are missing the point! Medusa Cosmetics sells make-up – and sometimes, that very make-up brings about inexplicable physical changes. Or should I say, 'mutations,' Miss Ghoorish?"

"Nonsense," she said, and she may very well have waved a hand dismissively, too. "You are raving like a talking parrot who has eaten a cracker covered with hallucinogenic mold. What utter poppycock!"

"Well then, cock your ears at the statement about to pop from my mouth!" I exclaimed. "I did a little digging ... a little rummaging around in the malodorous bottoms of certain long-forgotten filing cabinets ... and I learned this mind-reeling, little-known fact: Piranha Health Foods and Medusa Cosmetics are both owned by a corporation called SHATROCK Research. The very fact that SHATROCK is spelled in all capital letters has me aquiver with sinew-snapping terror."

"Then you scare easily. You simply must abandon this ridiculous line of inquiry. No good can come of probing so deeply down such dark, twisted passages."

I looked her straight in the supposed area of her eyes. "Be that as it may – but probe I must."

\* \* \*

The next night, as I was compiling some statistics at Piranha Health Foods, I noticed that Miss Blubb – who usually was cloistered away in her private office – was always doing some task within a feet feet of me. Had Miss Ghoorish mentioned my investigations to her?

Plus, when I went out into the lobby to get a candy bar from the snack machine, I espied a tall, thin figure standing in the shadows between the coffee machine and an especially tall potted plant with reddish-orange carnivorous blossoms.

I saw the figure a moment after I had slipped my money into the snack machine. I quickly made my selection and retrieved my purchase from the chute. But when I turned to address the loitering stranger, he was gone. I even went over to the coffee machine, to see if the interloper had slipped further into the shadows, but the person was gone, and the plant snatched my candy bar.

But that was not the end of my problems. When next I put in my time at Medusa Cosmetics, Miss Vreck always seemed to be hovering near, her alarming yellow eyes turned upon me. When my work was done and I was passing through the lobby on the way out, I thought I saw that same tall, thin personage standing next to a cut-out display of actress Magda Poppelopika holding a jar of Skin-So-Tite Anti-Wrinkle Cream. The figure slipped into the shadows behind the display. By the time I reached the cut-out, the lurker was gone.

I gazed with dread at the picture of the skin cream jar on the display, for that evening, I had managed to sneak a look at some ingredient inventories when Miss Vreck had tip-tapped off on her nail-thin stiletto heels to visit the little girls' room. To my horror, I had ascertained from examining the ingredient sheets that Skin-So-Tite contained a high percentage of the juice of the tikkuni berry.

* * *

Peaceful is the sleep of the blissfully uninformed, in that it is unencumbered by hell-wrought portents of doom.

Mad dreams swirled through my brain that night. My somnolent cranium was filled with images of happy housewives slathering their pleasant faces with loathsome dollops of moisturizing cream, which transmogrified their mundane visages into nightmarish clusters of tentacles, polyps, eyestalks, and other assorted googlies. Then – oh, the horror! – I dreamed of a certain vile, eons-old, praying-mantis-headed abomination. This uncouth monstrosity took rapturous delight in feasting on the outlandishly mutated flesh of those poor, innocent women.

Thank the merciful heavens it was only a dream ... or rather, a nightmare ... or who knows? Maybe a prophetic vision. At any rate, I woke up drenched in sweat, clutching at my pillow like a lovesick cheerleader.

Moonlight was streaming through the bedroom window ... but then, it was a one-room apartment, so it was also my kitchen and living room window. Outside in the yard, the wind whipped at the barren twigs of a lone catalpa tree. And beside the tree – There! Yes, there in the snow stood that strange, silent figure – that elusive messenger of doom from beyond the gateway of sanity – the Loiterer in the Lobby.

So I waved.

* * *

"You will have to forgive me for following you," the Loiterer said. "But I, too, am a seeker of ancient mysteries, and in my recent investigations of certain Arkham businesses embroiled in the ways and doings of certain extra-dimensional devil-gods, it came to my attention that you are employed by two such establishments, and so you might be privy to certain information that might be indispensable to a certain individual. Namely, me."

The Loiterer and I were in a coffee shop a few blocks from my home. The night before, when he had stood by the catalpa tree, I had gone down to meet him after waving to him, and we had then scheduled our little coffee klatch. Though to be sure, we would not be exchanging cinnamon roll recipes.

I was disconcerted by the fact that the Loiterer wore a veiled hood and black velvet gloves and would not tell me his name. The other patrons of the coffee shop seemed at ease with his eldritch presence, for as he told me before we'd ordered our coffee, he was a regular there, and sometimes he read his poetry on Open Mike Night.

He sipped his coffee through a straw he had slipped through the veil's folds. "I take it you are familiar with SHATROCK Research?" he whispered.

"I only know that they own both Piranha Health Foods and Medusa Cosmetics," I said. "I also have darker suspicions about their nefarious workings, but such matters may not be the stuff of polite coffee conversation."

"Oh, you mean the skin-eating atrocities of C'zog-Kamog," he said with a shrug. "Sure, we can talk about that. No problem."

For the next several hours, we chatted with dread about that grotesque and abhorrent devil-god. The Loiterer revealed to me that SHATROCK Research was in fact, an international conglomerate helmed by a secret society of rich, high-power C'zog-Kamog worshippers. In fact, he confided, the initials of SHATROCK stood for a message of unbearable horrificness: *So How About Trying To Resurrect Old C'zog-Kamog.*

"But what does this unspeakable conglomerate hope to achieve?" I asked. "There can't be much money in worshipping ancient Amazon abominations."

He dropped his fork – for he had been eating a piece of spinach pie (and had been doing an admirable job of navigating the fork through the veils to his hidden mouth). "Money? Ha!" He pounded the table with a gloved fist. "They care not for money. Their goal is to bring C'zog-Kamog back into this world and be his priests, and to honor him by feeding him great swathes of mutated flesh! C'zog-Kamong had dwelt on the Earth thousands of years ago, but the high-priests of a rival cult had exiled the god to another dimension. But those high-priests are long dead, and all the most evil stars are in alignment, Jupiter and Saturn are the right distance from each other, and more importantly, that big conglomerate just bought a nuclear reactor capable of generating enough energy to rip through the fabric of time and space, creating a dimensional portal big enough to allow the passage of something really big – like, say, one jumbo devil-god. In other words, the way is being prepared for the return of C'zog-Kamog!"

A pimply-faced coffee shop clerk walked up to the table. "You're going to have it keep it down, sir."

"I want to!" the Loiterer cried. "I want to keep C'zog-Kamong down! But how can I single-handedly battle an international conglomerate bent on turning civilization into a demon's all-you-can-gnaw buffet?"

Another young clerk with a problem complexion came to the table. "Sir, we're getting complaints."

"I would hope so!" the Loiterer screamed. "People *should* be complaining! Major companies are plotting their destruction! They are being sold make-up filled with tikkuni juice, designed to turn their flesh into mutated face-sushi for a hideous alien gourmet!"

A third clerk, whose face had more craters than the lunar surface, joined his coworkers. "Sir, I may have to call the police."

"The police won't be able to help!" the Loiterer howled. Then he grabbed me by the arm. "Come with me, Nathaniel. The shocking complexions of these three helpful young men have given me an idea..."

\* \* \*

An hour later, the Loiterer and I were in his midnight-blue sedan, parked on top of a cliff overlooking a valley filled with glowing, humming buildings. An illuminated sign identified the property as SHATROCK Research, and block-style letters under the heading stated: Soulfully Helping All The Really Old, Coughing Kangaroos.

The cunning devils! Surely theirs was the perfect cover operation!

Suddenly I saw two women moving across a walkway between two buildings. "Look down there! Do you see those two?"

The Loiterer nodded.

"Those are my bosses, Miss Blubb and Miss Vreck. And do you not see a third individual with them?"

Again he nodded.

"That absence of a person," I said, "is Miss Ghoorish, my supervisor at the temp service. How it pains me to think that she could be part of this whole sordid business. Ah, my loitering friend, would that you could not see, as I never saw, the undetectable twinkle in her eye. Assuming that she in fact has eyes as we know them." I sighed. "So tell me. Why did you call every pizza restaurant in Arkham when we stopped off at your place?"

"I told each to deliver a pizza to this cliff," he said. "The items I picked up at my house will help us defeat C'zog-Kamog once and for all."

I looked in the back seat. "A big box filled with jars of acne cream? Some old book? A peanut-butter sandwich? How are those going to help?"

"The peanut-butter sandwich is for me. That spinach pie wasn't

66

very filling. You will see how the cream and the book will assist us in due time." He reached back and grabbed the ancient text – the *Necrodermicon*, or Book of Dead Skin. "The nuclear plant in the valley will provide all the power we need. And, here comes the bait!"

So saying, he pointed to a fleet of headlights coming down a snowy, moonlit road in our direction. We got out of the car. Two-dozen pizza delivery cars and trucks parked behind us. The delivery men and women climbed out of their vehicles, all very much confused. The reflected glow of the headlights made their pimply faces gleam hellishly.

"The poor creatures," the Loiterer whispered. "Their youth, combined with the oily vapors hanging in the air of their pizza parlors, have given them the complexions of a legion of doomed souls."

"Oh, they're not that bad," I said. "Well, most of them aren't, anyway."

"Young people!" the Loiterer shouted, holding out the box of acne cream. "To reward you for making tonight's delivery, I would like to give each of you a jar of this special acne cream, which is flesh-tinted, to conceal even the most stubborn blemishes."

Tearful cries of happiness could be heard as the young people rushed to claim their jars. As they blissfully rubbed on the cream, the Loiterer began to chant from the book.

"H'ja C'zog! Trojdoth sloggog m'grob'lok!" he intoned. He then turned to me and whispered, "I'm opening a dimensional gateway. Look toward the nuclear plant."

I did as he said, and gasped with shock. Glowing ribbons of vibrant energy were swirling up into the sky, where they combined in a brilliant vortex of glowing green fire.

"Pretty," I said.

"N'kraa k'baal pthogg!" the Loiterer cried. "Praggola tazogg! Fghala p'taar!"

"Now what are you doing?" I said.

"I'm telling C'zog-Kamong that there's plenty of mutated skin down here, if he's hungry."

"I don't know if I approve of your use of innocent pizza delivery people as bait. And mutating their faces isn't very nice."

"No pizza courier is perfectly innocent," he said cryptically. "Besides, their complexions are so terrible, a little mutation might help. It sure couldn't hurt." Suddenly he cried out, "Kablog! Kablog! A'kee! P'tuui!"

"Was that a protective spell from the crypts of the pre-Atlantean serpent kings?" I speculated.

"No, just clearing my throat." He then raised his hands over his head. "Rog-Sagor! P'thall segrog panaka! C'zok c'zop C'zog-Kamog!"

I noticed movement down in the valley, and saw that Miss Vreck, Miss Blubb, and a gap between them that had to be Miss Ghoorish were all leading a band of armed guards out of the power plant. Miss Blubb pointed a plump forefinger directly toward us.

"You must hurry!" I urged. "Gun-toting foot-soldiers of doom are heading this way, and bullets have no place in my scholastic endeavors – or my body, for that matter."

As reply, the Loiterer simply pointly overhead.

The energy vortex had actually drilled its way *into and beyond* Night's yawming chasm, revealing a *darker darkness* – a *black blackness* – a *more abysmal abyss* beyond. And from out of that rip in the eternal void peered a horrifying alien visage, in a manner similar to that of a tiny tabby kitten peeking out of the pocket of a kindly grandmother's terrycloth bathrobe. Except, of course, a lot more evil.

The enormous praying-mantis head of Czog-Kamog gazed down at the greasy-faced pizza purveyors and licked its razor-sharp mandibles with an ichor-dripping forked tongue.

Meanwhile, the armed guards had found a narrow trail leading from the valley to the top of the cliff, and were ascending rapidly, led by those three maddened mistresses of mayhem.

"Danger of dangers! Horror of horrors! Monster of monsters!" I gushed. "My friend, how are you going to stop that rampaging blasphemy from beyond the ghoul-haunted corridors of time?"

"How? How, you ask?" The Loiter shrugged. "Like *this.*"

With those words, he slammed the book shut. The dimensional gateway instantly whipped shut as well, cleanly snicking off the head of C'zog-Kamog.

The oversized noggin plummeted to the earth, crushing Miss Blubb, Miss Vreck and I'm assuming Miss Ghoorish, too, just as they reached the top of the trail.

"We did it!" I shouted. "Or rather, you did it and I came along for the ride!" I grabbed the Loiterer by the elbow and turned him around to shake his hand. At that moment, a stiff winter breeze caught his hood, blowing off the covering and revealing his features.

"Hey, you guys," the Loiterer shouted to the armed guards, who now had no reason to shoot at anyone. "Want some pizza?"

* * *

So now the world is safe, and I'm out of work.

I keep searching the want ads, and the internet, too, but I haven't found anything. I don't want to participate in sleep studies being conducted at the Witch House. I don't want to tutor any twins born in Dunwich. And I don't want to model for some artist named Pickman.

But I do know this: whatever I do in life, wherever my adventures take me, I will never be able to forget the face of the Loiterer in the Lobby, revealed to me when that ill wind blew back his hood.

Apparently he had once been a user of some product of Medusa Industries, for his face was covered with grey and yellowish-brown bumps and unsavory open sores. But that was not the worst to be seen.

For back in the coffee house, the Loiterer had been eating a piece of spinach pie, and – God in heaven! – when he smiled at me on that cliff, I was uttered appalled to see that he still had *small bits and strings of green plant matter lodged between his teeth, with an especially large piece of leaf stuck between his two front incisors.*

Oh, and he had three eyes, too.

-

# My Friend, The Electrical Lint Squid

There's a creature made of lint living in my house. I think electricity brought him to life. I have really thick carpets and the littlest bit of walking stirs up all kinds of static (I live near a power plant – that might have something to do with it). The creature looks sort of like a squid. He stands about thirteen inches high and has five tentacles, two beaks, and one glowing eye that doesn't blink. He can really wiggle around pretty fast on those tentacles. It's fun to watch.

I'm working in a record store – for now. Mr. Parnell, the manager, gave me two weeks notice yesterday. I guess a lot of the customers were complaining about me. Just because I cranked up the store's sound system a few times. And I yelled at some people after I rang up their sales wrong and they started whining all over the place.

I told the electrical lint squid the whole sad story and this is what he said in his crispy little voice:

"Here's the plan, Buddy. I think you should stick me in your knapsack, take me to the record store and hide me in the back room. Then, after everybody's gone home, I'll come out and use my special lint squid powers to put static on all the tapes and records and CDs."

"Big deal," I said. "They'll just send all that stuff back to the factory."

The electrical lint squid chuckled through one of his beaks. "That's where you're wrong, Buddy." He wiggled into my lap and put a tentacle on my shoulder. "You see, it'll be this special static. It's like a dog whistle – really high frequency. The customers won't be able to hear it, but it'll screw up their brain waves. It'll make them all scatter-brained and hyper and well, just plain crazy. They'll start seeing things, too, like imaginary friends and stuff. So they'll go crazy and have imaginary friends and get all goofy and weird and you know what? They'll all probably lose their jobs. You bet. That'll teach'em, Buddy."

I thought for a moment.

"Now wait a minute," I said. "Maybe I'm crazy. Mr. Parnell told me I was. So did some of the customers. Maybe I'm seeing things, too. Things like, oh, I don't know... you, perhaps? Maybe you're only an imaginary friend – or maybe you're using me to make others just like you. Fill me in, Mr. Electrical Lint Squid. I mean, really: what's the deal here?"

"That's a good question, Buddy," my little friend said. "A really, really good question. Let me give it some thought and I'll get back to you, okay? Great!" A beautiful electric-blue glow sprang up in his eye. "Now help me find that knapsack."

# The Monsters Of Enlightenment
## (with Michael Kaufmann)

*Excerpts from the journal of Dr. Laochanon Carlyle:*

### April 1

No April Fool here! In fact, there are days when I think I may be the only truly wise person on the face of the Earth.

And of course, it would be selfish of me to keep all my wisdom to myself.

So I won't.

### April 2

Look at all the fabulous creatures of lore. Centaurs, satyrs, the minotaur – and that's only Greek mythology! Myths? Ha, we are sadly *myth*-taken! Some people say, "Oh, a centaur was probably the first guy who rode around on a horse, and everybody else didn't know what to think!" Were the ancients all afflicted with myopia?

Life was better in days of yore, when there were more monsters. Think about it. For back then, there were also more great warriors, sorceresses, and prophets, too. For every Grendel there was a Beowulf. For every Medusa, a Perseus. You couldn't walk down the street in those days without bumping into a legendary figure. Yes, people were happier and more enlightened, for the presence of monsters made them more willing to accept fantastical notions. And to believe all that is fantastic is to be as one with the gods!

Happy flesh is far more willing to adapt, and ultimately, take on new configurations. Just look at the evidence! Why do placebos work? Because people believe in them. Why are some mystics capable of walking across hot coals? Because they believe they can. They are enlightened, and so their flesh complies with their mindframe, healing joyously and instantaneously.

In ancient times, some individuals with happy flesh became monsters (beginning the cycle anew) while others became the afore-mentioned wizards and warriors. But what, I wonder, brought to an end all the earlier Ages of Monsters (for surely there were several, in different times, in various parts of the world)? I shall have to look into that, to make sure that history does not repeat itself.

April 4

Last night on Channel 4 News-4-U, pretty-boy Steve Slate delivered yet another thoroughly puerile health news report. I guess we are all supposed to overlook his mush-mouth speech impediment just because he has a Hollywood heart-throb face and eyes as blue as a summer sky. "Sshientishtssh sshay that they have now unlocked the human genetic code, and will sshoon be able to manufacture curessh for jussht about every human illnessh – even canssher." Hogwash! Yes, if ignorance could be turned into soap and water, I could easily wash a whole herd of swine in Sshteve Sshlate'ssh sshpit-sshpraying sshpielssh.

True happiness and enlightenment are the real answers to preventing or even negating cancer without going through nasty chemo treatments. And genetic problems like sickle cell anemia and Down's syndrome and maybe even mental illnesses like schizophrenia – all that nasty rubbish could easily be avoided, too. How? By unlocking the gates of bliss! Happy flesh can work miracles, and knows not the torments of disease. All the world could, should and must become happier and healthier.

Other scientists are ready to jump fully-clothed into the scary deep-end of the gene pool. But, alas, they will surely drown and take others down with them! It's time to set the world straight.

I, Dr. Laochanon Carlyle, heir to the Carlyle Pickle Factory millions, shall gradually and subtly introduce new monsters into society, so that I might:

A.) Re-introduce the concept of malleable flesh into the global mindframe;

B.) Show other scientists the error of their ways regarding gene-splicing as a societal quick-fix, and;

C.) Eventually take Humanity by the hand and lead it into a rapturous new Era of Enlightenment.

Let the world's huddled masses tremble! And at the same time, let them realize that trembling is a precursor to both pain and pleasure!

Still, I wouldn't want to drive Humanity into a suicidal frenzy by unleashing a veritable swarm of rampaging Godzillas and Mothras. One must start on a more manageable scale. And, based on ancient lore, it would seem that hybrids have always captured the imagination....

April 17

I called a certain zoo director I know – he's desperate for funding! – and have attained all the specimens I will need for my crusade. The subjects, as currently envisioned for gene-splicing, are as follows:

Crocodile plus African Cockroach will create the Crocoroach.

Dachsund plus Timber Wolf will create the Wiener-Wolf.

Golden Hamster plus Albino Vampire Bat will create the Beige Hampire.

Cousin Greg plus Gorilla will create the Gregorilla.

That last combination is pretty much for my own amusement, because reeeeally, Cousin Greg isn't that much different from a gorilla. A gorilla just has less hair on its back.

All my new guests are staying in lovely, spacious enclosures on the grounds behind the mansion, near the swamp. It was my dear old grandmother, Annabelle Carlyle, who genetically engineered the first Extra Crisp-O-Licious Carlyle Sweet Pickle – the world-famous pickle that gave rise to the family fortune. And while I cannot condone the garage-mechanic attitude she'd had toward genetic tinkering (she wasn't much better than the most of the idiots I deal with these days), I can at least be thankful she left me all her money and this big old estate. And I am thankful, too, for Annabelle's secret pickle-juice recipe. Not only does it make the tastiest pickles known to the cosmos, but it also serves as a marvelous genetic emulsifier. The amazing properties of that sweet yet tangy ichor – oddly akin to the primordial soup of our world's youth! – allow me to whip together the trickiest of gene combinations.

All this pickle talk is making me hungry. I'm going to have an Extra Crisp-O-Licious Carlyle Sweet Pickle right now.

April 18

The sheriff paid a visit today. From his election posters, I'd figured him to be a much taller man. But he only came up to my shoulder.

Evidently he saw the trucks from the zoo when they came to drop off my guests. It seems that it is not entirely legal for me to own an albino vampire bat, a crocodile, a timber wolf, and a gorilla in this state. And yet it's completely legal to have a Cousin Greg! Go figure.

74

I tried to explain to him that they are all housed here in the interest of science, but he was a stubborn man, and I think he fully intended to fine me.

Sadly, a demonstration of why crocodiles make questionable household pets was required. But happily, I saved a little money on pet food, and that jaunty sheriff's hat looks awfully cute on the gorilla. And now there's a police car parked, out of sight, out of mind, at the bottom of the swamp.

April 24

I've gathered DNA samples from all my specimens. Now comes the most difficult part – the splicing.

You know, most people don't appreciate the complexity of gene splicing. They think it's just as simple as hacking a DNA strand apart, sticking the new genes in, and gluing it all back together. But it's hard. Very hard. All that stuff puts the micro in microscopic, and the cutting and gluing have to be done with enzymes, and so your eyes are stuck to the electron microscope all day.

This evening I went to the club and noticed that people seemed to be snickering at me. At one point, I caught my reflection in the mirror behind the bar and saw, to my embarrassment, that I had dark bruises around my eyes from grinding my weary old sockets against the eyepieces all day! And worst of all, my glasses only magnified the size of the bruises. I looked like a bug-eyed raccoon.

Fortunately, the beautiful and brilliant Elizabeth Belasco wasn't there. I still haven't worked up the courage to ask her to the Geneticists' Ball. I really don't know why I even bother going. True, technically I am a geneticist, but I really don't think of them as one of me. They are all just a gaggle of bumpkins trying to fine-tune delicate Swiss watches with monkey wrenches. But I do need some social outlet – I can't stay locked in my lab forever! My Bunsen burners might make me sweat, but still I long to be set ablaze by Elizabeth's fiery kisses.

But lately, she has been spending more and more time chatting with that awful phony Sanderson. What is he thinking – a monocle in this day and age? How pretentious!

The worst thing about Sanderson is that he finds it amusing to call me "Loco-non" – or more often, just plain "Loco." Well, surely this Loco has the motive to wipe the smug smile off that idiot's face.

April 27

I went to the club again tonight, and was about to ask Elizabeth to the Ball when that ridiculous poseur Sanderson whisked her away. Ooh, I'll get him. Someday one of my spliced pets will make goulash out of him.

Truly my flesh will never be happy until it finds itself snuggled next to that of the goddess Elizabeth. Does that mean I am not completely healthy? I would suppose so! I simply must win over Elizabeth to ensure my continued longevity – and hers, too, for I am sure I will make her equally happy.

I still remember the first time I saw her. She was lecturing at Lockeford University, and she looked so delightful in her lace-trimmed pink lab smock. She was presenting the results of her research on recombinant DNA and mammalian limb regeneration. Her findings were inconclusive, but I knew that my lifelong search for love had ended.

Speaking of love – how I would love to release a herd of Crocoroaches upon Sanderson! Or colony? Or perhaps a pride? Certainly a flock of Beige Hampires. And a pack of Wiener-Wolves. As for the Gregorillas... How about a stupor? Yes, a stupor of Gregorillas.


May 1

Went to the Geneticists' Ball.
Stag.
Again.
Elizabeth looked simply divine in a black satin gown with a double-helix pattern of sequins up the side.
"Laochanon, so nice to see you all dressed up!" she said as she toyed with a lock of her flowing red hair. I think she was being flirtatious! "You clean up pretty well!"
"But don't I usually look ... okay?" I asked.
"Certainly you do – you are a very handsome man! – but sometimes..." Here she lowered her voice. "...For a man of your wealth, you really should try to dress more fashionably. You know, like that cute Steve Slate on TV. The change would do you good. No offense, but darling, you wear far too much brown corduroy."
"Do I? It's a sturdy material, but for your sake, I will buy a fashionable new wardrobe and throw away all that awful

corduroy...though it *is* hard-wearing and dependable."

She blinked those gorgeous green eyes of hers. "And while you're at it, perhaps you should get contacts, like me. Those heavy glasses hide so much of your handsome face."

Later, I wanted to ask Elizabeth to dance, but that phony-baloney Sanderson wouldn't even let me cut in. He thinks he's such hot stuff, just because he knows how to cha-cha. Since when have men of science deigned to cha-cha? Did Einstein ever cha-cha, or tango, or lead a conga line of physicists?

At last year's ball, I tried to work up the courage to ask Elizabeth to dance. But I had a few drinks first, and I fear they'd turned into a few too many.

Damn that Sanderson! I predict he will be doing the Tonsil Two-Step with my Crocoroaches soon enough!

May 13

For most of my monsters, I'm growing them straight from ova, the way Nature intended. But with Greg, I think I'll just keep injecting him with the juice, just to see what happens. I'm telling him it's a vitamin supplement. Ha! Vitamin M – for Monster!

Who knows? Maybe it'll raise his IQ. And then he'll be able to lend a hand raising the others. I've given them all enhanced metabolic rates, so they should grow pretty quickly.

The highpoint of the day was a call from Elizabeth! "I was a bit surprised you didn't ask me to dance," she said.

"I wanted to," I assured her, "but that Sanderson wouldn't let me get a foot in edgewise."

"Well, I don't want to spark a rivalry between you two," she purred, "but it's all about survival of the fittest, as well you know!"

I must remember to go out and buy new clothes and contacts.

May 17

Greg is definitely smarter than before. He seems to have gone through the procedure fairly well, and the gene splice appears to have been mostly specific. His knuckles drag and his forehead slants far back – those traits haven't changed. But his grooming is better now, and he tends to want to groom me, too, which I'm not overly fond of.

The Beige Hampires are due in two more days. If all goes according to theory, they should have flaps of skin between their legs

77

that will allow gliding (not outright flight; they're too heavy for that). They also will have a sonic squeal, pointy incisors, and a thirst for blood. Ah, yes, havoc will be wreaked, and horror sown – but to a manageable degree. It's all part of the plan, in order for the new Era of Enlightenment to begin!

## May 21

The Beige Hampires are two days old now, and are looking good. Still pink and ugly as all get-out, they do have their skin flaps, and are nursing well.

The Crocoroaches are hatching now. Reptiles and insects have such a cold-blooded charm. For me to combine them in one beast – well, as much as one hates to brag, I do have to admit it was an act of sheer genius.

Another two weeks until the Wiener-Wolves are due.

Greg is now a full-fledged Gregorilla. In addition to his grooming fetish, he now has even fewer inhibitions regarding autoeroticism. Who'd have thought that was possible?

## June 4

The Wiener-Wolves were born today, all six of them. A nice-looking litter. No noticable differences from normal Dachsunds – yet! But certainly, when they get older, their wolfish fury and sinuous Dachsund bodies, combined with my genetic enhancements, will make them grow into the canine equivalents of dragons. The Crocoroaches look very much like young iguanas, except darker and shinier. More insectile qualities will emerge with time. Crocodiles and cockroaches are both hardy, resilient creatures – so hungry and relentless! The snouts of the Crocoroaches have an oddly segmented look about them... I shall have to keep an eye on that.

## June 25

It is now time for the next phase of my plan: introducing my little terrors to the world!

I sold some of the Crocoroaches to a pet store. The owner had a sharp eye – he could tell they weren't regular iguanas. So I told him they were rare Viennese Iguanas. He wants me to bring in more!

I decided to celebrate by buying those new clothes, per

Elizabeth's suggestion. And contact lenses. Maybe I should buy a cane, mahogany with a fancy gold handle. But then, forty might be too young for such an austere embellishment.

My face feels naked without my old glasses, and I shall hate to throw away all my trusty corduroy, but I must be willing to embrace change, if I am ever to embrace Elizabeth!

June 27

Dropped some Beige Hampires off at another pet store today. They're furrier now, and I'm sure the sixtyish woman who ran the place didn't notice their glider-skin flaps or their teeth. She was too interested in trying to pinch my ass, the naughty old dear! She gave both sides a tweak.

Two pinches in one day, when before I've never had any! I guess Elizabeth was right about the corduroy.

Nothing to do now but wait until the animals are cuddled in the unsuspecting arms of the public... Oh yes, and make new batches of all my little terrors.

June 28

Dropped the Gregorilla off at Aunt Cora's today. I didn't stick around to see her reaction. She should appreciate how much cleaner he keeps himself, and now maybe she'll be able to teach him how to take out the garbage and use the toilet. I'm not betting the farm, though.

July 5

Stopped back at the pet stores. All my masterful mutations have been sold! My, but I do good work! Actually, great work. Fantastic work. What a pity I can't tell anyone except you, oh journal mine!

July 13

The Crocoroaches I kept for further study are growing rather well. They eat a lot of frogs, though. I'm sure the folks who bought some at the pet store are beginning to wonder. People can buy all the crickets and even baby mice they want to feed their pets, but when they start having to buy big old feeder frogs – that's when they start to get wiggy.

I figured out why their snouts have that segmented look. The snout opens up and down, like any animals muzzle – but it also opens from side to side when the creature becomes upset! I noticed that today when a couple of the Crocoroaches got into a fight. When they open from side to side, they also automatically curve slightly inward, like mandibles. One of the two fighting creatures is especially bullish, with very thick shoulders. I shall call him El Toro!

I am assuming that the various mutant pets around town are eating well. Apparently there are many neighborhoods where small pets are suddenly being reported as missing. Oh boo hoo, where did Fluffy go? So far, it's all just a mystery. Excellent!

July 24

I've been releasing new batches of mutants out in the wild. Just to spice things up.

Meanwhile, here in town, the story is out. Some Beige Hampires attacked a telephone company repairman. Alas, his line has been disconnected forever.

The news team at Channel 4 News-4-U has figured out that the Beige Hampires are mutants, but they are assuming that the mutants are a natural product of evolution. Ha! As if Nature would ever take a turn down so wild a cul-de-sac! I wonder how the authorities would react if my amazing gorilla-man ever went on a rampage? Would they try to attack him with model airplanes, like a scaled-down King Kong? Would Aunt Cora ever forgive me?

July 26

Sshteve Sshlate did a story on the Beige Hampires, calling them Vampire Gerbilssh. The fool! He doesn't even know the difference between a hampster and a gerbil! But the good news is, Crocoroaches everywhere are sprouting antennae and biting off people's fingers, and their bloody antics were all the rage on the Six O'Clock News. I knew I could count on Sshteve to tell the world we're all in mortal danger from sshuch sshtartling freakssh of nature.

August 3

Attacks on neighborhood pets by my monsters continue unabated.

But apparently, the owners of the deceased pets are not overly incensed. Intriguing. A pit-bull attacks a pet rabbit and gets put to sleep. A Wiener-Wolf takes down a prize-winning collie and the neighbors all stand around to watch the show. Clips have even been compiled into a new TV special, *When Mutants Attack!* I'm not quite sure how to interpret such unexpected developments.

August 22

I was in the mall today and saw a stand selling trading cards of my monsters. Trading cards! There were about twenty customers there, mostly smelly little boys but a few girls, too. My fantastic creatures were supposed to become Humanity's newest and greatest pantheon – harbingers of the Era of Enlightenment – not amusements for snot-nosed urchins. What next? Will one of the networks turn my hungry abominations into a Saturday morning children's show?

August 27

There was an article in the newspaper about my creatures. It seems that some of the owners of my voracious hybrids have banded together and formed an entertainment corporation, with agents and everything. They're planning some Expos, selling tickets at $30 and up, where people can come to look at the monsters. Of course, there are plenty of monsters on the loose, but anybody who gets to see one of them up-close will probably end up dead. After all, the Beige Hampires are now as big as watermelons, the Wiener-Wolves are all four feet high at the shoulders and seven feet long, and El Toro is now eight feet tall. Fortunately, he and I have bonded – he eats straight from the palm of my hand! – so I have nothing to fear.

And Cousin Greg? Aunt Cora called to say he's ten feet tall now, and he just signed (with a big sloppy 'X') a contract with a big genetics firm as their company mascot. I guess he hasn't told Cora that I'm the one who turned him into a monstrosity. But then, maybe he hasn't figured that out yet! I'm rather upset he has hitched up with that firm, though. Here I'm trying to unveil the Era of Enlightenment and he's working for a bunch of backwards science schmucks. And guess who's the owner of that company? Dr. Phony-Baloney Sanderson! I'll get him yet. I'm training El Toro to attack a dummy wearing a monocle!

September 5

Elizabeth called.

Sanderson has asked her to marry him!

"I haven't said 'yes' -- but I haven't said 'no' either. What do you think I should tell him?" she asked.

I decided that a bold move was in order. "Tell him you are in love with me!"

"Oh, Laochanon," she murmured. "Should I? Perhaps you and I ought to have a serious discussion about all this some evening. Perhaps over dinner. You really are very dear to me. But so is he. You're both quite enthralling. If only I had more female friends. I could go out for drinks with them on Ladies' Night. Then all my high-heeled friends could help me decide what to do."

"If I had any male friends," I told her, "I would certainly go with them to that bar on Ladies' Night so all my friends could fall in love with all your friends. It would be like one big happy TV show. I suppose. I don't watch television. Well, except Nature specials on public TV."

"Oh! Did you see that show about stick insects last Sunday?"

"Yes, wasn't that marvelous...?"

And so we spent the next hour pleasantly chatting about stick insects, and then it was time for her to go to bed.

Fortunately, I do have one brawny friend who can help me in my quest to win Elizabeth's heart. It is time to put El Toro to work – and take Sanderson out of the running.

I just phoned the big phony – El Toro and I are having the monocled moron for lunch tomorrow!


September 6

What a day!

I escorted Dr. Phony-Baloney into the dining room. "So what do you make of all these odd creatures running around these days?" he asked. What indeed!

"They're all quite fascinating," I said.

"One of those bloodsucking flying things almost hit the windshield of my car," he said. "And I saw some of those horrible long dog-creatures chasing a deer through a field. They're loose in the wild, too. I dread to think what they'll do to the eco-system."

"Yes, that's something to think about," I said. "But more

importantly, what sort of impact do you think they'll have on society as a whole?"

"None at all, I suppose," he said with an effete little shrug.

"None?" I tried my best to maintain a sedate tone of voice. "You don't think they'll ... change the way people think or ... live their lives?"

"No, not in the least!" he said with a breezy wave of his manicured hand. "People are quite *used to them* already."

"Used to them?" I was agog. "How can anyone get used to such nightmarish abnormalities – such monsters?"

"Really, Loco," he said. "They're in all the papers, on all the magazine covers, and they're always on TV. Just yesterday Steve Slate arm-wrestled my company's gorilla-man for charity. A monster isn't a monster after people get used to it."

After he said that, I finally realized why all the earlier Ages of Monsters had failed. Their creatures had become commonplace. Awe and fear would have fallen by the side of the road after that. After that, people had probably felt quite comfortable hunting them down.

"Just out of curiosity," I said, "do you suppose there's any sort of creature that Humanity could *never* get used to...?"

"One that constantly changed," he said. "A life-form that was continuously transmogrifying and evolving. You know, like the one Elizabeth has created."

What? This was news to me. My dear Elizabeth was sharing information on her experiments with Dr. Phony but not with me? Needless to say, I couldn't let him know that.

"Yes, Elizabeth's experiments! Remarkable, aren't they?" I said.

"Remarkable? They're absurd! She's a darling woman, and of course I love her, but –"

That was the last straw. I raced across the room and threw open the doors to the chamber that held my most insidious creation. "Say your prayers, Sanderson!" I cried. "You may love Elizabeth Belasco, but she will never be yours! You shall instead experience the none-too-gentle embrace of El Toro!"

"Wha– Wha–" He stammered with fear. Music to my ears! My mighty monster reared up on its hindlegs and advanced, waving its scaly mandibles. But then Sanderson said, "Of course I love Elizabeth. She's my half-sister. But she told me never to tell you. Don't you see? She's been using me to make you jealous, to make you take action, step up to the plate–"

He stopped talking after El Toro stepped up to the dinner plate and bit his head off.

The bones, random chunks and stringy bits that remained after my hungry pet finished eating are now locked up in the trunk of Sanderson's car – at the bottom of the swamp.

I repeat: What a day!

September 7

On the downside, I've killed Elizabeth's half-brother. But on the positive side, I now know that she really likes me!

But I'm afraid Sanderson was right. People are getting used to my monsters. In fact, I saw on *Hollywood Tonight* that one of the Wiener-Wolves has been sufficiently tamed and is going to have a role in the upcoming sci-fi horror movie, *Devil-Dog of Mars.*

I'm going to Elizabeth's place tonight. I just got off the phone with her. Oh, but I was sly!

"Say, Elizabeth," I said casually, "what's the worst thing about being a scientist?"

"Backing into a Bunsen burner?" she suggested. "Developing a new virus and then catching it, resulting in an all-over body rash and four days of vertigo and diarrhea?"

"Well, I must admit those are bad..." I said. New virus? Is she really trying her hand at creating new life-forms, like Sanderson said? "But I was thinking of the loneliness. The terrible loneliness."

"The loneliness is simply awful," she said. "Say, would you like to come over tonight, around seven? I can show you a little project I've been working on. I've been meaning to show it to you – but I guess I've been afraid you'll think it's silly."

I decided to test the veracity of Sanderson's comment about her experiments. "You know, Elizabeth, Nature can get so boring sometimes. Take animals, for instance. If only they changed their shape more often. Wouldn't that be swell?"

"It certainly would! Oh, Laochanon, I'm so glad to hear you say that. In fact, I'd like you to come over at six instead of seven. Is that okay?" She then gave me directions on how to get to her home, and what to do once I got there (she has rather unusual living quarters).

So! I'll be visiting Elizabeth tonight – and we shall see what we shall see.

September 8

It's four o'clock the next day, and my mind is still abuzz with all

84

that happened last night.

I arrived at her home carrying a large jar of Extra Crisp-O-Licious Carlyle Sweet Pickles. She lives in the upper levels of a large warehouse, where she does most of her experiments. I noticed that all the building's windows on the bottom two floors had been boarded up. I took the back stairs up to her door and knocked.

She opened the door wearing her lace-trimmed lab smock. "Laochanon, so good to see you – and you've brought pickles! Come right in!"

Upon entering, I became immediately aware of loud rumbling sounds coming from some lower level in the warehouse. "Sounds like the building has indigestion!" I said.

"Oh, that's just the cat," she said. "Come and see Kitty!"

She then took my hand and led me down a long hall, which led to a sort of combination laboratory and observation deck. The room held a desk covered with papers, a work station cluttered with test tubes and beakers, and a control panel on a waist-high stand next to a window. This window looked down upon a large experiment area, which reminded me of a gymnasium, with its open stretch of hardwood floor and steel support beams at the sides. In the middle of that expansive floor were a large pile of hay and a tub of water. And there, rolling around in the hay – was Kitty.

I took one look and wanted to cry.

*That* was the sort of creature I should have been working on all along. The beast presented a nightmare vision so complex that the very sight expanded one's consciousness. It was awe-inspiring, whereas my puny hybrids... By comparison, one could really only call them *interesting*.

*That* was *exactly* the sort of entity I needed to lead jaded contemporary Humanity into a new Era of Enlightenment.

How to describe it... Picture a well-stocked zoo that has been caught in a hurricane. Cover the swirling, constantly changing mass of muzzles, rolling eyes, gaping mouths and thrashing limbs with a light layer of striped orange fur. I imagine a pet tabby's DNA had figured into the mix at some point. Pinchers, prehensile tails, fins and even tentacles kept popping in and out of the roiling mass of flesh.

"I'm really not satisfied with it," Elizabeth said. "It's too – frivolous, I think. I need to make it much more frightening. Plus, it has taken too long to reach adulthood. I'm looking for quick growth if I'm going to raise an army of them."

"Frightening? Quick growth? Army?" I was utterly mystified by these comments. "What do you intend to do with it?"

"Why, take over the world, of course. Fortunately, Nature has been producing a spate of ridiculous mutants lately. I think adding some of their DNA will do the trick, since they're all so ugly, and have a rapid growth rate." She then pushed a few buttons on the control panel.

Mounted on the ceiling high above Kitty was a steel box. When Elizabeth pressed the last button, a small door opened in the box and a hypodermic needle on the end of a telescoping robotic arm emerged. The arm reached down and gave Kitty a shot. Elizabeth pressed more buttons, and more arms and needles emerged, giving Kitty even more shots.

"That first shot contained DNA from some bloodsucking flying furballs – perhaps you've heard about them on the news." She looked down out of the window, studying Kitty for changes. "The DNA in the other shots came from those roving monster dogs, and those insect-lizards, and also an ape-man who works for Sanderson's genetics firm. And also, a couple shots of your company's pickle juice."

"What? My Extra Crisp-O-Licious Carlyle Sweet Pickle juice?" I cried. How in the world had she unearthed that particular secret?

"You probably don't remember," she said, "but at last year Geneticists' Ball, you got drunk, and around midnight you started telling me how your grandmother's recipe was just like primordial soup." She leaned closer. "That stuff's amazing! And the pickles are delicious."

A thought suddenly occurred to me. "A minute ago, why did you call all those mutants *ridiculous?*"

She shrugged. "Because they are. Oh, they're bizarre and most can be deadly, but they're pretty goofy, too. They look like they were created by a backwards eight-year-old with a Junior Scientist chemistry kit. Fortunately, they shall provide the raw material necessary to improve Kitty!" She gave me a wink. "Oh, and I even mixed in some genetic coding from Steve Slate – I'm afraid it would make me blush to tell you how I obtained that particular DNA sample. Now it'll have those commanding sky-blue eyes!"

"And a sshpeech impediment, too!" I shook my head sadly. "Suppose this eight-year-old you mentioned had only good intentions? What if he was only trying to bring forth a new Era of Enlightenment...?"

"Ha! A runt with a Messiah Complex! Boy, that would take the cake–"

At that moment, the window of the observation deck shattered as an orange-furred gorilla hand on the end of a scaly tentacle burst through. There was no cake for it to take, so it grabbed Elizabeth instead, and pulled her down into the experiment area.

Evidently it was time to feed Kitty.

I wasn't about to serve myself up as dessert, so I left.

All the television networks today have been filled with "We-interrupt-this-program" news alert about the rampaging scaly, furry, incredibly hungry, blue-eyed behemoth that burst out of Elizabeth's warehouse to destroy civilization. It's huge and round and simply rolls, crushing buildings, grabbing people with its tentacles, devouring everything in its path with its hundreds of mouths. And all the while it is growing and growing and growing.

Elizabeth was a brilliant girl, but she hadn't realized that it wouldn't be necessary to create an army of such creatures.

One is certainly enough.

September 9

That whole Era of Enlightenment plan definitely needs retooling.

In the meantime, I suppose I'd better try to preserve the human race. Otherwise, there won't be anyone left to enlighten.

If I'm going to save the world, I'm going to have to create a fresh new species of voracious parasite that will drain the life from that rampaging Kitty. But that shouldn't be too hard. On the way out of Elizabeth's laboratory, I grabbed a box of disks and some notebooks off her desk. No sense in losing all her valuable research. Once I've created a big batch of the parasites and they've taken care of Kitty, I'll mutate the parasites into some really high-class monsters and set the gears in motion for a new and improved Enlightenment plan.

Now let's see. I'll need some DNA from a giant African leech (good thing I have a jar of them in the back room), and a barnacle, and a mosquito – how about a tick? – and maybe a praying mantis.

I think it's going to rain. I hear thunder, riotous thunder, drawing nearer like an enormous bowling ball.

# IV. HOUSEHOLDS OF HORROR

# Eye Dew

On Sunday they got married and became completely different people. Even though they had lived together for ten years before the ceremony.

That happens, sometimes.

They had decided not to go on a honeymoon, to save money. And really, after ten years, most of the lust was gone anyway. They'd only married because they were tired of relatives griping at them. "When are you two going to get married? The state probably considers you married anyway – that whole common-law deal – so you might as well just get it over with."

As soon as they arrived home that night, she peeled herself out of her wedding dress and flung herself into the shower, to wash away her make-up, hair gel, even the fine golden body-glitter lightly sprinkled on her shoulders and cleavage. He just stripped off his tuxedo and flung himself straight into bed. Though most of the lust had departed, a bit of random randiness remained.

She emerged from the bathroom with an oatmeal-based beauty mask caked on her face and her hair up in curlers. "Oh, honey," she said, glancing at the manmade tentpole jutting up under the covers. "I don't have the energy for that tonight. I'm completely exhausted. Weddings are hard on a bride. Be a dear and bring in the gifts from the car. We don't want burglars breaking into the car during the night and stealing all our wonderful gifts. Can you do that? Right now?"

So he threw on some clothes, went out and brought in the gifts from the car. When at last he returned to the bedroom, she was already asleep, snoring like a trumpeting elephant with a sinus infection.

He wasn't tired, so he went out to the living room and watched the cartoon channel for four hours, until he fell asleep slumped in his armchair. He dreamed of wide-hipped cartoon wives with crying babies clinging to their meaty legs. The wives kept chasing their scrawny, crazy-eyed husbands with rolling pins, screaming orders at them. "Take out the trash, you bum! Wax the car! Do those dishes! I'm too tired from raising these damned brats of yours!" The husbands could only reply with frenzied cries of "Yes, dear! Yes, dear! Yes, yes, yes!"

In the morning after shaving, he weighed himself – he did so every day – and was shocked to see that he'd lost six pounds. He used to have a little bit of a paunch, but now his stomach was quite flat.

At the kitchen table, she was eating a huge breakfast of bacon, eggs, toast and orange juice. "You'd better hurry up," she said. "You're going to be late for work."

"Work?" He stared down at the bowl of cereal in milk she'd set out for him. The cornflakes were now cornmush. "We're on vacation for the next two weeks, remember?"

She waved a strip of bacon at him dismissively. "Vacation? What for? The wedding's over. I called your office and told them you'd be in, same time as always. I gave my office notice two weeks ago, so I'll just stay home preparing our future. That's what wives do."

She got up, grabbed his breakfast bowl and poured its contents down the garbage disposal. "You won't have time for that if you want to make it to work by eight."

At the office, he found his black plastic in-box piled high with financial reports to prepare – plus, his boss wanted him to work on increasing the internet traffic of the company website, even though he'd never worked on that sort of thing before and had no idea where to begin. He wanted to cry, but what kind of a man does that?

"You have a family to feed now," his boss said. "Once you become a family man, you have to work harder than ever before. That's the way of the world."

When he arrived home after three hours of over-time, she greeted him at the door, waving a paint scraper in front of his face.

"How am I supposed to prepare our delicious future meals looking at those awful off-white kitchen walls? That terrible color is sucking the life out of me." She put the scraper in his hand. "Be a dear and paint the kitchen Springtime Periwinkle Fantasy No. 12."

"But I just got home from work and haven't had a thing to eat since lunch," he said, slapping his belly, which was now not merely flat, but actually sunken. His clothes felt loose, almost oversized. He slapped his empty belly again for emphasis, and the vibrations sent his pants flying down around his ankles.

"Oh honey, we don't have time for that now," she replied, gnawing on a roasted turkey-leg. Where did that come from? "Now please, get started on that kitchen. I'm going to look at new bathroom fixtures on the internet."

By two in the morning, he had the kitchen walls all scraped clean. He slept on the couch and dreamed of Amazons in aprons. When he woke up, he found himself seated behind the wheel of his car with his business clothes piled on the passenger seat. He managed to struggle into his shirt and pants – he couldn't get dressed in the driveway, what would the neighbors think? – then slipped on his socks and shoes and drove off to work. His clothes were looser than a circus clown's jumper, but there was nothing he could do to fix that. He certainly didn't have time to go shopping for new clothes – he was already five minutes late for work.

He spent the whole day working on financial reports and internet matters, and only had time for half a chicken-salad sandwich for lunch. He was so tired, he just wanted to curl up in a corner and cry himself to sleep, but that sort of thing takes time.

He painted the kitchen that night while she ate doughnuts and looked on the internet for a new mailbox – maybe one that had a pattern of baby ducks around the edges. Ducks were so cute.

He finished painting around three in the morning, then fell asleep on the kitchen floor and dreamed of bulldozers in Eva Gabor wigs. When he woke up, he was fully dressed at his desk, already working on a new batch of financial reports. His suit was so loose, he felt like a child playing dress-up in adult clothes.

Springtime Periwinkle Fantasy No. 12 turned out to be a nightmare, absolutely hideous, so she told him to scrape all that off and start over. He also washed all his shirts and pants in hot water that night, so they would shrink and fit him better.

The company website's traffic figures just weren't increasing fast enough, so that meant spending some weekends working on that, and the new kitchen color, Dainty Daisy Delight No. 7, turned out a little too greenish, too queasy, so he had to scrape it away, and he lost more weight and that meant boiling his clothes until they'd shrunk enough to suit him, and she ate chicken nuggets dipped in zesty barbeque sauce as she surfed the internet for pretty hand towels, and a new batch of financial reports came in and the car needed an oil change and Warm Autumn Ochre No. 8 looked like crap and so did Cool London Mist No. 10 as well as Enchanting Aqua Surprise No. 43 and his clothes needed more boiling and she bought more housewares and home improvements on the internet while eating pastries and pastrami and tacos and roast beef and one day, she turned to him and said, "Honey, we need to talk."

By then he was just a wizened, palsied little monkey, spattered with paint and dressed in crumpled, shrunken doll clothes, gnawing hungrily on some old paint chips – they looked so pretty and tasted so sweet, so yummy. But the toxins in the chips made him drowsy, *sooooo* drowsy. He felt himself falling asleep, and before his mind drifted into a black-velvet beddy-bye tunnel, he looked up and saw his five-hundred pound wife standing over him, her jowls flecked with pancake crumbs and dripping with maple syrup. And she whispered, "I'm bored. This marriage thing just isn't working. I want a divorce."

As his mind wended its way down into darkness, he pondered the fact that he could still feel his cheeks. He couldn't feel any other part of his body ... not even his lips ... but yes, he could still feel his cheeks, warm and wet with tears.

*  *  *

He woke up three weeks later in a chrome hospital bed. About a dozen thin plastic tubes spooled into or out of his body, nourishing him or removing wastes.

By the side of his bed sat a handsome, red-haired, thirtyish man with kind blue eyes.

"You're awake!" the man cried. "My prayers are answered."

Confused, he stared at the red-haired man. "Who are you?"

The man sighed. "Poor thing. You're still delirious. Just rest. I'm so happy you're awake! Soon you'll be all better. You'll see."

"I must be having trouble with my memory," he said. "I remember getting married to her and painting the kitchen ... painting it more than once ... and...."

The red-haired man laughed. "You really are delirious! But no wonder, after all you've been through. You must be starved – you've lost a lot of weight, so we'd better buy you some ice cream on the way home."

"Yes, I'd like that," he said.

"You've never been married," the red-haired man added, "and certainly not to a woman. You were painting our kitchen and you forgot to open some windows. The fumes got to you. The doctors were worried about brain damage, but I knew you'd be okay. Still, that didn't stop me from worrying night and day, and praying, too. I've been by your side this whole time, crying for you. Now you're better and we have so much to look forward to."

The red-haired man then began to cry. Copious tears of relief flowed down his face, landing on his lap and the floor with syrupy plops. He shed tears of Springtime Periwinkle Fantasy No. 12 and Dainty Daisy Delight No. 7 and Warm Autumn Ochre No. 8 and Cool London Mist No. 10 and Enchanting Aqua Surprise No. 43 and pretty soon the nurses rushed in to see why the patient was screaming.

# Don't Look In The Little Storage Room Behind The Furnace

Valgrumbo House brooded at the end of Doomthistle Lane like an angry chiropractor awaiting the arrival of his two-thirty appointment, who was already twelve minutes late. The building's spacious rooms and disturbing hidey-holes pulsed with lurid psychic energy, generated by the many hundreds of foul, soul-searing acts of violence and degradation which had taken place within its cobweb-festooned walls over the years. Yes, truly it was a malevolent structure, and because its labyrinthine passages echoed each night with the languid, unholy moans of those who had perished there, visitors to the doom-fraught domicile often stood rigidly at attention, paralyzed with nerve-jolting terror – straightening their spines in the process. But was Valgrumbo House, like the afore-mentioned metaphorical healthcare specialist, awaiting a tardy visitor?

Most certainly.

Every day, the house hungered for new souls, fresh victims, to step over its dread-haunted threshold into its entry hall of blasphemy. And so days gathered and became weeks, which in turn snowballed into months, years and decades – but just as that inconsiderate chiropractic patient did eventually arrive for his adjustment, so did the Pelterbank family show up in the fullness of time to take up residence in that architectural abomination of abysmal apprehension.

"Oh, sweetie, it's beautiful!" Twyla Pelterbank enthused as she climbed out of their tan-and-pea-green station wagon. She brushed a wavy lock of flowing blonde hair out of her eyes to get a better view of the massive, austere house, with its black-shingled gambrel roof, columned porch and coffin-lid front door. "It looks so Old-World and elegant, like a fairy-tale castle or a spinster's skull. And to think, it's all ours!"

Her chunky, red-haired husband Rusty threw open his car door and struggled out of his seatbelt, which had worked its way down into a particularly hefty fold of belly-fat. "You know," he said, "it really was lucky for us that one morning, a dusty, time-yellowed document appeared out of nowhere on my lawyer's desk – a document proclaiming that the grandson of murderess Ezrabeth Pelterbank should inherit this house. And I am that grandson! What are the odds?"

Both backdoors of the car opened and out clambered the Pelterbank children – introspective, adolescent, dark-haired, willowy Letitia and scampish, towheaded, eight-year-old Petey.

"This is our new home?" Letitia moaned. "Even though I have not yet entered its shadowed recesses, already I can tell it reeks of death ... of unearthly secrets ... of terrors from beyond the grave..."

"Yeah, it stinks like your butt!" Petey said, running across the yard to get a closer look at a small pond near the house ... a small pond filled with big secrets...

"The moving vans will be here with our furniture and boxes this afternoon," Twyla said brightly. "Kids, now's the time to stake your claim, room-wise!"

Petey stopped in his tracks just five inches from the edge of the pond ... and two inches away from something cold and ancient just beginning to emerge from the pond's tar-thick muck ... something that sensed Petey had stopped, so it returned whence it came amidst a light gurgle of primordial goo...

"I want the attic!" Petey shouted, racing toward the house of nightmares.

"No, I do!" Letitia cried, heading the same way.

"Now kids, don't fight – there are plenty of rooms for everyone!" Rusty said with a jovial chuckle, watching his children hop into the gaping maw of the stygian abode.

At that moment, a tall, dark, bone-thin figure stepped out from between some stickle-bushes beside the house, and Twyla shrieked with surprise, terror and a little more surprise.

"Well, I'll be a possum dipped in flapjack batter and deep-fried in canola oil!" snarled Old Man Sarples, who lived in a ramshackle hut just over the hill from the Valgrumbo property. "Ain't you city-slickers ever seen a quaintly rustic yokel before? I is your neighbor Jeremiyuh, and I heard you was a-movin' in and figured I'd better sashay over here to warn y'all – a'fore it's too late!"

"A warning?" Rusty raised a paternal eyebrow. "Does the place have dry-rot? Termites? Excess dust build-up in the ventilation system?"

"Worse! Much worse!" Jeremiyuh howled. "At least two-hundred and seventy-eight times worse! Can't you sense the brain-addlin', bowel-voidin' gruesomeness of this here rat's-nest of revenants and devils?"

"Did he say, 'rats'?" Twyla whispered.

"I also said, 'revenants and devils,'" Jeremiyuh added.

"Yes, I know," the suburban wife said with a polite smile. "No offense, but that just sounded like 'crazy old man' talk."

"Missy, I do indeed take offense. I don't like to be called a 'crazy old man,'" said the crazy old man. "I prefer to think of myself as a mature, reality-challenged individual."

"Well, I don't like to be called 'Missy,'" said Twyla, "since that was the name of my twin sister who died at birth and whose spirit may still haunt me, for my umbilical cord choked her to death during labor. But it wasn't my fault. *It wasn't my fault.*"

"Now, angel," said Rusty, slipping a pudgy, comforting arm around her waist, "I'm sure the nice wacko wasn't trying to upset you with memories of your twin sister's hideous death. He didn't know, that's all. Just as he doesn't realize that I, too, am haunted by the fact that sadism and murder run in my family, and I pray I never bring harm to you and the kids. But really, the only thing that could do that would be–" He gave the matter a moment's thought. "Oh, I don't know. I suppose, say, living in a house filled with grim avatars of despair might drive me to murder – but hey, this is the real world, we know that won't happen any time soon. I wonder what the kids are up to? They've been in there for quite a while."

"Don't you want to hear the shocking secrets of this here old house?" Old Man Sarples said with a pout.

"We're kind of busy right now," Rusty said. "First day in the new house – lots to do. Can you come back tomorrow?"

"Oh, sure." Jeremiyuh smiled, revealing a mouthful of crooked, half-rotted teeth. "I'll bring doughnuts."

*   *   *

Inside, Letitia and Petey wandered through the mazelike halls of Valgrumbo House. Their race to see who could claim the attic first was completely forgotten, for each was mesmerized by the paintings, antiques, medieval weapons, sundry knickknacks and bric-a-brac littered hither and yond throughout that mortifying museum of moldering monstrosities.

"Hey, I found a really cool old book!" Petey shouted, assuming Letitia could hear him from wherever she was in the building. "It's called the *Nec– Necrono–* Just a second, I'm trying to figure out how to pronounce this... The *Necronomicon!* It's got funny pictures of some squid-headed dude in it. Hee heee!"

"Shut up, ya dumb squirt!" Letitia shouted back. "I'm busy looking into this weird mirror. The frame has little horned skulls on the corners. My reflection looks like a creepy old woman with white

94

hair, beckoning for me with a bony finger."

"That's silly!" Petey giggled. "Now I'm looking at some goofy thing covered with hair. I think I've seen this before. I wish I knew what it was."

"I'm a monkey's paw," said the hairy thing, which was indeed a monkey's severed and dried paw. Its voice was composed of the various creakings of its desiccated joints and sinews. "I can grant three wishes to whoever is holding me. And that's you, kiddo. You've got two more to go."

"Boy, I wish I'd been holding you a couple weeks ago, when I was at the toy store with Dad," the boy said. "I saw a toy just like you. It just popped up out of nowhere, but Dad had already bought me a Turbo-Transformin' Kung-Fu Kommando, so he didn't get it for me."

"Yeah, that was me," the paw said. "That was the result of the second wish you made just now. I showed up at that store but you didn't realize why I was there, so you didn't use your third wish to purchase me."

"Wha–? You should have said something at the time."

"You father would have heard me, and I can't talk in front of non-wishers," the paw stated matter-of-factly.

Petey's usually adorable brow furrowed in impish exasperation. "So I've wasted two wishes on nothing!"

"Maybe you should save me for the future, in case you need my help during your stay in this house of evil," suggested the primate appendage.

"Hmmm, maybe... Hey, did you say this place is evil?"

The paw extended its forefinger and thumb, forming an 'L' for 'Loser.' "Duh! The pond has an omnivorous shoggoth in it, the attic contains a transdimensional gateway to the Land of the Damned, and you just got done looking at the *Necronomicon*, the ultimate book of cosmic horror and demonic worship. What do you think?"

"You're just a monkey meanie!" Petey said, sulking. "I wish you'd go to H-E-double-hockey-sticks."

"Oh, crap!" cried the monkey's paw, disappearing from the face of the Earth.

Petey walked through the house until he found his sister. "Hey, Sis," he said, "you can have the attic."

"The attic–? Oh yeah, I'd forgotten about that," Letitia said, looking up from the Aztec sacrificial dagger she'd been admiring. "You mean it? The attic is mine? No arguments, no crying to Mommy, nothing?"

Yep, it's all yours!" Petey said. He looked around – this room was fairly large, with a fireplace, several shelves packed with exotic oddities and whatnots, and a huge, basalt Egyptian sarcophagus etched with jackals and winged scorpions.

"Totally rad!" he said, gazing with wonder at a dead praying mantis on the floor. Then he took another glance at the sarcophagus. "That's kind of cool, too."

Twyla and Rusty entered the room. "So have you two figured out who gets the attic?" Twyla asked.

"Yeah, Sis can have it. I want this room!" Petey said. He pointed to the sarcophagus. "I want to sleep in that – so I can pretend it's a race car!"

"I don't know, scout," Rusty said. "It looks foreign-made. It might not be one-hundred percent safe. What if its enormous stone lid slammed down in the night, sealing you in an airtight deathtrap? You'd be sorry then."

Twyla poked her husband in his ample side with her shapely elbow. "Oh, stop teasing the boy! You can just take off the lid. Or prop it up with a tennis racket. Of course you can have this room, Petey! Enjoy the royal slumber of a long-dead king of the Nile."

"I'm gonna go check out the attic," Letitia said. "I bet there's lots of awesome stuff up there."

Petey smiled. "Yeah, out of this world, Sis!"

\* \* \*

In his tumbledown hut, Jeremiyuh cooked up a new batch of doughnuts, using his finest roadkill flour, made from dried and pulverized roadkill meat, and roadkill oil, rendered from only the very best roadkill fat. He looked forward to spending time with his new neighbors, the Pelterbanks.

Would they all become great pals, eventually? Would they invite him over for ice-cream socials and debutante cotillions? That would give him an opportunity to finally wear the roadkill tuxedo he'd made last September. A lot of skunks had been run over that month, supplying him with plenty of luxurious black material. The contrasting white stripes provided added elegance. Perhaps someday, the Pelterbanks would help him get a big-city job, enter polite society and leave behind forever his pathetic world of bumpkin squalor.

*So what you gonna tell them city-slickers when you see them tomorrow-day?* said the voice in his head – Or was it just in his head? Who can say? – that he called 'Maw.' He turned to the wizened cadaver in a paisley sundress slumped in a rocker in a shadowed

96

corner of his miserable shack.

"Good question, Maw," he said. "I reckon I'll tell them their cozy homestead in the country is in fact a gosh-darned bubblin' cauldron of imps, restless spirits, and boogeymen. I'll inform them that their long-dead kin-woman Ezrabeth was not only a murderess, adulteress and writer of bad checks, but also a sorceress whose main goal was unleashin' the forces of blood-spillin' wickedness upon this entire county and the world beyond that." He gave the corpse a decisive nod. "They have a right to know."

*Boy, you're dumber than a big-city plastic grocery bag filled with rotten pork-chops,* screamed the voice in his mind – but was it really just in his mind? *You fergit, I can look into that sad, rotten peach you call your brain, and I know whats you is really thinking. You want them to make you into a big-city fancy-lad. You think they'll go to all that bother fer a hick like you – 'specially after you tell them their house is pretty much the Devil's poopchute? Do ya, boy? Do ya? Hmmm?*

"Maw, I've told ya before – keep yer dead-lady powers out of my brain-pan!" Jeremiyuh roared. "If you do that one more time, I'll stick yer dried-up twig-bones in the pot-bellied stove and use you to boil my coffee-water, ya nosy old crone!"

*I do have one more question fer ya, boy,* the Maw-voice murmured. *This here's a very important question, so I hope ya cleaned the wax outta yer hillbilly ears. Did ya tell them city-slickers about ... the little storage room behind the furnace?*

"No, Maw, I hadn't mentioned that yet," Jeremiyuh said. "But believe you me, I will!"

*Oh, ya will, will you?* Maw said.

"That's the plan!" asserted the pastoral psychopath.

*Well then, I guess now's as good a time to tell ya as any,* the voice thundered. *I, yer dead Maw who you kilt, is in fact the second-cousin of Ezrabeth Pelterbank, and her all-powerful witchy presence is tellin' me, I gotta stop you from blabbin' that infer-mation to her kinfolk, 'cuz she has very special plans fer them – and if you spoil things, she'll make sure you and me both suffer in a million unspeakable ways, most involving flames, for all eternity. And that's a Hell of a long time, boy!*

"How, pray tell," Jeremiyuh asked, "are you gonna stop me, you crummy old bag of bones?"

Immediately, an enormous cleft opened up in the ground, right under the dilapidated hut of poor, lonely, crazy, dentally disadvantaged Jeremiyuh Sarples. He screamed as he fell down through the chasm, right into a stream of molten lava about a quarter of a mile down. The cleft then slapped shut just as quickly as it had opened.

*Like that,* Maw declared.

*       *       *

Up in the attic, Letitia stared at a rectangle of green light that shimmered on the west wall of what was now her new room. She had no way of knowing it was a transdimensional gateway to the Land of the Damned. She figured it was probably just a big patch of mold, or maybe alien slime.

"Hi," she said to the rectangle. "Are you mold or alien slime?"

The glow did not reply.

"Come on," she said. "Talk to me! I'm very sensitive and Goth and probably psychically receptive. If you can't talk to me – who *can* you talk to?"

"I can talk to Maw," said the glow. "But that's more of a psychic thing, not really actually talking, like what we're doing right now."

"Oh!" Letitia was genuinely surprised to receive an answer. "Who's Maw?"

"You don't know her," the glow said. "I don't talk to Maw very often. She's not very well-educated, and dead, too. There's not much we can talk about. Though she did send me a little message about a minute ago – she just killed her son."

"Really?" Letitia moved a little closer to the rectangle. "Wow, I've been here less than an hour and already people are getting killed and I'm talking to a creepy glow. What are you, anyway? Am I caught in some kind of supernatural web of intrigue?"

"I'm a transdimensional gateway," said the glow, "and yeah, you're definitely caught in that web you mentioned. It could mean death to you and everyone you hold dear, so maybe you ought to be peeing your pants right about now."

"Whoa!" Letitia cried. "You don't know me well enough to talk that way, so bring it down a notch, okay?"

The glow considered her words.

"Honey," the glow said, "I'm a sentient threshold to the Land of the Damned, while you're just some teen Goth chick. I'm eternal and incredibly intimidating and you're just a skin-bag of bones, living meat, hormones and attitude, okay? I wouldn't mind being your friend, since you're an outsider and I think outsiders are neat, but don't be gettin' up in my grill."

"Sure, okay," Letitia said. "Really, I didn't mean to be

disrespectful. All this is just very new to me." She flashed a big smile. "I think this whole gateway deal is pretty amazing. I want to know more."

"Fair enough." The voice of the gateway switched from bitch-on-acid to sitcom-Mom in three seconds flat. The supernatural is nothing if not flexible. "Hey, you want to visit the Land of the Damned? It's the sort of trip that would render any average mortal totally insane, but I think you can handle it. Waddayah say? Can I pencil you in ... right about now?"

Letitia nodded. "Let's do it."

"Hang onto your giblets," the voice announced, "because –"

The glow swelled out from its rectangular boundaries and poured over Letitia, who found herself swimming and swirling in an ocean of death, past, present, future, congealed blood, death, rot, brittle bones, death, pain, madness, condemnation, death, nightmares, unforgiving stone, hysteria, death, and ultimate corruption. But it smelled great. Kind of like chocolate-chip cookies baking on a Sunday afternoon.

"Love the cookie smell," Letitia called out. "Good job!"

"Oh, you noticed!" The voice giggled just a little. "Thanks – it's something I've been working on."

\* \* \*

"So what do you think Letitia's doing up there?" Rusty said.

The Pelterbank parents and Petey were now checking out the kitchen, which featured an overhead rack cluttered with pans and kitchen implements, enormous stainless-steel sinks, a walk-in meat locker and curiously, a walk-in oven.

"Oh, I imagine she's up there trying on quaint old opera gloves and feathered hats," Twyla trilled. "She acts all tough, but deep down, she's really just a sweet, feminine girly-girl, just like her mother!" She pointed to a swastika etched on the blade of a meat-cleaver hanging from the rack. "Sweetie, I don't recognize this logo. What company made this?"

Rusty moved to her side to take a look at the chopper in question. "Gosh, darned if I know! A lot of those old blades and big scissors have that same logo. Must be part of a set."

"Redrum!" Petey cried out.

"What did you say, sport?" Rusty asked.

"Redrum!" the innocent tot uttered again.

"What an odd pair of syllables for a child to cry out, apropos of nothing!" Twyla commented. "It sounds like he's saying a word backwards – which would be a nutty thing to do, even for one so young. Petey, what are you trying to tell us?"

Petey smiled. "I was just thinking, I want to be a drummer when I grow up, and that'll mean a lot of practice. I'll have to drum and redrum over and over, to make sure I'm getting it right."

"What an interesting observation," Rusty said. "And speaking of observations – I think it's time we all went into the basement, to see what kind of neat stuff the previous owners left behind. I bet that's the way down there." He pointed to a heavy metal door at the far side of the room. "I wonder why somebody scratched a big '666' above the knob?"

Twyla squinted at the mysterious message. "Are you sure those are sixes? Maybe those are three lowercase italic b's. That must mean the door has been approved by the Better Business Bureau."

"Well, they could have just put a little sticker somewhere, instead of making such big scratches." Rusty shrugged his plump shoulders. "Oh, well! Guess this town is just really, really proud of its Better Business Bureau. Now let's go check out that basement, gang!"

"You want me to go get Letitia?" Petey asked.

"Oh, no," Twyla said. "I'm sure she's having the time of her life. Let's not disturb her."

\*    \*    \*

The Land of the Damned reminded Letitia of a theme park modeled after a dead pig's guts. She once had to dissect a dead baby pig in science class, so she knew what porcine innards looked like.

All around her, three-eyed, lime-green demons whipped at doomed zombies with wet guts they'd torn from other doomed zombies. The buildings here were all slaughterhouses, crematoriums, mausoleums, and pizza restaurants. Looking into one of the windows, she saw that in this place, they had an entirely different mind-frame about what ingredients to use as pizza toppings.

The sidewalks here were cobbled together out of skullbones and kneecaps, bound together with tar. Rats, iguanas, three-legged cats, and wind-up, spark-shooting toy robots rushed up and down the streets. The streetlights reminded her of huge lightning-bug asses. They were in fact human asses, inset with colored bulbs.

Every now and then she would pass a pit in which zombies were receiving some sort of unspeakable punishment. Each pit held a different torment, and she had to admit, whoever had designed all that nastiness had been pretty creative. In one, the zombies were forced to eat macaroni and cheese, nonstop. That might not seem so bad, but in this case, the macaroni was uncooked, so the hard noodle shells tore into the gums and tongues of the undead feasters – and, the cheese was Limburger.

In a different pit, the lime-green demons surgically whittled and reshaped each zombie down into a cute little zombie kitten. Then they reversed the process, sewing and hot-gluing back the material they'd pared off, turning each victim into a full-sized zombie again. At no point were the zombies allowed to enjoy being kittens. They didn't even get to play with any balls of yarn or catnip toys.

In yet another pit, the demons chopped up the zombies and made them into pies, stews and other foodstuffs, which they then ate up quickly. The demons were always eating their victims, and always pooping them out, too, and the zombies squealed in a thoroughly loathsome, blubbery fashion as they were excreted from the scaly rears of their three-eyed tormentors. The demons would then take the squealing poop, pour it into enormous steel molds and cast new zombies, to begin the torture cycle anew.

Suddenly a ball of glowing green light appeared at Letitia's side. "Hello!" said the voice of the transdimensional gateway.

"Hi!" the teen replied. "Shouldn't you be back up in the attic?"

"Most of me is still in the attic. This is just a little ball of me I've sent into the Land of the Damned, to see how you're doing." The ball drifted over the pit of pooping demons for a moment, to see what was going on down there. Then he drifted back over to Letitia. "Yuck! These demons have too much time on their claws. Have you noticed that none of the demons or zombies have attacked you?"

"Now that you mention it, you're right." She smiled at the glowing ball. "Okay, tell me what you did."

"I made you invisible!" the voice said. "I really only have about four or five powers, but that's one of them, and it's a pretty good one, too. They can't hear you, either. It was really nice of you to mention the cookie smell ... and, well, I don't have that many friends, since I spend all my time in a long-forgotten attic ... so I thought I'd treat ya to a little invisibility, so you didn't get torn to ribbons. Hey, do you want to see your great-grandmother Ezrabeth Pelterbank, the murderess?"

"Sure, why not? Is she around here? I don't want to rush you, but I should be getting back to my own dimensional pretty soon, so my parents don't worry."

"See what huge, blackened husk of a cathedral over there?" The voice-ball wiggled a little to the left to indicate direction. "She's in there, readying her ravenous troops of the undead to take over the world."

Letitia gasped. "Oh no! We've got to stop her!"

"We?" The voice laughed. "I don't get involved with anything that crazy old bat does. I've kept my existence a secret from her ever since she moved into Valgrumbo House, years ago. Whenever she used to come into the attic, I'd stop glowing so she wouldn't notice me. I'll help you get a closer look at what she's doing, but that's it. You're on your own with any big plans to save humanity, honey."

"Fair enough." Letitia marched toward the cathedral, and the ball drifted right behind her.

"So is it fun, having a body?" the voice said.

"I guess so – I've never been disembodied, so I can't really compare." Letitia suddenly caught sight of something moving near her feet. "Hey, what's this...?"

\* \* \*

Back in Valgrumbo House, the rest of the Pelterbank family explored the basement. "Look at all these wonderful antiques!" Twyla said. "Look at this big, funny metal trunk, shaped like a woman. It has spikes inside – isn't that weird? It wouldn't be much good for storage. Sweetie, I've been meaning to ask: your family name is Pelterbank, so why is this place called Valgrumbo House?"

"This was my grandmother's house, and Valgrumbo was her maiden name," Rusty said. "Pelterbank was actually the last name of a powerful and wicked sorcerer she married, who eventually taught her about the dark arts."

Twyla sighed softly. "You know, I'm a little disappointed you didn't tell me you were related to a murderess and a sorcerer before we got married. I mean, I would have still married you, because I love you – but it would have been nice to know you trusted me enough to share things like that."

"I'm sorry, angel." Rusty took her slender hand and kissed a delicate pinky knuckle. "I guess I didn't want to scare you off! I mean, I was amazed a gal as pretty as you would want to marry a guy as big as me. I didn't want to screw things up by throwing insanity and devil-worship into the mix."

"Sweetie, nobody's perfect! I mean, I accidentally killed my twin sister at birth, remember?" Twyla then noticed another curious feature of their new home. "Gee, I thought the walk-in oven was something. But a walk-in furnace...?"

"Look what's behind the furnace!" Petey said.

"A door – must be a little storage room," Rusty observed.

102

"Should we look inside?"

"Of course we should," Twyla stated. "Nothing bad could ever come from looking inside some silly old room. Yes, let's all look inside the little storage room behind the furnace!"

"Maybe it's full of toys!" Petey cried. "And drums! Redrum! Redrum!"

"There's a big cross nailed to the door," Twyla observed. "I wonder if it has any special significance? If I were superstitious, I'd think it was protecting this world from some sort of evil force – a force located just beyond that door."

"Fortunately, we're not the least bit superstitious," Rusty said. "Petey, I'll let you have the honor of opening the door of the little storage room behind the furnace."

"Sure thing, Dad!" The precious, vulnerable child rushed with glee to the door ... grabbed the knob ... twisted the knob while pulling on it ... and in just a few seconds, the door to the little storage room behind the furnace flew open, to reveal–

"At last! At long last!" shrieked Ezra Pelterbank. The white-haired, desiccated, undead witch cackled with shrill gusto as her lime-green demon-servants pulled Rusty, Twyla, and yes, even little Petey into the sub-basement of the blackened husk of a cathedral in the Land of the Damned. "My evil plan shall now bear hideous fruit! Finally, the door to Earth has been opened and my slavering battalions of the undead shall soon surge forth and destroy everything and everyone – and nothing can stop me!"

Twyla turned to Rusty. "One of your relatives, right?"

"Don't destroy Earth!" Petey pleaded. "It's full of butterflies and rainbows and Turbo-Transformin' Kung-Fu Kommandos and stuff!"

"Oh, rest assured, I will personally destroy each and every butterfly and rainbow and–" The witch stopped in mid-rant. "What was that other thing? A turbo-foamin' kung-fizzy whatchamawhoosie?" She turned to the nearest demon. "Any of that ring a bell with you?"

The creature shook its three-eyed head. "The kid lost me at 'butterfly.'"

"Yeah, we don't get too many of those down here." The witch turned back to Petey. "I like you, kid. You remind me of me, back when I was small and obnoxious. I'll turn you into one of my demon minions. As for the butterball and his sappy wife – they shall be thrown into the nearest pit of eternal torment! That would be the one where the demons eat you up and poop you out!"

103

"I object!" Rusty shouted.

"Sweetie, I don't think this is a court of law," Twyla said. At that moment, she spotted Letitia, entering the sub-basement from a passageway behind and to the right of the demented hell-hag. "Look, Rusty!" the perky wife whispered. "There's Letitia! What's that funny little thing she's holding?"

Letitia walked right up to her family. "Hey, you guys, long time no see. So like, wow, we're in the Land of the Damned! These devils and zombies can't see or hear me. I love it!"

"Maybe they can't see you or hear you – but I can, what with me being a witch and all!" roared Ezrabeth Pelterbank. She grabbed Letitia by the wrist. "Now I have you, my pretty, and you're going straight in the poop-pit, along with your parents!"

"Hey, Sis – you found the monkey's paw!" Petey shouted.

Letitia held up the hairy, shriveled talon. "Yeah, it was crawling around outside and I thought it looked pretty cool, so I –"

"Whoever holds it gets three wishes!" Petey cried. "Quick, make some wishes and save us!"

"Hey, that's mine!" bellowed the undead witch, reaching for the paw. "I bought it back when I was alive, but it crawled off before I could make any wishes. Give it here!"

"No way!" Letitia kicked the hag in the shin. "Stop bugging us! I wish you were a pile of dog-turds, you old scum-bucket!"

With a sad little plop, Ezrabeth Pelterbank promptly turned into a small mound of poodle feces.

"That wasn't a very ladylike wish!" Twyla scolded.

The three-eyed, lime-green demons backed away from Letitia, shivering with dread.

"I don't have any gripe with you guys," the teenager said. "But I do wish you'd stop torturing all those dead people and learn to live in peace with them."

Throughout the Land of the Damned, countless centuries of torment finally came to an end. The demons apologized to their former victims, and they all started talking about what could be done to turn their realm of nightmares into a really snazzy hangout.

The green ball drifted into the sub-basement, right up to Letitia. "I was waiting in the passageway – I didn't want the witch to see me. Where'd she go?"

"I made a wish and turned her into crap," Letitia said. "This is my family. Family, this is the voice of the transdimensional gateway in the attic."

"The monkey's paw can talk, too," Petey said. "But he can't do it in front of non-wishers. That's probably why he didn't say anything to you before, if you were with that glow-ball."

Letitia stroked the bristles on the back of the silent claw. "Monkey's paw, since you saved me and my family, I'll use my last wish on you. I wish you were done giving out wishes, so you can just be yourself and talk whenever you like."

"Thanks," creaked the paw. "It would have been nice if you'd used that wish to bring back the rest of my body – but it's the thought that counts."

The Pelterbanks, the voice-ball and the monkey's paw then left the Land of the Damned, now known as Happy Acres. They closed the door of the little storage room behind the furnace and returned to the living room. Letitia told her parents and Petey about her adventures, the glow-ball shared some of the house's history with the family, and soon everyone was up to speed.

"You know," said the voice-ball, "now that the witch has been turned to crap–"

"Let's say, 'laid to rest,'" Twyla suggested.

"Yeah, that's better. Now that the witch has been laid to rest, Valgrumbo House feels ... friendlier." The ball pulsed with happiness. "It used to give off waves of evil menace. It was as if the house hungered for new souls, fresh victims ... but now, the place has a really cheery vibe to it, fresh as a daisy! The evil energy has dissipated and the ghosts of Ezrabeth's victims have departed. Though you're probably going to have to do something about the shoggoth in the pond. If you have a copy of the *Necronomicon* laying around, you'll find some suggestions in there. I'll also need to have a psychic conversation later today with your next-door neighbor, a dead witch called Maw. She's been doing her best to stay out of the Land of the Damned, since she's always been afraid of Ezrabeth. She'll be happy to know Ezrabeth is dead and the Land of the Damned is a really nice place now, so she'll probably scoot on down there as soon as she can, so she can start meeting other dead folks. She really needs to get out more."

"Hey, what's that I hear?" Twyla crossed to the window and looked out. "The moving vans! Our furniture is here! And all our boxes. So much to unpack!"

"Can I lend a hand?" cried the monkey's paw.

The Pelterbank family all broke into laughter. "Monkey's paw," trilled Twyla, "you're the greatest!"

105

"And so are you, voice of the transdimensional gateway!" Letitia added.

The glowing ball pulsed with happiness. "Thanks, honey."

"Monkey's paw and voice-ball," Rusty said, " You've both been so helpful, I'd like to invite you to be a part of the Pelterbank family for as long as you like. How does that sound?"

"Fine with me," said the voice. "I live here anyway!"

"Yeah, so do I," said the paw. "The voice and I will probably outlive all of you, since we're supernatural and pretty much immortal, but it'll be nice to have a family until you all eventually die and rot to dust. So hey, count me in!"

"Oh, but first things first, you two," Twyla said. "Folks living under the Pelterbank roof need names. Voice-ball, you definitely sound like a Dana. And monkey's paw, I think you're more of a Steve. So welcome aboard, Dana and Steve Pelterbank!"

"A name!" A gentle sob of happiness escaped the glowing ball's nonexistent lips. "At long last, I have ... a name..."

"Actually," replied the monkey's paw, "my name's Kevin."

# You Shall Have This Delicacy

## 1.

From *The Fine Art Of Living*, the unpublished autobiography of Erika Finlay Pennywhistle Nelstrom Wong Vultaine:

It's hard to believe I was ever a baby. I'd like to think I simply popped full-grown out of my father's forehead, like Athena, but birth is never that tidy. And of course, if I had gone the Athena route, I could have avoided my mother entirely.

Father was a warm, albeit nondescript teddy-bear of a man. Mother was loud, needy, and a terrible drinker. No, wait – technically, she was very good at drinking. But it made her a terrible person.

I learned about addiction from her. She was addicted to booze, a variety of drugs, and stupid men. Losing her looks was the best thing that ever happened to her. I've fallen in and out of addiction many times. You know how it goes: you discover a new thrill, so you try it every now and then. Before you know it, you are starting and ending the day with it, until it sickens you. At one point, I was addicted to dried Peruvian spiders – I would chew them, make coffee out of them, and spend the whole day in a silken spider-buzz. My fifth husband Osbo helped me through that whole mess. Osbo, what a wonderful man. The very mention of his name brings back such delicious memories.

Whereas mother was not a picky person, I have made it my life's work to be as discerning as hell. I'm a survivor, and survivors should be rewarded. If others won't reward me, well then, I'll just pamper myself. So I have allowed myself one special addiction: the need to be surrounded by luxury. Exquisite jewelry. Fabulous outfits by genius designers. Exotic taste treats from strange lands. Rare books. And of course, the ultimate luxury: magic.

There will come a day when I will have to give up the clothes and the jewels, but the magic will always be a part of me. My last two husbands – one of whom was dear Osbo – were leading experts in that particular discipline. Since it is a secret discipline, they had to live in the shadows.

But they lived well.

\*   \*   \*

Mrs. Vultaine had invited six to dinner; invited them with crisp black cards, the message embossed in gold leaf. Each guest had been instructed to bring one companion. Thirteen at table did not fret the hostess: this was a woman who had survived strange diseases, stranger travels, and far too many years of perilous existence. Thirteen? Pshaw. Just another number.

The widow walked tall through the dining room, observing, correcting, at times praising her servants during preparations for the evening. She wore black silk pants and a matching blouse with the shoulders cut out. She knew this was a very young fashion, but no matter. She had a beautiful face, regally angular and as pale as milk; long, silver hair; even, white teeth; and soft, fine-boned hands, anointed with expensive creams. And she still had smooth, lovely shoulders: this the world had a right to know, and she refused to hide them.

A sad-eyed maid with delicate features poured nuts into a crystal dish.

"Just a moment, my dear," Mrs. Vultaine said, her voice an imperious warble. Her right hand fluttered at eye level, punctuating, emphasizing. "Cashews? Oh, no, no, no. Certainly my guests would not care for cashews."

"We're out of morroka seeds," the maid whispered. "I found these in the servants' pantry. They're very good. And they look the same."

"And you look like a melancholy puppy. Does that mean I feed you scraps and make you do your business outside?" The widow rolled her eyes and sighed. "If you like them so much, take them to your room. And set out praku berries for my guests. I know we have buckets of them somewhere."

The maid picked up the dish and walked a few paces. Then she stopped and turned around. "Please don't fire me. I know I'm common. But I can't help it."

Mrs. Vultaine stepped forward and placed a cool hand on the girl's cheek. "Your tastes are common. But you ... you, Vexina ... are not common." She ran her fingers lightly over the servant's coiffure – a pinned bundle of thick auburn hair. "I would never surround myself with common sorts. Now off with you, puppy. There's work to be done."

The maid flashed a nervous smile and hurried off.

The widow turned her attention to the table settings. Five forks, five spoons, three knives per plate – and such plates. Plates of glass, gold, silver and polished bone: no two were alike. Green lizard-fat candles. Napkins with a pattern – goats, moths and daggers – matching that of the tapestries on the walls.

She entered the great hall to make sure the display was in order. The curious objet, or perhaps objets, d'art would amuse and surely disconcert her guests. This pile of gleaming metal appeared to be composed of parts from a disassembled golden harpy. A wing and a ribcage topped the pile; around the edges, one could detect a spine, a hip, and some extravagant clockwork organs.

She went into the library and strolled down a long row of books. How she loved books; they were her sturdy, silent friends, always willing to share. Many of these were first editions, signed by the authors. Here was an especially rare one – *Listen to the Weeping Dead,* a book of poetry by Augustus Fygg, the cannibal. And here – *The Hidden Power of Maps* by Benson Phelps. How ironic that he died while lost on safari. There was only one cookbook in the library: *A Pinch of This, A Smidgen of That* by Jacob Nelstrom, her third husband. And then there was the privately published *Worlds of Splendour: The History of the Family Vultaine*, by her last and most beloved husband, Osbo. His love had made her the happiest woman alive. Would she ever be that happy again? Perhaps, perhaps. She was not one to rule out any possibility.

Mrs. Vultaine settled in the lace-draped corner of an overstuffed couch by the fireplace. On a small table by her side rested a stack of small boxes, a roll of black wrapping paper, tape and scissors. She picked up a box and smiled as she shook it by her ear.

That tiny squealing was absolutely precious.

2.

From *The Fine Art Of Living*:

I did a lot of traveling back when I was an adventurous single girl, and one of my boyfriends was a spy named Nicos. We never talked about marriage, but we became very close. Nicos sold secrets to the highest bidder, regardless of the consequences. I helped him on a few of his assignments, just for the thrill of it. But it was a dangerous game, even by my extremely liberal standards. He was found disemboweled in the backroom of a French bakery. I later found the microfilm in a croissant.

I learned a lot from him, and my efforts eventually turned from espionage to politics. I met and trysted with many powerful men, most of whom were married – and I kept records. A tiny camera was hidden in my loofah sponge.

Ah, when it comes to romance, men of power are merely puppets. They can be weak, foolish. I went through a rather long phase where I delighted in pulling their strings. I wasn't even using magic.

These facts help explain why I do not pay taxes ... why I do not need a passport to travel the world ... why there are no public records of my marriages, or even of my birth. I am a woman of countless secrets. Even the address of my luxurious home is a secret. That particular secret was devised and maintained by the Vultaine's. His family created a sort of visual labyrinth around the house – quite an achievement, when you consider that the building is bigger than most cathedrals.

Of course, my friends all know how to find the House. Most also know how to keep quiet. Friends who become too loud ... well, they learn to quiet down soon enough.

I do want to stress that I don't use magic every day. Months can go by without my even thinking about using it. I can be resourceful in my own right. I like solving problems and figuring out why people do the strange but interesting things they do.

Of course, magic doesn't give a person permission to do absolutely anything. There are limits. Magic is nothing more than a reality booster. I can't tap an evil person on the shoulder and say, "You are now good." I can't just point up and say, "Let all the money in the world rain down upon me." No, no, no. I must first find a way, set the wheels in motion, turn up the dial on the old booster – so to speak! – and then hope for the best. Nothing is absolutely certain for *anyone*.

\* \* \*

The guests – all pale, dark-haired chain-smokers – arrived on foot. They all had to leave their cars parked a mile away, inside an abandoned warehouse. Each guest received a glass of reddish-gold champagne upon entering the basalt immensity of the House of Vultaine. They mingled, laughing and gossiping, in the great hall. Overhead, a full moon shone through an enormous skylight. The window had been levered open to let in the night air.

Vexina refreshed the plates of praku berries while her sister, Osmette, hefted a large platter of hors d'oeuvres. Osmette was a thick-waisted cherub with small dark teeth. She had no idea what sort of delicacies she carried, and had no desire to taste them.

All eyes turned to the grand staircase as Mrs. Vultaine made her

110

entrance. She still wore the silk blouse and pants, and her hair was piled high into a shining nimbus, with wispy tendrils snaking down along her slender neck.

She circulated among her guests, listening to speculation regarding the golden display. "My dear Silhouetta," she said to a sliver of a girl with limp black hair and nervous eyes. "So good to see you. Hope you've brought an appetite. You *are* eating these days...?" For six years, this wee girl had lived off of various ointments smeared onto her skin.

Silhouetta snatched a brandied trilobite from a tray. "Afraid so. I found out the hard way that intestines, like muscles, need their exercise."

The widow spotted a tanned man with a white streak in his reddish-brown ponytail, and tapped him on the arm. He smiled enormously as he embraced her.

"It's been years, Erika," he whispered into the pale shell of her ear. "Can't we just send all these awful people home?"

"Tinder, you are incorrigible," she whispered back. "Imagine, flirting with a woman who will soon be gone."

Tinder gazed into her eyes, shocked. "What are you saying?"

She shrugged. "Nothing less than the truth." She put a finger under his chin and shut his gaping mouth. "Now come to dinner."

The silver-haired woman walked to the table, arms outstretched, beckoning with her fingers. The others followed instantly – even those whose backs had been turned to her.

Mrs. Vultaine took her place at the head of the long table. Once the guests were seated, the servants brought out, per instructions, baskets of black bread and small bowls of grasshopper bisque. They filled the wine glasses with a vintage as clear as water.

For a few minutes, the widow watched her guests dip chunks of bread into their soup.

Silhouetta nodded toward the widow's glass. "Look, she hasn't touched her wine." A reedy giggle fluttered from her lips. "Maybe she has brought us all here to poison us."

The old woman sighed. "I never hold a dinner party without an occasion. But mass murder is not on tonight's agenda. I haven't touched my wine because alcohol no longer thrills me." She smiled alarmingly. "I have gathered you all here to say goodbye. Soon I will be gone. I will be done with this world, and this evening, I shall share my arrangements with you."

## 3

From *The Fine Art Of Living*:

I remember something very unusual, and absolutely *pivotal,* that happened to me during my childhood. We were living on a outskirts of a small town, near a wooded area. My parents had gone off on some errand, and had left me alone. Back then, parents weren't worried about things like 'bad strangers.' And it was the afternoon: bad stuff only happened at night in those days. At any rate, what happened to me wasn't bad. It was meant to happen. Some men – or rather, manlike beings – came up to me while I was playing in the backyard.

Based on what I have learned over the years, I now think they had once been human, but years and years of magical living had made them quite different. They told me that they could tell I was a very special young lady. I was flattered by this, but also a little scared. I saw one of them had a lump moving around under his skin, and I remember saying, "Oh, are you sick?"

"Oh, no. We each have one. See? We gave them to each other." And so I sat in the backyard, looking at the busy lumps as they moved around their arms and across their chests.

They seemed very happy with their lumps. They then told me exactly what the lumps do. The explanation would be too hard to convey in words – their expressions told most of the story – but the entire experience can be summed up by saying: some gifts are more special than others.

\*   \*   \*

As Mrs. Vultaine enjoyed her bisque (with a spoon: no dipping and dripping for her), she noticed many of her guests casting small glances about the room, taking in the paintings, the statuettes on the side tables, even the chandelier of pale rose crystals and rubies. She didn't mind.

"I have one possession," she stated, "that is exceedingly dear to me ... one that should be bequeathed to a special someone. If any one of you can prove you are that someone, why then, you may have it."

"I cannot believe what I am hearing," Tinder said.

"Incredulity is the calling card of the simple-minded. Or so some say." Mrs. Vultaine finished her last spoonful of creamy bisque, then deftly pointed a pinky toward her empty bowl. The servants cleared away the soup course. They began to bring out salads made from seven-pointed leaves and strands of pink seaweed.

A young man with a round face and shaggy eyebrows turned in his seat toward Tinder. "Are we to assume you are more worthy of Erika's affection than the rest of us?"

Tinder flashed his large-toothed smile. "Erika and I know each other quite well, Moyan. You wouldn't understand."

The young man returned his smile. "Oh, but I would."

With a cry of outrage, Tinder grabbed a knife and sprang across the table, upsetting wine glasses and toppling salads. Moyan yawned, pulled a small pistol from a jacket pocket, and shot the toothy man in the left eye.

At the widow's sign, the servants cleared away the doomed salad, carted off the body, and presented petite servings of flavored ices.

"After that unpleasantness," Mrs. Vultaine said, "we must cleanse our palates."

More courses were served after that, and the guests took pains to compliment her at length on the selections. She simply nodded and observed.

At one point, Osmette brought out a tray piled high with boxes wrapped in black. Vexina helped by setting one box in front of each guest. Many packages remained.

"My servants also may take one each," the old woman said. The maids and butlers moved quietly but eagerly to claim their gifts.

"Now, unwrap! Unwrap!" Mrs. Vultaine clapped her hands like a delighted schoolgirl.

Shreds of black paper sailed through the air. Box lids flew open. A few gasps were heard, then many screams.

The widow continued to clap. She giggled as thumb-sized larvae with human faces and crablike pincers sprang forth to burrow into their recipients. The faces of these tiny creatures resembled that of Mrs. Vultaine in all but one detail: the silver-haired woman did not have the ringed, razor-fanged mouth of a lamprey.

Chairs fell backwards and bodies toppled. Before Silhouetta slumped to the floor, she forced a wretched smile and cried "Thank you" to her hostess.

"You're welcome," the widow said. She then tiptoed past the writhing bodies and out of the dining room.

4.

From *The Fine Art Of Living*:

It makes me sad, whenever I meet some poor young woman who feels she will never be able to catch a man.

Men! Men are notoriously indiscriminate. Given the right set of circumstances, men will link up with – you name it. Produce, household appliances ... There are men who are desperately in love with hot water bottles. Marsupials. Cacti.

Catching a man is about as hard as catching a cold. Let us look at how I caught some of my husbands:

Mr. Finlay: At this time of my life, I was still a little too much like my mother – too needy, too man-hungry. I used sex to snare this one. I basically just tossed myself at him. We had a few good years, but then I started concentrating on magic and we grew apart. I still feel sad about – and yes, somewhat responsible for – the way he died. We'd had an argument, so I told him to go to Hell. I may have been using a little magic without realizing. And, he may have had a buried self-destructive streak, which I'd inadvertently unearthed. The next thing I knew, I looked out the bedroom window and saw he was pouring gasoline all over himself in the backyard. I shouted for him to stop, but that only caught the attention of our nosy next-door neighbor, who came over to see what was wrong. And she was a smoker.

Mr. Pennywhistle: He was very handsome and very rich. I captured him with elegance and attitude. He was also very work-oriented, and spent a great deal of time at the office. We had servants, so I was able to concentrate on my own interests, and of course magic. He had no idea: he was wrapped up in meetings and reports and mergers and cocktail parties. I was his beautiful trophy wife, and he never knew that his trophy could work wonders. He had a terrible heart attack, and as he sat by his hospital window (he refused to stay in bed) dying, I told him everything about myself. He said, "Darling, don't be silly," and then he was gone. So I brought him back and kept him alive for a few seconds, just to show him a thing or two. That took some effort, but it was worth it.

Mr. Nelstrom: He was a very serious fellow. He was a chef, and he taught me a great deal about the art of food preparation. One begins with the finest ingredients, and then works from there. Timing is also incredibly important. That flavor peak won't last forever! But as the years passed, my Mr. Nelstrom began to miss a few dinners, and my eyes and ears in the community told me he was seeing a crude young thing with an enormous bosom and tiny brain. Can you imagine how that made me feel? My dining room gourmet was a bedroom gourmand. Unthinkable. So I told him in a very stern voice to go away. But, there was a problem much like the episode with Mr. Finlay. He walked away – and never *stopped* walking. Again, I must have tapped into some sad inner defect of his. Eventually I divorced him. I caught up with him on a road in Italy – he was just a scrawny thing, walking, always walking – and trotted by his side, holding the papers as he signed them.

Those were my first three husbands, and I will admit, I had a small advantage since I am a person of magic. But really, every person – every living creature – has some degree of magic. They just have to learn to find it. To embrace it. And of course, to *use* it.

*    *    *

Four hours later, Mrs. Vultaine came back into the dining room. She smoked a clove cigarette as she waited for her party to resume consciousness. When at last the guests returned to their chairs, she instructed five of her groggy servants to fetch the main course.

"I had to prepare the entree myself," she said, "and I don't mind saying, it took a bit of doing."

Vexina leaned against a sideboard. She put a shaking hand to a raw, bloody hole below her collarbone. "What have you done to us?"

"Oh, that," the old woman said. "A little something to remember me by."

The maid pressed a finger tentatively against the wound. "Oh! I think it has healed up already." She took a deep breath and said to her employer, "I'm frightened."

The widow laughed. "Fright is simply a symptom of ignorance. Note that I am not calling you 'stupid.' Rather, I am bringing to your attention the fact that there is much you do not know. You are young and inexperienced. You must learn to trust. Certainly you can trust me. I have no reason to destroy you. I am too jaded to do it for amusement! Therefore, if I do anything *to* or *for* you, it will probably help you. Do you see?"

Vexina nodded slowly. "Yes, I think I do. I'm still scared, though." Her eyebrows raised a little. "But please, don't worry about me. The fear will go away eventually."

Mrs. Vultaine smiled warmly. "You are trying. Genuinely trying. I like that." She then addressed her guests. "Next is the main course. The specialty of the house! After that, you may all take whatever of my gewgaws and trinkets you like. Load them in your cars. Call for trucks. Fight over them if you must."

"I must say, this is all very..." Silhouetta searched for a word.

"...impromptu!"

"For all of you, yes. But I have been planning this evening for quite some time," the widow said. "I suppose I do have a weakness for springing surprises on others. And why not? I've had enough sprung on me over the years, and they've all made me a better person. And speaking of surprises: there is an utterly enormous safe in the basement. You will find the combination etched onto the handles of the dessert forks. For my treasure, dear ones, is your dessert. But first..."

She clapped her hands lightly, and the servants brought out several covered trays, which they set at intervals on the tables.

"Bon appetit," whispered Mrs. Vultaine.

The servants raised the tray lids, revealing large, steaming chunks of roasted meat. Vexina and Osmette began slicing at the savory mounds with curved knives.

"As for my most cherished possession..." The widow studied her guests. "I still don't know who should have it."

## 5.

From *The Fine Art Of Living*:

So how did I catch my last two husbands – the magical ones?

Mr. Wong: A very handsome, exotic man – half Chinese, one-fourth French, and the last fourth...! His grandmother on his mother's side was a circus reptile woman. He had wonderfully sculpted features, and a slight greenish cast to his skin. He was always hungry, so I captured him by making him wonderful things to eat. I will admit, most of the recipes were Mr. Nelstrom's. Mr. Wong preferred raw meat, so I had to make a few adjustments.

Mr. Wong showed me how to make animals understand human words, and also, he taught me to slow-dance. That second skill isn't really magical, but no one had ever shown me how to do that before. It was fun. Sexy. It made me feel young.

But in time, I tired of Mr. Wong. He became more reptilian with the years. He grew bigger – not fatter, just proportionally larger. He was still good-looking, but huge, and cold to the touch. Eventually, all he wanted to do was eat and bask. So we separated. I hear he now has a tail.

Mr. Vultaine: Ah yes, Osbo! He was the only one who ever caught *me!* I met Osbo Vultaine at a film festival. He saw I was a woman of power and he simply had to have me. He was a fantastic

116

man, and very handsome and virile for a fellow of three-hundred. When he showed up at my door with *The Book of Thoth*, I knew that he was the one for me. We traveled to lands which most people think are mythical, and met people who had no business being alive. Did you know there is a valley in Canada where everyone has yellow eyes, and a plateau in Argentina where the women have four breasts? They say technology is making the world smaller – don't you believe it! It's still big enough to have plenty of hidey-holes. Osbo and I had many exhilarating adventures. But best of all, we could talk, share concerns, figure things out – and laugh! We had seventeen marvelous years together. And then the Night-Birds came and carried him away.

I tell people I'm a widow, but I'm still not sure. Someday, I will go to where the Night-Birds roost and see what I can discover. The thing is, that's not the sort of place from which one can return. But for Osbo Vultaine, I would do anything. Even the impossible.

\* \* \*

A murmur arose among the guests. Suddenly Moyan stood up. "I have killed to prove my love for you! Your cherished possession should be mine."

Silhouetta cleared her throat. "What about me? At least I say 'thank you' when I receive a gift."

Other guests voiced their reasons, their desires, their concerns. The widow simply nodded. So much greed. So many social climbers. But still, she had to pick one, and soon.

"Maybe I ... " murmured a small voice.

Mrs. Vultaine looked about the room. It took her a moment to realize it was Vexina who had spoken. "You? Tell me more, puppy."

The sad-eyed servant slid a slice of meat onto the nearest plate. "I've worked so hard for you. Even though you scare me to death."

"True." The widow rose from her chair. "You are a survivor, and survivors should be rewarded."

Slender metallic wings ripped through the back of Mrs. Vultaine's silk blouse. She tore away her clothes, slowly, delighting in the sharp *rrrrrrip* of the fabric. She stood naked before her guests, revealing golden arms and legs, golden breasts and hips. The display from the grand hall was now her body, new and improved. Of her own flesh, only her head, shoulders and hands remained.

She picked up a rounded lump of meat from a tray and offered it to Vexina. "Take it, my dear. Take my heart."

As always, the servant did as she was told.

117

Mrs. Vultaine stared into her servant's eyes. "A trite gift, but the right gift. You are a sad, sickly creature. You shall have this delicacy and it shall nourish you." She brought her lips close to the servant's ear. "There is a manuscript in my nightstand drawer. It contains all the dreams and secrets of my life. Read it, learn from it, and then burn it."

She then spun round to face the table. "As for the rest of you... My useless old body is yours." She gestured toward the meat. "You must forgive me for foisting that little nap upon you earlier, but in meal preparation, timing is everything. Try the roast and I think you will agree: one cannot accuse me of being tasteless."

The widow's metal wings flapped slowly, once, twice. Then they began to beat in earnest, speeding to a golden blur. Protective golden sheaths slid over the hands, and shields rose up from her back, covering the shoulders.

"I'm coming, Osbo," she said.

More curved shields sprang up, sliding together as a sleek helmet around her head.

Erika Finlay Pennywhistle Nelstrom Wong Vultaine soared out of the dining room, into the great hall, and up through the open skylight.

Vexina sat on the floor, chomping on her gift as though it were an apple. But yes, oh yes, it was sweeter by far. She removed the pins from her coiffure, shook out her long, lustrous hair and laughed and laughed and laughed.

# V. FIVE BRANDS OF ZOMBIE

## It Isn't What You Gnaw, It's Who You Gnaw

Wilma Website: Yeah, I was a Deathquaker. I suppose I still am, but I really can't call myself one, since Dandy Voorhees isn't around anymore.

The Deathquakers without Dandy? Unthinkable! That would be like the Youthquakers from the Sixties without Andy Warhol. Everybody knows that Dandy modeled his every movement, every utterance, every moment of his existence after Andy Warhol. Andy was an artist and a genius, and so was Dandy. But Dandy gave everything a dark twist – a Goth sensibility – so he could take it one step beyond and call it his own.

Andy had a hangout called The Factory, with everything spray-painted silver. Dandy had The Funeral Parlor, with everything draped in black velvet. Andy had his paintings of Campbell Soup cans and his Brillo box sculptures. Dandy did the same thing with formaldehyde bottles and clove cigarette packs. Andy looked like a pathetic corpse – and Dandy...?

Like I said. He had to take everything one step beyond.

Koko Fantastic: I was Dandy's first friend in his town without pity, make no mistake! I was actually at the bus station when he arrived. But I wasn't there to see Dandy. I didn't even know who he was. No one did.

No, I was arguing with my boyfriend at the time, whose name I will not even allow to cross my lips, because he was leaving town and he still owed me at least three or four thousand dollars. I was just yelling and yelling at him, telling him I was going to hunt him down like a dog, when out of the corner of my eye I saw this scrawny little white-haired man-child with sunglasses and skin three shades whiter than an onion. He was wearing some kind of tattered black-velvet suit that was falling apart at the seams.

I looked at that little piece of ghost-meat and said, "Freak, what's your story?"

He just pointed behind me and said, "Gee! That guy's getting away."

I turned around and sure enough, the bus was pulling away from the curb. I just sank to the ground and started crying, and damned if that skinny-assed albino shrimp didn't sit himself down next to me and start crying, too.

"Oh, now don't you start," I said. "You're so skinny, you'll leak out all your water and turn to dust. Why are you crying anyway? You don't know me. "

"I can't help it," he said in that soft ghost-voice of this. "Gee, you're just so beautiful I can't stand to see you so sad. What's your name?"

I told him my name. My real name, that is. He shook his head. "That's all wrong for you. Your name should be Koko Fantastic. A beautiful lady should have a beautiful name."

Well now, of course I know I'm beautiful. But sadly, most folks don't appreciate that fact. They think a woman over three-hundred pounds has just gotta be – shall we say, less than pleasing to the eye. I thought little ghosty-boy was really sweet ... and very observant ... so I told him he could stay at my place for a few weeks. I took that name he gave me, and it turned my life around. His stay turned from weeks into years, but that was no problem, because by then, he was a force to be reckoned with, and I was high and mighty among his Chosen Ones – the Deathquakers.


Arabella Cream: He came to town with ten bucks and a suitcase full of home-made Goth clothes and a headful of dreams about Andy Warhol. I forget where he was from, but it was some little ditchwater burg in the Midwest. Kansas? Iowa? Nebraska? One of those really flat states.

I was managing the Saunders Gallery and living in a crummy apartment building about six blocks away – a real rat's nest filled with crazy artists. But it was close to work and I hate to drive, so it was fine for me at the time. Plus, I had a little act going on at the coffeehouse across the street – performance poetry every Wednesday night – so it was a really convenient location. My neighbor across the hall was this hugely fat Southern gal – a massage therapist who had these totally impossible dreams of being a great actress. Dandy was staying with her. She'd found him at the bus station and so I guess she'd sort of adopted him. Like a stray kitten.

He started going around to all the ad agencies, trying to do freelance work for them. Andy Warhol did that back at the beginning of his career, you know. And like Warhol, he was as pale as a ghost, with patchy white hair, and so eager, so sensitive ... so unearthly. I had a couple agency friends at the time, and we called him Andy

Wannabe for a few weeks. Dandy was into the whole Goth thing, but I guess that made sense. If Warhol were alive today, he'd be loving that whole lace-trimmed doom scene.

I saw Dandy pretty often, because after all, he lived right across the hall. We'd talk every now and then. He couldn't hold a real conversation: he'd either just mumble a few words or else ramble on about his latest obsession. He showed me his drawings and paintings and photos. He wanted to buy some silk-screening equipment so he could do pictures that way – just like Warhol.

Eventually I let him do a show at the Saunders Gallery – half out of pity and half because he really did have some talent. Eventually he started hanging out with a group of artist types and he became their leader. Amazing, really, when you consider how socially awkward he was. But he did have a knack for finding people who could help him reach the next stage – whatever that stage might be.

Xavier Y. Zerba: I met Dandy at the coffee shop across the street from where he used to live. Goth men are usually so chic in their own grim, counter-culture way, but Dandy just looked ghoulish. But still, he had some definite magnetism, and I found myself spending more and more time with him, listening to him go on and on about all kinds of nonsense. He was convinced that he was the reincarnation of Andy Warhol. He said that living and dying as Warhol had given him unbelievable insights, and that this time, he was going to tilt everything at just the right angle so that his work would live forever.

Back when he was Warhol, he said, he'd touched upon the ultimate truth when he did his remakes of those old Dracula and Frankenstein movies. The truth that lurks beyond life. He just hadn't lingered long enough on those themes – not long enough to learn anything substantial.

You know, when you think about it, it really is odd that a pop-culture guru like Warhol would ever have remade a couple of creaky horror movies like that. The things Dandy said gave the whole situation a perfectly logical rationale. I found myself nodding whenever I listened to him.

His work started selling pretty well at the Saunders Gallery. I hitched him up with a few other opportunities in the city – I know everybody who's anybody. If I don't know them, they aren't worth knowing. I introduced him to politicians, newspaper columnists, club owners – even the S&M cult-freaks who run The Absinthe Martini. I was the one who introduced him to Taffy Belasco. Crazy rich girl with too much time on her hands. She had loads of old-money friends, all perfectly eager to throw cash at somebody if Taffy deigned to give that person the nod. She funded quite a lot of Dandy's projects – his silk-screening projects, his art films – she even paid the rent at The Funeral Parlor, before Dandy started making money hand over fist.

Taffy Belasco: Dandy was simply, simply, simply divine. I wasn't attracted to him in any sort of physical way – but really, that's just as well. Sex would have ruined our relationship. We had something better than sex. We had rapport.

He was like my daddy, my brother, sometimes even my mother, all rolled up into one. People used to tell me, "Taffy, he's just using you for your money. He's sucking on you like a leech. Wake up and smell the coffee!" But I would just laugh. For a crazy little man who looked like death, he made me feel so alive! So I helped him out. I was the one who helped him set up The Funeral Parlor. He was living with Koko Fantastic, but I thought he needed some additional work-space. Her place was just so small – but then, maybe it just looked small in comparison to her. At The Funeral Parlor, Dandy finally had enough room to really launch some fantastic projects. A lot of his little movies were made there. I paid the bills early on, and in Dandy's defense, he did eventually pay me back. With interest, which is some-thing leeches never do. Eventually I let him study the Crowley papers – though looking back, I suppose that might have been a mistake.

Wilma Website: Dandy once told me, "I can't be around common people. They make me nauseous." So he picked his own family of uncommon folks – the Deathquakers. He was our pseduo-Daddy, and eventually Taffy became our pseudo-Mommy. And The Funeral Parlor was our spooky tree-house.

Dandy and Taffy, Taffy and Dandy – the society columns were all abuzz at the time. Who is this pale mystery man squiring everyone's favorite spoiled-little-rich-girl hither and yon? I first met Dandy through Taffy – I was designing her website, and she introduced us at a party. He took one look at me and said, "Those cheekbones! I've just got to put you in one of my movies!" He'd started making art-films. At that point, he'd only made two or three. One of those early ones was called "Fish" – they showed it at that party. It was just forty minutes of Koko Fantastic chopping up dead fish. Every now and then she'd stop to read their guts. I guess some people can read fish-guts. Sounds like pretty boring reading, though.

There can't be much of a plot.

Koko Fantastic: I was the star of Dandy's first movie, "Fish." I didn't even have to act – I just read entrails for him, since he'd always been fascinated by the fact that I could do that – that <u>anyone</u> could do that. My mama taught me how to do it, and her mama taught her, and I suppose her mama taught her, on down the line all the way back to Eve.

That puny rich girl he used to hang out with, that Taffy, she's related to Aleister Crowley. You know who that is? Weird old black-magic guy. Born 1875, died 1947. A member of the Hermetic Order of the Golden Dawn. He was Taffy's great-uncle or something like that. He designed a set of mystic tarot cards once. Whenever Taffy couldn't make up her mind, she'd break out those cards and do a reading. One of those cards showed a golden woman holding a giant snake – or maybe she was wrestling with it, I couldn't tell. And there was this big eye shining golden light onto that snake. Yeah, I remember that one. It was the Universe card.

Taffy used to let Dandy look at Crowley's old papers – she has a bunch of them tucked away in the library at her Papa's mansion. I said to Dandy one day, "What do you want with that kind of magic? It's too evil. Too powerful. Don't look at that stuff any more."

He said, "Ask the fish guts if it's okay for me to look at Crowley's work. I'll do a film of the reading. Gee! It'll be marvelous! Just marvelous!"

Well, I've always wanted to be an actress, so I said "Sure," even though I didn't think people would be too interested in watching me read fish entrails. But I did it, and I'll tell you this: the fish-guts never lie.

The guts told me that death would come walking, and that's just what happened.

Arabella Cream: Dandy started making those art-films of his, and before long, they were the talk of the town. Everybody wanted to be in a Dandy Voorhees movie, just like everybody wanted to buy a Dandy Voorhees painting or go to a Dandy Voorhees party. The whole city was all wrapped up in Dandy Voorhees.

After he'd been making those movies for about four or five years, I said to him one day, "Dandy, I've been good to you. Why don't you put me in one of your movies?"

He fixed his goofy stare on me and said, "Gee! What a great idea! How about this? We'll remake 'Macbeth,' except we'll make it

123

modern and interesting. You and Koko and Taffy can be the witches in the big cauldron scene. Xavier can be Macbeth. How about that?"

I had to bite my tongue to stop from laughing. Hmmm, apparently Shakespeare wasn't interesting, but Dandy was going to take care of that. Then he said, "You won't have to memorize any Shakespeare. Actors should never memorize anything – they should always put the lines in their own words. You know what might be fun? I'll see if we can work in the Chant of the All-Seeing Eye somehow."

I told him, "Never heard of it."

"No one has. But gee! It's really exciting!" he said. "It's something Crowley picked up during his travels. He found the original inscription in the tomb of the Red Pharaoh. He was going to publish a whole book about it, but he only ever got around to writing a couple chapters – Taffy has them up at her house. Crowley realized you had to combine science and religion to attain the ultimate truth of the Universe, and the Chant of the All-Seeing Eye was the way to do it. The chant reconfigures the brain so that it can see beyond good and evil. And the best part is, we'll be the first people since ancient times to use it, since Crowley never got around to publishing it."

Something seemed wrong with what Dandy was saying. "So you're saying this Crowley guy never used this chant thingy himself?"

Dandy nodded. "Yep."

"Even though he's the one who discovered it? Even though he was writing a book about it?"

He nodded again. "Yep."

"And that doesn't bother you?"

Dandy just shrugged. "Gee, why should it? Maybe he never got around to doing it. A lot of people are like that. They mean to do stuff, but then they just forget."

Dandy may have been an artistic genius, but you know, that doesn't mean he was *smart*.

Xavier Y. Zerba: Dandy was going to make a movie called "The Legend of Macbeth and the All-Seeing Eye," and he asked me to play the part of Macbeth. But as it turned out, I had to be out of town on the weekend he was starting production. He was disappointed that I wouldn't change my plans for him, so he said in a really bitchy voice, "Fine, I'll play Macbeth myself."

I was a little pissed off myself, since he was giving me so much attitude, so I said, "While you're at it, change the name. Your movies aren't long enough to have big titles like that."

"Well, gee! What should I change it to?" he whined.

"Use something from the show." I thought over what little I knew about 'Macbeth,' and finally suggested, "Well, there's a line that says, 'boil your oil, toil and trouble' ... or something like that. Call it 'Toil and Trouble.' Or maybe just 'Trouble.'"

Dandy's face lit up like a jack-o-lantern. "Gee! That's a great title! Thanks, Xavier. I'll call it 'Trouble.'"

"Yeah," I said, "You do that."


Taffy Belasco: Well, you know I simply adored Dandy. But 'Trouble' certainly lived up to its name. I wasn't too happy with Dandy while he was making that picture. How was I to know it would be his last?

The problem was, Dandy got it into his head to play Macbeth himself, and he was terrible. I mean, he'd recruited some pretty far-out characters to play in some of his films, but he was about ten times worse than any of them. I tried to help. I told him: Dandy, I'm sure Macbeth never used the word 'Gee!' – but of course that advice went right over his head, since he wanted all the actors to say the lines however they pleased.

The sets were just hideous. Most of his movies had funky, kitschy sets – usually rooms in The Funeral Parlor, and sometimes steam-rooms, alleys, fire escapes painted purple, you name it. But for this one, he decided to build a cemetery out of cardboard, like in the movie 'Plan 9 From Outer Space.' He built it in a big, smelly warehouse – the stink was awful, a nauseating combination of burnt plastic and ammonia.

Plus, Dandy was the only person running the camera, which meant he had to rush in and out of the picture all the time, to change the angle whenever somebody moved too much. Ridiculous! He'd say, "It'll get fixed in editing." He kept talking about this chant he was going to do as part of the movie, but he said he'd be doing it last, when we weren't around. He wouldn't explain why.

He really dragged out the witch-and-cauldron scene – that probably takes up half of 'Trouble.' I've never seen the whole thing, so I wouldn't know. The other parts of the movie didn't take that long to shoot, since the rest was just a super-abbreviated version of 'Macbeth' with a few scenes of a homeless woman doing some sort of spastic go-go dance. He saw some weird old woman dancing outside of the warehouse, so he put her in the movie as Ophelia. I didn't have the heart to tell him that Ophelia was from 'Hamlet.'

So finally, when it came time for him to do the big chant scene, he just sent all of us home. Just like that. He told Arabella and me to take the homeless woman with us. He gave us twenty bucks and asked us to buy her dinner somewhere. All the frustration I'd felt making that movie melted away as soon as Dandy asked us to do that. That was so sweet of him. So we bought that old lady a steak dinner at a nice little diner. And while she was eating she said, "That guy, he's the gate. He's gonna open the gate." She said that about five times.

Finally Arabella said, "He's the gate <u>and</u> he's gonna open the gate? What does that mean? He's gonna open himself?"

The old woman nodded and said, "Exactly." As soon as she finished eating, she got up, said "See ya!" and walked out of the restaurant. We never saw her again, which is probably just as well.

Wilma Website: Dandy died filming the chant scene of 'Trouble.' And apparently he'd made some secret arrangements with some people. The camera and sets were gone but the body was still in the warehouse. Two months later, the film premiered at a Goth art gallery called The Absinthe Martini.

The body had been discovered by some guy who'd been looking for old copper wire to sell. Dandy didn't have any ID on him – typical Dandy – but he had my business card in his pocket. I'd given it to him the day before, since my phone number had changed. So the copper-wire guy called me on a cell-phone! I told him to call the police, too. Then I drove straight down to the warehouse. It wasn't that far – only twenty minutes away from my studio. I arrived ten minutes before the police. The copper-wire guy was gone by then.

The body had turned an awful shade of sky-blue. I identified it as Dandy's, and answered a few questions about him for the police – and right in the middle of the questioning, the body scrambled to its feet in a jerky, puppet-like way, and Dandy croaked out, "Gee!" in a sad, dry, raspy voice. His eyes were shining with bright golden light. An officer stepped right up to him, and Dandy seized him by the throat and actually *fired* golden beams out of his eyes, burning two holes into the officer's face.

It was the *damned*est thing.

Another officer started firing at him, so Dandy shot those golden beams at him, too – and burned two spots as big as quarters into the guy's throat. He ran over and started chewing on the second cop, who was very good-looking. We're talking Brad-Pitt-good-looking.

Then Dandy slowly turned to stare at me, and started licking his lips. Licking his pale-blue lips with a dark-blue tongue.

So of course I turned and ran. I'm no idiot.

Koko Fantastic: The Absinthe Martini is run by a weird little clique that's into S&M, so none of us Deathquakers ever went there, even though it was Goth. Xavier knew those folks, but even he never went to their place. No sirree. But I guess Dandy went there. They were the ones who ended up with 'Trouble,' so I suppose he had some kind of thing with them. An agreement. An alliance. I don't know what you'd call – what they had. I'm sure they were the ones who took away the sets for the movie after Dandy died. They left the body because they knew what it was going to become.

Eventually the police figured out a way to load him into a truck and take his zombie ass away. That's what he was, you know. A zombie. And not your garden-variety, me-want-brains, Dawn-of-the-Dead-style zombie. He was some kind of freaky primal thing, cooked up out of that damned Aleister Crowley magic.

Poor Dandy. Poor man-child.

Poor thing.

Arabella Cream: That chant, that's what did it to him. But you know, I don't think it did what it was *supposed* to do. That Dandy – he never could stick to a script.

But evidently his rendition of the chant was caught on film. I can just see him, setting up the camera, getting everything ready, then running in front of it to do his bit. Mr. Do-It-Yourself. None of us Deathquakers went to the premiere of 'Trouble' – we never went to The Absinthe Martini and besides, we weren't invited. But it's just as well. The film turned everyone in the audience into zombies. Which leads me to wonder how the film was *edited*...? Maybe different people took turns editing different parts. Maybe it was edited out of sequence. Or maybe zombies edited it. I don't know.

You know, I'm really sick of art. Running the Saunders Gallery was hard enough, having to deal with whiny diva artists. But having to contend with art-film zombies – that's just too much. One of these days I'm just going to move to some small town, find me a hunky gas-station attendant and settle down to a quiet, fat, frumpy life with a few brats and a station wagon.

I'll even start using my original first name again. Darla.

Xavier Y. Zerba: You know, I was supposed to go to the

premiere of 'Trouble.' The gang at The Absinthe Martini even sent me an invitation. They were a strange little group. Pale, tattooed men who always wore leather. And that was management – you should've seen the bartenders. All of them had names like Toad-Scar and Crow-Claw and Barbed-Wire Joe. They'd have been the first to admit that they loved stirring up – trouble! I guess that made the movie's title especially apropos.

I always told the other Deathquakers I never went to The Absinthe Martini, but yeah, sure I did ... all the time. Just for fun. I took Dandy once, just for fun. I think he had more fun than I realized.

But I wasn't able to make it to the premiere because I was sick – stomach flu, puking and diarrhea all night. I've been pretty lucky. If I'd have played Macbeth in that movie ... or gone to that premiere ... I'd be a zombie now.

There were probably about a couple hundred people at that premiere – The Absinthe Martini can be standing room only on a good night. Now all those folks are zombies, roaming the streets day and night, blasting chunks out of people with their eye rays. I hear some of them have managed to turn other folks into zombies – not sure how, but I'm not sticking around to find out.

Luck only lasts for so long, so I'm getting out while the getting is good. I'll be on the first plane taking off tomorrow morning – I don't even care where it's going.

I've had a lot of fun in this city. Now I'll have fun in another city. Sans the living dead.


Taffy Belasco: Papa has connections, so this morning, I asked him to find out what the authorities are doing to Dandy's zombie. He made a few calls, pulled a few strings – Papa's wonderful that way. He found out that Dandy is being tested at some sort of institution. They've got him locked up in a concrete room, and they're running all sorts of tests on him – which isn't easy, since he can fire those eye-beams. In fact, Papa's taking me to the institute next week. He said I can watch Dandy on a monitor. Dandy on TV, at long last! Yesterday he managed to turn one of the guards into a zombie – he recited that chant to him. So Papa said he'll have them turn down the sound on the monitor while we're watching Dandy.

The police are having a terrible time hunting down all those zombies. The horrid things don't care about bullets at all, and they can shoot that burning light out of their eyes. They're kind of like movie projectors, aren't they? They shoot out beams that make a lasting impression! It really was naughty of Dandy to use that Crowley chant to make so much mischief. So much trouble. 'Trouble' begetting trouble. I wonder if he really knew what he was doing? This whole affair stinks of an experiment gone wrong.

But you know what's the funny part of this whole mess? Well, of course, the zombies attack anyone who attacks them – that's human nature, even if the human in question is one of the living dead. But if they're left to their own devices, they'll only attack and eat good-looking people. It isn't what you gnaw, it's who you gnaw! Isn't that a stitch? The media has really picked up on that – especially since some zombies have already attacked two health spas and a beauty salon. So ugly people and fatties have nothing to worry about. Ha, I guess that means Koko Fantastic is safe!

The other night, the Channel 17 Action News gal, Sharla Fontaine, was doing a report on the whole zombie scene from the street when suddenly one of those creatures rounded the corner – and marched right past her. Oh, but she was flabbergasted! She practically threw herself at it – did everything but stick her head in its mouth – but that zombie just wasn't having any of <u>that</u>, thank you very much! It was delightful! But you know, I've always thought she should do something about those teeth of hers. And those crow's-feet! A little Botox wouldn't hurt.

It seems those awful creatures have a lot of Dandy in them. Not his sweet side, which I must admit was pretty puny most of the time – but certainly his discerning nature. So maybe the meek will inherit the Earth after all, if these zombies take over and the beautiful people are turned into fodder.

Of course I still have all the Crowley papers. I've checked, and the chant is still there. Dandy didn't steal it – he must have just copied it. I bet he screwed it up. He probably left out some words when he was writing it down. And knowing him, he probably added some lines and said "Gee!" too many times while reciting it for the movie.

I'm tempted, you know. I really am. Tempted to go into the library, dig out those papers again, and recite that chant perfectly. Perfectly. Perfectly.

Just to see what happens. Or rather, what's *meant* to happen.

But not today.

I'm sure there will come a day when – horror of horrors! – my beauty will start to fade. My curves will sag. My limbs will ache and my eyes will bag.

Maybe then.

# Zombies Are Forever

"So what'll it be?" asked the bartender, a bald, muscular man with pockmarks and a scar over his right eye.

On the party side of the bar stood a handsome man with thick black hair and a wry smile. His eyes were large, black and alert – almost childlike. His skin was pink and smooth, without even a single wrinkle. He wore a black tuxedo with a white rosebud pinned to the lapel. "Carrot juice," he said, "if you have it. Tomato juice if you don't."

"Sorry, no carrot juice. Bugs Bunny drank the last of it." The bartender started shaking a small can of tomato juice. "How about a Bloody Mary?"

The handsome man wrinkled his boyish nose. "Why ruin some perfectly good tomato juice with alcohol?"

The bartender laughed. "Isn't it time for church, choir boy?" He poured the tomato juice into a plastic cup and set it on the bar. "Here ya go. On the house. Are you even old enough to be in here?"

The handsome man put a five-dollar bill in the tip jar and took his drink. "I don't know. Do you serve forty-year-olds?"

"Forty!" The bartender looked the man up and down. "Hell, I'd have guessed twenty-two, twenty-three tops. What's your secret?"

"Clean living." The man in the tuxedo turned back toward the party and walked over to the buffet table. He leaned slightly over a huge silver bowl of jumbo shrimp on ice and sniffed, once, twice. A little off. He picked up a radish from a vegetable tray and munched on that.

He studied the other partygoers. Politicians, tycoons, all sorts of folks with too much money and too many bad habits. They all looked so tired ... so unhealthy. There were plenty of beautiful trophy wives wandering about, but theirs was an artificial beauty. Their sagging flesh had either been pulled tight or plumped up with implants.

A pink-cheeked, sixtyish woman walked up to him. She wore a pinstriped suit, high-heels, no make-up and a white rosebud pinned to her bun of steel-gray hair. "Good evening, Pi," she said softly. "How are you enjoying the festivities?"

"For a birthday party, it's rather depressing," he said. "These people all look so sickly. Nice suit, Omicron. Where's the guest of honor?"

"Senator Phelps is in a private meeting right now, but he should be here shortly." She glanced at her wristwatch. "We'd better start heading toward the balcony. It's almost time to meet our new friend."

Pi smiled. Omicron always used such charming euphemisms.

As they moved through the party, Pi noticed that many of the older men turned to give Omicron the eye. And rightly so. She was lovely and perfectly fit. She didn't need make-up to enhance her stunning patrician features. One could tell just by looking at her that she was a strong, confident woman.

Pi was proud of her, but he was a little peeved at the men. He didn't like it when guys ogled his mother.

The balcony doors at the south end of the room were locked, but Omicron had the key. She opened them and Pi walked through. Omicron undid the ties on the curtains of the French doors so that they covered the glass. Then she passed through, locking the way shut behind her.

Out on the balcony, a woman stepped out of the shadows behind a large potted plant. She wore a blue-velvet hooded cloak. The hood was up, so that all Pi could see of her face was the tip of her nose and the gleam of her eyes. "You're right on time," she said. Her voice was raspy, like that of a chain-smoker.

Omicron smiled. "Of course we are. Hello, Olive."

"Can I see some identification?" the woman asked.

Pi handed her a small leather case containing his badge. He noticed that she was wearing long gloves.

Olive opened the case and looked inside. "Unhip."

"Excuse me?" Pi said.

"United Nations Health Investigations Program. The initials spell out 'unhip' – that's funny." She handed back the case.

"Just a coincidence, I'm sure," Omicron said. "You have the papers we discussed...?"

"Yes, and photographs, too." Olive reached behind the potted plant and picked up a black leather valise. "There's enough evidence here to have Dr. Loki put away forever."

"Let's hope so." Pi took the valise from the woman.

"We'll be leaving now," Omicron said. "Will you be rejoining the party?"

Olive laughed, though it sounded more like the crunch of autumn leaves underfoot. "I didn't come in that way. Parties are a thing of the past for me." So saying, she threw back the hood of her cloak. At one time, she had been a very beautiful woman. Certainly the left side of her face was beautiful. But the right – that was a horrid mass of livid yellow scars and orange lumps. She pulled off her gloves, revealing hands and arms streaked with yellow and orange. Her palms and fingertips looked like they had been coated with lime-green paint. She hurried toward the wall, kicked off her shoes and jumped.

Pi gasped – for a split-second he'd thought she was jumping off the balcony. But no, she was in fact flinging herself onto the wall. She stuck to it by her hands and the tips of her toes. Then she quickly scuttered away along the vertical surface. The only sound to be heard was a faint squelching sound, oddly reminiscent of suction cups.

"Could I borrow your handkerchief?" Omicron said.

Pi handed her a square of white silk from the breast pocket of the tuxedo. "Catching a cold?"

Omicron walked over to the wall and used the cloth to wipe a bit of slime from its surface. She then folded the handkerchief neatly and handed it back to her son. "Silly boy. I've never been sick a day in my life. You know that. Give that little keepsake to the lab folks."

She opened the balcony doors and they returned to the party. They only stayed long enough to grab some more radishes and carrot sticks from the buffet table. On the way out, they walked by the table of Senator Phelps, a tall, stocky man with a deep tan. Omicron nodded to the politician and he gave her a smile and a wink.

"Nice fellow, that senator," Omicron said to her son as they walked out of the building, into the cool autumn night. "He asked me out to dinner while we were arranging tonight's social call."

"Oooh, is he going to be my new daddy?" Pi said with a laugh. He tucked the valise under his arm, since its thin leather handle was starting to dig into his hand.

"I've yet to meet the man who could replace your father. He was the –" Suddenly she stopped. "Over there." She pointed across the lawn.

Three figures emerged from a group of trees and began to move toward them. They moved quickly, hunched down so that their hands touched the ground as they scrambled forward. Their yellow and orange skin gleamed in the moonlight. One of them gave voice to a raspy howl, revealing a mouthful of jagged yellow teeth.

Omicron and Pi both reached into their jackets, pulled out lightweight gas-masks and slipped them on. Omicron removed her high-heels. She flipped the silver buckles on the shoes, which were in fact safety catches. She then pressed small, flat buttons on the sides of the heels, releasing a spray of fine mist toward the creatures.

The gas should have paralyzed their assailants on the spot. But still they kept coming, so Pi handed the valise to his mother and rushed forward. He grabbed the foremost creature by the arm and swung it in a circle, back at the other two creatures.

Suddenly, a thin young man rushed out from behind a nearby parked car. He wore a black fedora with what looked like a raven feather tucked in the hatband. He took the feather and flung it like a dart at Omicron.

Quickly, Pi pushed one of the creatures into the path of the projectile. The monstrous thing squealed as the feather pierced its shoulder. Suddenly its flesh began to bubble, releasing billows of steam. The bubbling spread from the shoulder to the entire body, reducing it to a pile of bones mired in thick, reddish mush. Frightened, the other two creatures ran back into the woods.

Omicron pulled out her gun. The thin man jumped into the car and drove off.

"Shoot out his tires," Pi said.

His mother fired several silent shots at the car. But it just kept racing down the road.

"That ought to do the trick," she said.

"But you missed!"

Omicron shook her head. "This gun isn't loaded with bullets. It's got magnetic tracers instead. They'll broadcast a signal that we can trace back to Dr. Loki."

Pi frowned. "But what if Brimley had jumped you?"

"Brimley? Jump me? That pipsqueak wouldn't dare. He's just a coward – that's why he only attacks from a distance. No, I knew he'd run the moment he saw a gun." Omicron pointed to the feather, which now rested on the skeleton's shoulder blade. "Another souvenir for the lab folks. We'd better give them a call."

\* \* \*

The next day, Pi and Omicron visited the office of their supervisor, Gamma. The cluttered room was filled with filing cabinets and piles of newspapers and videotapes. In one corner was a cardboard box with a pregnant cat sleeping on a pillow.

It was against department policy to bring in pets, but Gamma was a widower with only cats for company, so nobody complained. Besides, he was the head of the department.

"You two did some fine work last night," Gamma said. He was a heavyset man with wavy white hair and thick glasses. "So did the lab folks. They had that mess in the yard cleaned up before any of the

133

Senator's guests had started heading for their cars. I looked over the evidence in that valise. This thing is bigger than any of us would have dreamed."

"Well, then," Omicron said, "don't keep us in suspense. Give us the lowdown."

"I think today's the day." Gamma sat on the floor by the cardboard box and stroked his cat's belly. "This will be Lulu's eighth litter. At this rate I'm going to have to buy a bigger house! Or maybe just move out into the country, so the cats can wander around. They'd like that."

"That's great," Omicron said, "but I was talking about the case."

"Oh, sorry." Gamma sighed. "It's hard to concentrate when the little ones are on the way. Well, Balthazar Loki is still bent on world domination. No big surprise there. I mean, what else is an evil genius billionaire going to do? Open a hardware store? That woman you met with last night – Olive Mylove – used to be his chief assistant. She's an expert in biochemistry, and she helped him to develop two deadly compounds.

"They call the first compound Gecko Juice. Silly name, but what the stuff does – not so silly. It's made with DNA from three different types of Brazilian rainforest lizards. These lizards have incredible powers of regeneration. Hack off a leg and it grows back in a week. Olive and Dr. Loki spliced DNA from those lizards with that of a fast-growing slime mold.

"If some of that Gecko Juice comes in contact with a human – that nasty genetic cocktail gradually combines with the person's own DNA and grows over them and into them. Eventually it kills them. After a day or two the new DNA completely saturates the body, just as mold works its way through anything rotten, and brings it back to... Well, not life, but a damned active form of death. The flesh becomes more reptilian, and so does the brain. The person becomes a sort of reptilian zombie. The body is still rotting, and the mold lives off the dead tissue – basically the creature is eating itself from the inside. But if it eats something living, the mold lives off of that instead, and if it gets enough nourishment, the lizard regeneration factor kicks in: it actually strengthens the body and repairs some of its damages. So basically, the more these zombies eat, the stronger they get. If they're starved, they'll eventually shrivel away to dust.

"Also, they have a unique mutant power. Their hands and feet can exude a tarlike, adhesive substance that gives them remarkable climbing abilities. You saw Olive in action with that. I guess the poor gal got some of that Gecko Juice on her in the lab. It hasn't killed her yet, but in about a week she'll be ... you know. One of them."

"But I touched one of those creatures," Pi said. "Am I–?"

"No, don't worry, you're not going to turn into a zombie. Their skin is dead and dry – no Gecko Juice there. But if one of them bit somebody, and some of their active DNA got into the bloodstream... That's a one-way ticket to Zombieville. Omicron, the paralysis gas in your pretty heels didn't work because zombies don't breathe. Like the slime mold that animates them, they have no use for lungs." Gamma tickled his cat under the chin. "Isn't Lulu a real cutie-pie? Have you ever seen a cuter cat in your entire life?"

"Adorable," Omicron said. "So what about the other compound?"

"Dr. Loki gave that stuff the delightful name of Piranha Spit," Gamma said. "They stumbled across that formula while they were making Gecko Juice. It's a super-activated form of slime mold that eats away flesh, living or dead, in record time. He lets his flunky Brimley use it to get rid of his enemies. He gave you a lively demonstration last night. I found out something interesting about Brimley while going through those papers. He's Dr. Loki's son."

"What about those tracers that Omicron fired at the car?" Pi said. "Do we have a fix on Dr. Loki's headquarters?"

"Yes," Gamma said. "But I can't tell you where it is. You two won't be going after him."

"What?" Omicron cried. "I thought this was our case!"

"It was – but now it's time to call in the big guns. The military." Their supervisor gave them an apologetic shrug. "One of the documents in that valise mentioned Project WILD – World Insurrection of the Living Dead. We've recently received reports of zombie outbreaks in China and Australia. Sounds like Dr. Loki is giving his plan some test runs before going global with it. We're here to protect the health of the planet – and in this case, that's going to take troops. But you two collected some valuable information, and I'll see that you're commended for that. Next week I'm sending you on a new assignment in Morocco. You did your part to help defeat Dr. Loki, so please – go celebrate. I know you two don't drink, but in this case, I think you should crack open a bottle of champagne. That's what I'll be doing after Lulu has her babies!"

In the elevator on their way out, Pi said, "I think Gamma's about ready for retirement."

Omicron gave him a hard look. "Why? Because he likes kittens? Gamma is brilliant man. A fine leader. He just gets a little – overenthusiastic – about cats. That's all." Then she grinned. "And after all, Lulu is sooo cuuute!"

Mother and son went down the street to a quaint little coffeehouse called Bean There, Done That. Coffee was their beverage of choice when it came to celebrating.

Pi ordered a cup of French Roast and Omicron decided to go all-out and have a latte. They sat in a booth under a painting of Elvis on velvet.

"I know I should feel happier," Omicron said, "but still, I'm a little disappointed. I wanted to be there when Dr. Loki was defeated. You and I have been chasing him for ten years. Before that, your father and I chased him for twenty years. I still sometimes wonder about the way your father died... Was Dr. Loki responsible?"

"I don't think so," Pi said. "He slipped in the bathroom and hit his head on the tub."

"Yes, but maybe your father was distracted, thinking about what to do about Dr. Loki, and..and..." Her voice trailed away. Then she said, "Listen to me. I've completely demonized Dr. Loki in my mind. Ridiculous. He's only a man. An evil, filthy-rich megalomaniac – but a man just the same."

"I know what you mean," Pi said. "Everywhere I go, I think I see him. Like that man by the counter, looking at the big cookies. I keep thinking, 'Is that Dr. Loki?'"

Omicron glanced toward the cookie display case and gasped. "Keep your voice down," she whispered. "That really is Dr. Loki." She turned away from the counter but continued to watch the billionaire in the mirror of her compact. There was no make-up in the silver case. Instead, it held a small communications device. She pressed a small red button, sending a distress signal to headquarters.

Pi picked up a menu sheet and pretended to read, watching Dr. Loki over the top of it. "What's he doing in here?"

"Looks like he's buying some big cookies. They're putting his order in a sack. It's to-go. I've signaled headquarters. We've got to stay on his trail, so when they find us – they'll find him, too. Hey, what's he doing? Is he coming over here?"

Dr. Loki was a tall, silver-haired man with black eyebrows and almond-shaped blue eyes. He walked up to their table and waved the to-go sack in front of them. "Hello, Margaret. Hello, Perry. Want some cookies? I followed you here from your secret headquarters. I hope you don't mind. Actually, I've known the location of your head-quarters for years – not much of a secret, I'm afraid. Would you like to come with me and see *my* secret headquarters? My car is right outside."

"I suppose we don't have a choice," Omicron said.

"Of course you do." the billionaire said. "I'm not pointing a gun at you. Brimley isn't here pointing a feather at you. Now come along, please. Aren't you even the least bit interested in my latest diabolical plan?"

*       *       *

They sat in the back of Dr. Loki's limousine, eating big cookies. Brimley was driving with one hand and holding his big cookie with the other. He was still wearing his black fedora, with a fresh feather tucked in the hatband.

"I do wish you'd drive with both hands, son," Dr. Loki said. "Put down that cookie."

"It'll get crumbs everywhere," the young henchman said.

"So what? We have one of those handheld vacuum thingies at the garage." Dr. Loki sighed with exasperation. "I don't want to get in a crash, okay? Now put down the cookie. You can eat it later."

He turned to Omicron. "Children. They need guidance every minute. I do admire how well you and Perry work together."

"You have a funny way of showing your admiration," she said. "You sent Brimley and some of your zombies to exterminate us the other night."

"Oh, I knew they wouldn't kill you," the billionaire said. "You're much too clever for that. I just wanted to distract you so that Brimley could get that valise back. I was very disappointed that he failed." He turned toward his son. "*Very* disappointed."

"Yeah, Dad. I heard you," Brimley said.

"Well, that was very civil of you, not really wanting to kill us. I guess." Omicron crossed her arms. "But why this great show of kindness all of a sudden? You're not trying to make me switch sides again, are you? You try that every five years. When a woman says 'No,' she means 'No.'"

Dr. Loki laughed. "Ah, you know me so well. Yes, my dear woman, I'm afraid I am. But this time I have a different sort of alliance in mind. Look what we have here. You, me, two fine young lads. Rather like a family. You and I have known each other for what, about thirty years now? Isn't it time we got married?"

"You've got to be joking!" Pi cried.

Now it was Omicron's turn to laugh. "I can't believe what I'm hearing! Me, marry you? You've been trying to ruin the world's health and enslave the masses for years! Right now you're trying to turn people into zombies! Plus, if the smell of this car is any indication, you smoke. I could never love a smoker."

Dr. Loki thought for a moment. "I would be willing to give up the cigarettes. Ah! We've arrived."

Pi looked out the window. They were in the parking lot of Yummy-Cream Doughnut's corporate headquarters. "So you're in the doughnut business now?"

Omicron shook her head. "I don't approve of doughnuts, either. All that sugar."

A few minutes later, they were in the main lobby of the building. Dr. Loki led them down a hallway lined with offices, through another small hallway cluttered with cardboard boxes, to an elevator with an 'Out Of Order' sign on it.

Brimley took off the sign and pressed the Down button. "Dad likes classical music," he said.

No one said anything.

He gestured toward Omicron. "I was hoping you liked classical music, too. Maybe you two have that in common."

Again, no one responded.

The henchman shrugged. "Well, excuse me for trying to make small talk."

The elevator doors opened and they entered. Brimley flipped up a panel above the floor buttons, revealing a small keyboard. He pressed several of the multi-colored buttons in rapid succession. The elevator began to descend.

"By the way, we found those tracers you fired at that other car," Dr. Loki said. "That vehicle is currently parked outside of a Presbyterian church."

"Earlier, you claimed you knew the location of our headquarters," Omicron said. "Why haven't you destroyed the place?"

The doctor smiled. "Because my greatest spy has ready access to that building."

"You don't mean Gamma!" Pi said.

"No ... his cat Lulu. His veterinarian has been on my payroll for years. Gamma brings Lulu to work whenever she's sick or pregnant. And she always wears a lovely pink flea collar installed with an equally lovely listening device." Dr. Loki tapped Omicron's purse. "Oh, and that compact you were using in the coffeehouse...? A homing device, perhaps? You never wear make-up, my dear."

"A squadron will be invading this cover operation any minute now," Pi said. "So you might as well give up."

The elevator doors opened and Dr. Loki led them out, down a long white hallway. "That's fine with me," he said. "Right now all the friendly Yummy-Cream Doughnut employees are driving home, and their offices are being filled with reptilian zombies. Your people have quite a surprise in store for them. And even if they get past the zombies, they'll never be able to get down here." He pulled a small metal box out of his pocket. He lifted its lid and pressed a button. A thunderous roar echoed behind them. "That elevator shaft is well and truly 'Out Of Order' now."

The hall soon ended in stainless steel double doors with a row of multi-colored buttons above one of the handles. The doctor stabbed a finger repeatedly at the buttons and a loud clack sounded. He then pulled open the doors and ushered the group through.

They now stood on a railed metal platform high above a cavernous work area. On the floor below were dozens of huge cages, each containing a group of the orange and yellow zombies. Metal tunnels led from the backs of the cages to the far wall, and presumably beyond. Workers in lab coats moved between the cages, throwing red chunks from buckets into the cages. They reminded Pi of zoo-keepers throwing meat to the lions. Some of the zombie-keepers were almost as homely as the creatures they were feeding.

"It really is quite a chore, keeping them supplied with the sort of nourishment they crave," Dr. Loki said. "They'll rot to nothing if they don't get fresh meat regularly. Fortunately, the world above us is teeming with homeless people, druggies, prostitutes, all sorts of walking tragedies. Project WILD will help to clean up the streets."

"I see. Dr. Loki, the great humanitarian." Omicron stared at the billionaire with contempt.

The doctor stepped up to a dais in the center of the platform. There he stood before a large control panel with several view screens. "See those tunnels behind the cages? They connect with the city's sewer system. They're closed off now, but I can open the way for my hungry darlings just by pressing a few buttons. I think you'd better agree to join forces with me, Margaret. It's really for the best. I can release zombies to routes leading to various sections of the city. They'll be swarming out of manholes everywhere. The people they don't devour will soon become zombies, too. Now let's see..." He pointed down toward the work area. "That cage leads to the park area. That one heads straight for a hospital zone..."

"Get away from those buttons," Pi said, rushing toward the

139

doctor.

"Not so fast!" Dr. Loki pulled out a gun. "I have a lot of state-of-the-art toys, but this old thing works pretty well, too."

Omicron slipped to the side behind Brimley, twisting the thin henchman's arm behind his back. She then put one of her own arms around his neck. "Come on now, Balthazar. You don't want me to snap your son's neck."

"I see we're at an impasse." Dr. Loki sighed wearily. "What shall I do now? I think the park could use a bit of color..." So saying, he pressed several buttons on the control panel. Below, a metal squeal sounded, as a tunnel gate began to open behind one of the cages.

The squealing became louder, almost deafening – and then stopped entirely. The zombies remained in their cage.

"I don't understand," Dr. Loki said. "Why didn't it open?" He stared down at the cage.

Suddenly Pi heard a faint, familiar squelching sound. He glanced up.

Olive Mylove was clinging to the wall six feet above him. She wore filthy jeans and a ripped sweater. She was almost completely transformed by the compound. Only one eye and part of her forehead appeared to be human.

She jumped down to the platform. Dr. Loki fired his gun at her, hitting her in the chest and shoulder. She didn't even flinch.

"Nice try," she said, "but I'm already more dead than alive. Now it's my turn." She removed Brimley's hat, pulled the feather from the band and flung it with deadly accuracy at the doctor's throat.

The billionaire screamed as his flesh was quickly eaten away by the voracious slime mold. His head lolled to one side, and then his neckbones gave way as the tissue connecting them was dissolved. His head fell off, hit the floor and began to roll.

Straight toward Omicron and Brimley.

Omicron quickly let go of the young man and scrambled back. Brimley was too terrified to move. Then Olive grabbed the head by the hair, and the henchman breathed a sigh of relief.

"Here. Play catch with Daddy," she said, tossing the grisly prize.

He caught it without thinking, streaking both of his hands with the bubbling gore at the stump. The pestilence spread quickly – to his wrists, his arms and onward until his entire body was consumed.

Soon Dr. Loki and his son were both nothing more than steaming piles of bones and human sludge.

"Thank you, Olive," Pi said. "You saved our lives. How did you get down here?"

"I know a secret way through the sewers," she said. "I jammed all the tunnel gates so that the zombies couldn't get into the sewers. I came back while I was still me to deal with Dr. Loki and his brat."

"Can we do anything to help you?" Omicron said. "Is there some kind of cure? An antidote?"

Olive let loose with a hard, rasping bark of a laugh. "This isn't something you can undo. Once a zombie, always a zombie. Zombies are forever. Now that I'm going to become one, the only answer is complete destruction of the body. For me–" She pointed down toward the work area. "–and for them. Even the people feeding them. Most of them have been bitten. And even the ones who haven't been bitten... They're traitors to the human race. They don't deserve to live."

Olive shambled to the dais and pressed some buttons on the control panel. A section of the wall opened up, revealing another white hallway.

"Dr. Loki's secret escape passage," Olive said. "He always tried to plan for every contingency. That will lead you to the bottom level of a nearby parking garage. You might as well take his sports car. Cherry red. Beautiful." She picked something up from off the dais and threw it to Pi. He caught it in mid-air: a metal ring with car keys on it.

"But we can't just leave you to...to..." Pi wasn't sure how to finish the sentence.

"To destroy myself?" Olive whispered hoarsely. "I assure you, oblivion is the best thing for me right now. I believe in reincarnation. I'll try to come back as something simple and helpful. Maybe a bee. A wonderful bee that only wants to make sweet honey." She nodded toward the exit. "What are you waiting for?"

"How are you going to – end this?" Omicron said. "I think we should know."

Olive smiled. "Yes, I suppose you should. You'll need to file a report, I'm sure. It's a two-part solution. The first part is *this*." She pushed some buttons on the control panel. Down below, cage doors opened into the work area. The zombies rushed out and began to attack their keepers, tearing into them with ravenous zeal.

Olive stroked the panel next to a large, square black button. "In a few minutes, I'll push this particular button exactly three times. That will activate the sprinklers."

Pi and Omicron both looked up. The expansive ceiling of the chamber was crisscrossed with metal pipes, with a nozzle at every intersection.

141

"Can you guess what's in those pipes up there?" Olive said.

Pi looked at the pile of bones and slush that had once been Dr. Loki – and nodded. Omicron nodded, too.

"Good." Olive said. "Now go."

Without another word, Pi and Omicron stepped over the threshold of the escape route. The wall panel slid shut behind them.

For a moment, mother and son stood in silence, lost in thought.

"So," Omicron said at last, "Dr. Loki is dead."

"Are you happy now?" Pi asked. "You even got to see him die. And next week, we're off to Morocco. Business as usual."

"Sure, I'm happy... It's strange, I had no idea he wanted to marry me. Do you think he actually loved me?"

"Does it matter? You could never have returned his love."

"I know that," she said with a sad smile. "But I suppose it's flattering. He was a handsome man. And smart. Rich, too. Pity he was so evil..."

They began to walk down the white hallway, toward the parking garage. Pi jangled the car keys in front of his mother. "Here you go. A souvenir."

"Oh, thanks." Omicron took them for his hand. "You know, maybe it's time for me to start dating. After all, Dr. Loki seemed to think I was hot stuff."

"Dating? But your work – a lot of guys might have a problem with that."

"There is one man who has asked me out a few times. I've always turned him down, but maybe that was a mistake. He's very sweet ...about my age...and he doesn't have a problem with my career."

"So who's–" Pi stopped walking and stared at Omicron. "Hey, wait a minute. Are you talking about Gamma?"

"As a matter of fact, I am." Omicron smiled and shrugged. "He's goofy about cats, but he's very nice and he thinks the world of you. He could never replace your father, but he's charming in his own way. I think I'll have dinner with him after we get back from Morocco. Is that okay with you?"

"Wow. I didn't see this coming." Pi took a deep breath. "Sure. I just want you to be happy. And Gamma is a great guy. He treats Lulu like a queen, so I bet he'll spoil you rotten. Flowers and mushy stuff."

"Probably." Omicron nodded. "But a little mush can be nice." She cocked her head to one side. "You know, maybe you should start dating, too. I wouldn't mind being a grandmother someday..."

Pi rolled his eyes. "Oh, Mother!"

# The Voice of the Pangyricon

I was onboard the Pangyricon when Velasko's Crane scooped up and deposited its most hideous prize. Perhaps you've seen the movie based on the incident – *Attack of the Space Zombies*. That studio paid me big bucks to act as a consultant for that project, but they didn't stick with the facts. They had the zombies talking, shooting guns – the creatures didn't do any of that. The movie didn't even mention Daniel, which really surprised me.

Let me tell you what really happened.

My name is Leon Sybek, and I was one of two-hundred Care Technicians on space station Pangyricon. Care Technician – a great title, but it only meant that I helped take care of the animals. A glamorized farm-hand.

Before that, I was loading dishes in the washers at SpaceTech Industries. A kitchen goon. So when I found out that Project Hermes needed folks with agricultural experience, I signed up. I grew up on a dairy farm, milking cows and feeding calves. As a child, I'd hated the work because it was so lonely and boring. But I figured, maybe farming would be more interesting in space.

And it was.

Sure, the tasks never changed from day to day. But it was thrilling to be up in space as part of a big mission – that made me feel pretty important, even though I was only tending to livestock. Plus, the other Care Technicians were friendly and liked to talk about all sorts of things, like books and current events and of course, Project Hermes.

Hermes was the messenger of the gods in Greek mythology, but I don't know why the project was named after him. Basically, the goal was to prepare Mars for colonization by Earth. That meant building enclosed work communities on the planet surface, changing the atmosphere, integrating flora and fauna, and thousands of other related objectives. I suppose they chose the name Hermes because we were delivering a message to Mars: Hey, we're moving in.

Of course, Mars was the Roman name of the Greek war god Ares, so they should've called it Project Mercury, since that was the Roman name for Hermes. Maybe they named it Hermes because there was already a planet Mercury – and Earth wasn't about to colonize that sun-scorched chunk of real estate.

143

Mars was a dead planet, but a clean one, too. Clean and dry. No lava, no sloppy oceans of liquified poisonous gases. Mars was *workable*.

The Pangyricon is a revolving space station in orbit around Mars. It's shaped like a giant wagon-wheel, with a huge spherical hub and five spokes that serve as hallways to the circular outer frame. Us workers lived in the hub and carried out our duties in the frame, where the supplies and animals were housed.

The hub contained a machine known as Velasko's Crane. I'm not a scientist, so I don't completely understand how it works. Here's what I know about the machine and the man who invented it:

There used to be a brilliant man named Daniel Velasko who was like a space-age version of Thomas Edison – always working, rarely sleeping, and coming up with incredible ideas on a regular basis. His greatest invention was the Crane, which made it possible to transport matter across great distances instantaneously. He'd named it after a carnival game he'd enjoyed as a child. The game featured a glass booth with a toy crane surrounded by prizes. The player used a crank and maneuvered the crane's scoop to grab at the little trinkets.

I once got to play that game at a retro outdoor festival that tried to recreate the old carnival experience. The glass prizes were always the hardest to grab because they were so slippery.

Velasko's Crane had three parts: a chamber that housed the control panel and power unit, and two rectangular platforms, each as big as a full-size mattress. One platform was set by the chamber and the other was taken to the final transport destination. When something needed to be transported, the item was placed on the platform by the chamber. The operator would make the appropriate calibrations, hit the right buttons and in a flash, the item would disappear and then show up instantly on the other platform, wherever that had been placed. Any platform could send or receive, but it needed a nearby chamber to send. Without the chamber, it could only receive.

I know all that because Daniel told me the details. Or rather, Daniel's electronic persona. Velasko had been one of the designers of the Pangyricon, and he'd loaded his memories, personality and intellect into its main computer decades ago. These elements had been integrated into the computer's behavioral programming to create a logical but friendly thinking machine. The space station didn't have a captain – it had a board of directors back on Earth, but no one person at the helm, symbolic or otherwise. It didn't need one, with Daniel looking after things.

Daniel was the voice of the Pangyricon, and he used to chat with me while I did my chores. A person could talk to the computer from any point on the station. Unlike a real person, he could talk with hundreds of different people at the same time. He always came across a smart, helpful friend who was both interesting and interested in what you had to say.

I remember the day he told me about the early days of Velasko's Crane. I was feeding the calves, which hopefully would spend their adult years grazing on the surface of a greener Mars.

"Attention, Daniel," I said. You had to start any conversation with those words to get the computer's attention. "How long did it take to come up with the Crane?"

"It only took me a few seconds to 'come up with' the idea," he said in its low, firm voice, which had a very slight metallic buzz. I liked that he acted like he was his own inventor. "It took much longer to actually make it work. Thirty years. With a few mistakes along the way, too. But that's to be expected."

"Yeah? What kind of mistakes?"

He laughed. "Where do I begin? Hmmm. Let me put it this way. Some substances transport better than others."

"You mean like glass?" I then told it about my own experience with the carnival crane game.

"That's the right idea," he said. "But it's easy to transport glass with my Crane. Glass sits still."

"I suppose any crane works better when the cargo isn't moving around," I said.

"Yes! Exactly!" His voice rose a couple notes when he was pleased or excited. "Right now the process of transportation is practically instantaneous. But in the early days, it used to take a few seconds. After if the cargo item was not absolutely still... It would either show up damaged or just not appear at all. Living things usually died – even if they weren't moving on the outside, their organs were still active on the inside. Like their beating hearts."

At that point, a few other Care Technicians came by to ask if I wanted to join them for lunch. One of them was Quinn, a young woman who liked me quite a lot. I enjoyed talking with her, but I wasn't attracted to her because she was very skinny and nervous. She reminded me of a hungry hummingbird in need of a nectar fix. "Gotta run," I said. "Talk to ya later, Daniel."

"See ya later, alligator," he replied. The computer ended most conversations that way. Just like the real Daniel Velasko, I suppose.

145

Later that week, we were scheduled to receive two new calves – holsteins, which are black and white and grow to be quite large. The calves already onboard were smaller, yellowish-brown jerseys.

Most of our coworkers were in the main leisure area, watching a broadcast of a baseball game. Quinn and I weren't big sports fans, so we'd agreed to take care of the livestock transport at that time. The platforms were phenomenally expensive, which was why we only had one onboard. Two or three would have been more convenient – especially in the livestock quarters – but that sort of expense just wasn't in the budget.

"Why holsteins?" Quinn asked as we stood by the platform. "Holsteins get too big! And they're not as manageable as jerseys. They're just big and stupid."

"They're only sending two," I said. "And they're just calves. It's probably part of a feasibility study. They do need to consider holsteins – they give more milk, and its low-fat, too. If they don't work out, they probably won't send any more. Don't get all upset about it."

"I have a right to be upset," Quinn said. "I grew up on a farm with holsteins on it. That information is in my personal file–I'm well-informed on the matter. I wish somebody had thought to ask me."

I ruffled her hair. "Well, if I was ran this banana boat, I'd run every major livestock decision your way."

She gave me a very sweet smile.

"Okay," said Remson, the Transport Technician. He was in the chamber, speaking over the room's audio system. "Here they come, fresh from the dewy fields of Earth. Ready?"

"Sure," I replied. The calves would arrive harnessed within a metal stall, so it wasn't like we'd have to catch them.

We stood by the platform – but nothing happened.

"What's wrong?" Quinn said.

Through the glass of the control chamber, I could see that Remson was talking on a communicator. Apparently he'd turned off the audio system so we couldn't hear what was being said.

Remson finished his call and then stepped out of the chamber. He walked up to us and said, "I don't think the calves will make it."

"Hooray!" Quinn shouted.

Remson gave her an angry look. "This is serious. I'll tell you what happened, but you didn't hear it from me, okay?"

"Maybe you shouldn't tell us at all," I said. "Daniel will hear you telling us." I looked up at a small black box in the far corner of the

146

ceiling. That box housed Daniel's eyes, ears and other sensors for that room, as well as his voice.

Remson smiled. "Daniel sees and hears everything. But so long as no person or property is being injured, and nobody says..." He then mouthed the words 'Attention, Daniel,' "...it doesn't become part of the permanent log. So don't say – you know what."

"Okay already," Qinn said. "What's up with the calves?"

"One wasn't harnessed right," Remson said, "and it broke out of the stall just before transport and ran – bang! – right into the side of the chamber in mid-transmission."

Quinn laughed. "See? Holsteins are nothing but trouble."

The Transport Technician continued. "The other calf and the stall were sent, but – well, they're lost. Who knows where. Just like Valesko."

"Whoa!" I said. "What does that mean – 'just like Velasko'?"

Remson shrugged. "That's how he disappeared. No body ever showed up. Didn't you know that? There was a big court case long ago. Somebody even made a movie out of it – *Murder By Crane*."

"I saw that," Quinn said. "Velasko's wife used to help him in the lab, and she had a boyfriend on the side. She wired a chamber so it would switch off in mid-transmission the next time hubby traveled by Crane, leaving him out in..." She gestured vaguely into the air. "Wherever."

"Yeah," Remson said, "and that's where that calf is right now. Wherever."

Suddenly a sequence of beeps issued from the transport chamber. Remson ran back inside and picked up the communicator. He listened for a minute and then said to us over the audio system. "They've managed to lock onto the transport coordinates again. They're going to try and finish the transmission. You two ready?"

"I don't like this," Quinn said.

I ruffled her hair again. "Oh, give it up, holstein-hater. Yeah, we're ready!"

I once read that a long time ago, a fire devastated the city of Chicago after a cow knocked over a lantern. Who'd have thought another rambunctious bovine could kick-start a catastrophe in space? I was there to see the first step.

And it literally was a step. The metal stall appeared, its pipework structure drenched with blood. But there was no calf to be seen. And something horrible stepped off the platform.

It was a corpse. A walking corpse with blue skin, streaked with

147

dust and what looked like thick strands of yellowish-green cobwebs. Its eyes were tightly squinted shut. Its face was smeared with blood and strings of meat still hung from its broken teeth.

"Attention, Daniel!" I screamed. "Daniel, help us! Activate security systems!" None of us had any weapons. There had never been any need for them.

"Interesting!" the computer said in its higher voice of excitement. "I've completed a brain-scan on this being and though the organ is profoundly altered, I can detect familiar patterns. That is my original body."

"Don't just scan that thing!" Remson said as he came out of the chamber. "Activate security systems!"

"Yes! Look what it did to the calf!" Quinn cried.

"I detect animal blood, but no animal," the computer said. "I cannot activate security systems based on an external occurrence."

The creature's eyes slowly opened, revealing twin milky-white orbs. Apparently it had needed some time to get used to the light. It rushed to the door, which slid open, like all work area doors when somebody stepped up to them. The thing then raced down the hall.

Remson ran into the transport chamber and got on the communicator. Quinn went to the emergency intercom by the fire control equipment and tried to summon a Security Technician.

I looked around the room for something that might be used as a weapon. I noticed the wall-mounted fire extinguisher – a long metal cylinder. Good enough.

"Attention, Daniel!" I screamed as I ran out of the chamber, holding the cylinder over my head. I was ready to bring it down on that dead thing's skull. "Where did the creature go?"

"Creature?" Daniel said.

"Your body. Where did it go?"

"My body is simply moving through the station. It has not injured any person or property." The computer's voice was low and steady, as always. "You, however, appear to be acting in an aggressive manner. You are holding that extinguisher in a position that suggests attack."

I lowered the extinguisher and cradled it in my arms. "Sorry, Daniel. I just wanted to see if I could lift it over my head." I hated having to lie, but this was a desperate situation. "Can you tell me where your body went? I want to welcome it onboard and show it how this fire extinguisher works."

"It is now leaving elevator 7 on level 3," Daniel said.

"Quinn! Remson!" I shouted into the transport chamber. "That thing just got off the elevator by the laundry area. Let Security know!"

I then hurried to elevator 6, which opened onto the third level near the medical area. I wanted to warn those folks before going to the laundry area, which was probably empty, since most workers were watching the baseball game. The Security Technicians were probably enjoying the game, too. They had communicators, but of course, those only do the job if their users are carrying them. We only had two people in Security, and they also had other duties onboard, Daniel being fully equipped to take care of most defense issues. They really just served as a backup in case of a computer failure or malfunction.

Once I was on the third level, I ran to the medical area, where a young male nurse named Duane was looking at a magazine centerfold. He blushed when he saw me.

"Take your porn and get out of here," I said. "There's an – an intruder onboard." I had been about to say 'monster,' but I'd figured he wouldn't believe that.

"An intruder?" he said. "Attention, Daniel!"

"Yes?" the computer replied.

"Is there an intruder onboard?" the nurse asked.

"No," Daniel said. "I am familiar with every person currently onboard."

The nurse stared curiously at me.

"Attention, Daniel!" I said. "Is there a person with white eyes, blue skin and blood on his face wandering around on this level?"

"Yes, there is," the computer said. "He is now in the laundry area."

A scream echoed from down the hall.

The nurse grabbed his magazine and ran out of the room.

"Find a Security Technician!" I called after him. Then I ran toward the laundry area. When I got there, I found, slumped in a corner, the body of Kitchen Technician Barnes, a middle-aged, heavyset woman. A strand of that strangely colored cobweb was stuck to one of her legs. Her left hand had turned blue and even as I watched, the color began to creep slowly up her wrist.

"Attention, Daniel!" I screamed. "Your body has killed Barnes! Activate security systems!"

"My body took Barnes by the hand." Daniel's voice was in the higher, excited mode. "It was interesting! He did not appear to be hurting her, and yet she made a noise of alarm. She then moved to the floor."

"She's dead!" I screamed. "Your body took a living person and

149

made her dead. That is personal harm, Daniel! Activate security systems!"

"I have scanned Barnes." The computer's voice rose yet another note. "I can still detect brain-wave patterns. The organ has been altered, but it is still functional. Also, I can still detect cellular activity. Barnes is becoming more like my body."

"But that's bad!" I said.

"Define 'bad' in this instance," the computer prompted.

"I give up!" I said. "It's no use talking to you."

"Very well," he said, back in his lower voice. "See you later, alligator."

"No, wait! Attention, Daniel!" I looked down at Barnes. Her arm was now blue from the fingertips to the elbow. "I have a funny question for you. What would you do if I manually activated the lock on the laundry area door?"

"The manual locks are only for fire or security emergencies during times of computer failure," Daniel replied. "I'm fully functional, so there'd be no reason to do that. We are not experiencing any emergencies. I would unlock the door."

"Can I ask another funny question?"

"I don't understand your sense of humor, but sure. Ask."

I watched the blue creep slowly up Barnes' arm, toward the shoulder. "Actually it's a three-part question. Part one: if you saw anybody hurt someone else, what would you do?"

"Well, I have defense mechanisms in place throughout the Pangyricon," he said. "If I detected somebody acting in a violent, aggressive manner, I would incapacitate them."

"Part two: what would you do if I bashed in her head with this fire extinguisher?"

"I would incapacitate you, using one or more of several methods, such as electric shock or sedative gas."

"Now for part three: what would you do if your body tried to touch me while I was unconscious?"

"Nothing. That would not be a problem."

"But don't you see? Your body is carrying some kind of energy force, or plague or pestilence, or...or..."

"I cannot detect any such radiation or microorganisms," Daniel said.

"But it's something you've never encountered before!" I shouted. "Damn you, Daniel! I can't tell you what's wrong with your body because I don't know. But something is very, very wrong! Why can't

150

you believe me?"

"I am sorry you're upset," the machine said. "But if I believed every single thing any person told me – without the subsequent presentation of supporting data – I would be of no use to the Pangyricon. I require some form of documented verification."

I ran out of the laundry room. I didn't want to be in there when Barnes got up. I had the horrible feeling that she'd want to take me by the hand. "Attention, Daniel. Where is your body now?"

"In the dining area." That was at the other end of level 3.

"Has it touched anybody else?"

"Yes. It has touched thirty-five crew members. All are currently resting. Now thirty-six. Thirty-seven. Thirty-eight."

"That's enough."

"See you later, alligator."

I decided the only thing to do was escape – to get back to Earth and tell the authorities what was going on. So I took the elevator back down to level 2 and the transport room.

Remson and Quinn were both in the chamber with its door closed. When they saw me, they came out. "Leon, you're okay!" Quinn said, rushing up to hug me.

"What's happened since I left?" I said.

"Security isn't responding and Daniel refuses to acknowledge that anything is wrong," Remson said. "He won't even let us lock the door of this area because there isn't a fire. And to make matters worse, the entire Crane system is shut down. Earth has it turned off on their end. Same with the colonies on Mars. So we're here stuck in the middle. The folks at SpaceTech want to talk to Daniel before they do anything else, but he sees no reason to involve them."

"Why is the Crane shut down?" I said.

"Velasko wasn't the only one to get lost in the Crane over the years," he said. "There have been about nine or ten others. We should never have told them what happened. Now they're afraid those other zombies will escape from whatever void they've been in all this time."

"Zombies?" The term, at that time, didn't mean much to me. I thought it meant somebody who was extremely stupid, or just walking around in a daze. "Who's calling them that?"

Remson nodded toward Quinn.

"I collect old horror films," she said. "Some of those movies had zombies in them."

"Well, I don't watch scary movies," I said. "What are zombies?"

"Zombies are dead bodies that have come back to life," she said.

"They eat the flesh of the living, and if they bite somebody, that person turns into a zombie, too."

I looked at the dried blood on pipes of the metal stall. "Why didn't the zombie go after any of us when it got here?"

"It wanted to get the Hell out of here," Remson said. "Away from this equipment." He nodded toward the transport platform. "That's the only thing that can send it back to the void. Not that the machine can do us any good now."

"Maybe those movie zombies eat people, but this one hasn't bitten anybody." I then told them about Barnes and my frustrating conversation with Daniel.

"Perhaps it doesn't eat humans," Quinn said. "I think it just wants to convert them. Maybe they hunt down their food in packs. I wonder what kind of animals live in that void of theirs...?" She picked up a length of cobweb draped over the edge of the platform. "Look how fat this strand is. If this is from some kind of spider, it must be as big as a horse." She flicked the sticky thing off her fingers. "That zombie wouldn't need much help to hunt here on the station. All the animals are in pens. Completely helpless. I hope it hasn't found the livestock yet."

"Attention, Daniel!" I said. "Is your body still in the station's central hub?"

"Yes. In the main leisure area."

Quinn's eyes went wide with horror. "Oh my God!"

I dreaded asking the next question. "How many people has it touched?"

"Three-hundred and thirty-six."

Remson rushed to the transport chamber. Quinn and I followed him. "Attention, Daniel," he said. "Bring up the leisure area on my main monitor."

"Sure thing," the computer said.

The image sprang into view on the screen, along with a chorus of echoing screams. The zombie simply wandered through the auditorium, which was filled with people running and shouting. Every now and then it would place its hand on someone. That person would instantly stop moving and slowly sink to the floor, as though suddenly very tired. There was nothing violent or aggressive in anything the creature did.

"Are any of the people who have been touched by your body moving around now?" Remson asked. "And if so, how many?"

"Yes," Daniel said. "Seventy-three. Now seventy-four. Seventy-

152

five."

"Shut up," the Transport Technician said.

"See you later, alligator," the computer replied.

"Well, isn't that great," Remson said. "While we're having ourselves a nice cozy chat, that monster is turning this space station into zombie-land. People are probably wondering why the Hell nobody's helping them. And Daniel's just sitting back, watching the whole damned freak show. He won't even let us fight back."

"Because he hasn't got a clue," Quinn said. "Follow me!" So saying, she left the chamber and ran out of the room.

Remson and I ran after her. "Wait up!" I called to her. "What's going on?"

"I know what I'm doing," she yelled. "Just follow me!"

So we did. What else could we do?

As we ran, we passed an empty meeting room that had recently been used for a retirement dinner. I noticed a pile of soiled tablecloths on one of the chairs. "Wait a second!" I shouted. I ran in and grabbed the whole stack.

"Put one of these around you," I said, handing out tablecloths. "That way a zombie can't touch your bare skin."

"Great idea," Quinn said. "Now let's get going."

There were two left over, so I decided to carry them in case one of us lost our covering. We followed her down the hall, and I soon realized we were heading toward the workers' living quarters. Just as we reached an intersection with another hallway, a group appeared directly in front of us.

A group of zombies, with the Velasko creature leading the pack.

Daniel Velasko's ghastly head tilted slightly to one side. The corners of his mouth drew back in what might have been a smile. The rest turned their staring white eyes toward us, and reached out with writhing hands. The group included several Care Technicians and both Security Technicians. Barnes was there, too, her face as blue as a summer sky.

I ran ahead of Quinn and flung a tablecloth over them. One of the creatures reached out for my shoulder, but it only grabbed a handful of linen.

We went around them and continued down the hall. The creatures simply followed us, and the only sound they made was the brisk shuffle of their feet moving down the hall.

At another hall intersection I saw another group coming our way. "I hope you know where we're going, Quinn," I said.

153

"Through here." She gestured toward a small game room. After we entered, she closed the door behind us. Then we cut across the room to a door leading into another hallway, which was clear.

She pointed two doors down. "There. My room."

"Your room?" Now I was completely confused. "What's in there?"

"Please, don't ask questions," Quinn said with a tight, almost grim smile. She opened her door and we followed her in. Then she locked up behind us. We piled the tablecloths by the wall.

She opened the door of a closet and pulled out a wheeled cart with an old-fashioned movie projector on top. She plugged it into an outlet with a special adapter.

Quinn grabbed a reel of film off a lower platform of the cart. She installed the movie on the projector and spent a few minutes rolling the reel around, looking closely at the frames until it had reached a particular spot. Finally she set up a screen on the other side of the room.

"All set," she said, picking up a pen from her coffee table. She turned down the lights and switched on the projector.

The scene that popped up before us depicted decayed, blood-spattered corpses chasing a screaming couple through a field. She'd mentioned that she collected old movies – this had to be one of them. An old horror movie with zombies in it.

"Attention, Daniel!" Quinn called toward the black box in the corner of her living room.

"Yes?" the computer said, helpful as always.

"Look at the screen," she said. "Evidence of the living dead going after humans. That's just what's happening here. That's what those creatures are – walking corpses. Zombies. Look, damn you! Documented evidence! Just look!"

The couple on the screen raced down a country road – only to find themselves stumbling into a cemetery filled with the glassy-eyed horrors.

"I am unfamiliar with this data source," Daniel asked in his high, excited voice. "What is this I am watching?"

"Archived news footage," she lied. Quite convincingly, too. "The information was suppressed by the government so that people wouldn't go into a panic. I have the last remaining bit of evidence. Look, Daniel! That woman is crawling out of a grave. The dead aren't supposed to come back to life. You know that!"

"You'd better do something about all this right now," Remson said. He'd obviously picked up on Quinn's plan and was proving himself to be a fine actor. "Do something right now before more people are turned into zombies."

"Zombies," the computer repeated. "I have no data files regarding that subject."

Quinn stood directly between Daniel's box and the projector, and I saw her quickly jab the pen into the workings of the projector. The image on the screen froze as the film began to bunch up inside the machine. She turned it off. "Damn!" she said. "This stupid old clunker isn't working right." Quinn had thought through her plan well. It wouldn't do for Daniel to see too much of the movie. One bad special effect and he'd realize that the evidence was questionable.

Quinn turned toward Daniel's box. "I think you've seen enough. You saw them, right? The zombies? You saw how scared the living people were, right? They were scared for their lives – just like us!"

For a moment, Daniel was silent.

At last he said, "This situation requires further investigation. In the meantime, I will seal off all rooms and hallways containing the zombies." He paused, as if to give the matter more thought, and then added, "I will vent liquid nitrogen into those sectors to cryogenically freeze them. If there are any unaffected humans in with them, they can be sorted out and revived later. I will contact my board of directors on Earth and tell them that we need additional assistance."

"Great idea, Daniel," I said. "You do that."

"See ya later, alligator," he said.

Now you know the real story behind *Attack of the Space Zombies*.

At the end of the movie, I was named the captain of the Pangyricon. Sorry, but that didn't happen. The writers did get one fact right: Quinn and Remson fell in love, got married and moved to a Martian colony.

I went back to Earth and made some big bucks with that movie studio I mentioned. Eventually I opened a pet store with the money.

The Daniel persona was removed from the Pangyricon and according to Remson, is now being used on a hydroponics farm on Mars. Daniel now makes daily recommendations regarding the nurturing of okra, asparagus and tomato plants.

Some of my old coworkers drop by my pet store when they vacation on Earth. They tell me that the big decisions on the space station are now being made by actual human beings.

Imagine that.

# Z.W.A. (with Michael Kaufmann)

It would not have been entirely accurate to say there was tension in the boardroom.

Tension would have implied a strong level of interpersonal feeling between the room's occupants – and although all the executives worked together closely, none of them really cared much personally about the others. It's hard for zombies to feel. They just don't have it in them. But they do have a keen sense of survival – at least the brighter ones do – and so conflict and competition still exist in their day-to-day afterlives.

The deceased but ambulatory executives gathered in the boardroom at DedCo headquarters had been sent copies of the latest annual growth report the previous week. Something needed to be done, that much was clear: the document had stated, quite simply, that there had been no growth in the previous year on which to report.

Mr. Corpus, jowly, shockingly pasty – even by zombie standards – and hair-plugged, sat at the head of the long, well-polished mahogany table. He had been the chief executive officer at DedCo for as long as anyone could remember ... and for the undead, that's a long time. A visionary, he had steered the global zombie community through good times and bad. He had been instrumental in the zombie movie boom of the 1970s, giving certain directors access to actual zombies. That outstanding strategy had proven quite successful in raising both the profile and reputation of the undead in those early years, and Mr. Corpus had enjoyed nearly unprecedented popularity.

Then – as so often happens to visionaries – he'd made a significant mistake wholly attributable to his expanding ego. The undead actors decided they should be paid scale, and he backed them. The directors simply went to living extras caked with makeup, and once again, real zombies were dead to Hollywood.

The quality of the films went down, of course, with only a couple of notable exceptions – but by then, nobody seemed to care. Zombie movies were a niche market with a devoted following that would watch whatever came out, just for the sake of watching people being devoured. Mr. Corpus survived the unrest that followed, but sadly, he was forever chasing the glory years.

Ms. Scuhl sat to the right of Mr. Corpus. Tall and cadaverously (of course) thin, with deep-set, glowing eyes that seemed to bore right through you, she was the heir apparent to the head of DedCo. She still

156

had a nose, undoubtedly because she'd had some work done before becoming a zombie, and that well-sculpted nasal triumph was the envy of many at DedCo, though they'd never admit it.

There were rumors, as there always will be in such situations, that Ms. Scuhl and Mr. Corpus were more than just colleagues, but it was doubtful there was any substance to such hearsay. After all, they were zombies, and erotic dalliance was not a particularly high priority. Mr. Corpus didn't have a problem with keeping his personal parts stiff. The challenge rested in keeping them from falling off.

Ms. Scuhl prided herself on being the smart, reasoning voice of caution, not easily swayed by the latest trends. She had warned against supporting the actors' demands for scale back in the day, fearing that even if they got it, they'd get too big for their funereal britches and DedCo would lose its sway with them. She'd come out looking good when the whole movie deal fell apart completely, and she had leveraged that success into her current seat at Mr. Corpus' right hand.

Meanwhile, to the left sat Mr. Dullaird, a dim-witted flunky who seemed to come to meetings mainly for the food. He was just bright enough to realize his continued suckling at the DedCo executive teat was solely at Mr. Corpus' pleasure, so he was always encouraging Mr. Corpus' meanderings down the golden path of yesteryear, quick to defer to Mr. Corpus on all issues, and eager to give Mr. Corpus loud huzzahs whenever the doddering chief opined on anything.

Incredibly, those toadyish tactics actually worked for Mr. Dullaird, whose seemingly infinite capacity for concurrence was matched only by his insatiable appetite for the finer comestibles regularly sampled at the DedCo executive table. It was he who first broke the silence with a predictable refrain as Paolo, the corporate chef, wheeled in the day's delicacies.

"Good, Paolo, yes, very good," the obsequious corpse wheezed through corpulent chops. "What do we have today?"

Paolo lifted the gleaming silver lids off the serving platters. "Brains on the half-skull, cerebellum cutlets on rye, and spinach-ganglion dip with Hawaiian bread. And a lovely 2001 blush that I think you'll enjoy." With that, he uncorked one of two rosy-hued bottles and filled a glass for Mr. Corpus.

"Brains on the half-skull, my favorite," Mr. Dullaird enthused, loading his plate.

Ms. Scuhl made a face. Getting rid of Mr. Dullaird was high on her to-do list once she acceded to the head chair.

157

Mr. Corpus sipped the wine, and nodded vaguely toward Paolo, who smiled, tipped his head forward, and left the room.

Mr. Reiper, chief financial officer of DedCo, got up and lurched to the catering cart. He had a fondness for Paolo's spinach-ganglion dip – the sweet bread contrasted well with the slightly tangy flavor his discriminating palette savored in the ganglia. He was in no hurry to start this meeting. His report on the organization's finances was no better than last month's, which had been disappointing at best. Better to enjoy Paolo's excellent fare than to rush into news that would take him nowhere.

Just as he returned to his seat, in strode young Mr. Nekro. Fashionably late, as usual, and sporting the latest business casual, he was the very picture of a new generation, ready to take on new challenges and push, push, push the envelope of acceptability.

"Good morning, everyone," Mr. Nekro said. His glittering black eyes took in the room; they locked with Ms. Scuhl's for an eternal instant, then moved on. Sniffing the air, he turned to the food cart. "Ah, our favorite finger-foods," he observed. "Paolo is catering to our every whim, as usual." Then his brow furrowed and he wrinkled what was left of his shrunken nose. "A blush? *With cerebellum cutlets?* How gauche. A pinot noir would have been far more appropriate."

"I like the blush," Mr. Reiper snapped. "It goes well with the dip." He had little patience for young Mr. Nekro and his airs. Twenty years earlier, maybe even ten, he'd have given Mr. Nekro what-for and sent the upstart packing. But times had changed, and the balance of power was shifting. Mr. Reiper didn't care for that, but what could he do?

"But really," Mr. Nekro said, "nobody drinks blush anymore."

"Well, they should," Mr. Reiper muttered. Nobody heard him. He dropped into his chair in front of his plate and took a long pull from his glass.

Mr. Corpus called the meeting to order as his executives fed on the gourmet spread. Mr. Corpus himself rarely ate in front of his subordinates. To him, feeding was a vulnerable time, when one was chiefly concerned with satisfying one's cravings. Mr. Corpus eschewed even the appearance of vulnerability.

"Today's agenda concerns recruitment and retention," he announced. "As you are all aware from that lamentable growth report, the former is more urgent than the latter. However, a concerning number of members have had their heads separated from their bodies somewhat prematurely, as compared with historical norms. As this is more quickly addressed than recruitment, we should start there. Ms. Scuhl?"

"Thank you, sir," Ms. Scuhl said as she rose gracefully from her chair. She clicked a button on a remote control in her hand and images sprang to life on a flat-screen monitor mounted on the far wall. "As you can see from the graph, the average period of post-existence has been relatively stable throughout the ages. Our population experienced a shortening of that period when zombie stories were popularized in the general media, with resultant widespread dissemination of methods to end post-existence. We quickly countered that unfortunate trend with a zombie education campaign, instructing our legions on ways to be more prudent in their choices of meals. Our current difficulties..." She clicked to the next graphic, which broke down the statistics for recent post-existence terminations into various categories. "...can in all likelihood be resolved in a similar manner."

"Very good, Ms. Scuhl," Mr. Corpus said, nodding. "What stands in our way?"

"Currently, only funding. Over the past two years, we have seen our education budget decline by 27 percent. That simply is not enough to sustain our population in the current climate. This has been discussed before, but no action has been taken by the appropriate department."

Mr. Reiper nearly choked on his spinach and ganglion dip. Had he possessed a working heart, his face would have been red with anger. He glared at Ms. Scuhl. "That money was diverted from the education fund to the legal fund at your request, Ms. Scuhl. I believe the record will show that I voted against that decision."

"I believe, Mr. Reiper, that the record will tell a different tale. The vote to which you refer concerned increasing the legal budget but had no recommendations attached concerning which budget said monies should come from." Ms. Scuhl's voice was steely, her gaze direct and unforgiving. "When it came to this board's attention that you had indeed appropriated monies from the education budget, rather than some less-pressing initiative, a recommendation was made to readjust the budget accordingly. Has that happened?"

Mr. Reiper ground his teeth. He had expected pressure about the bleak financial position of the organization, but not an ambush placing the blame for the retention decline squarely on his bony shoulders. "Many important fiscal agendas have complicated reassignment of monies – including the project to initiate an internship program at DedCo," he said pointedly. Two could play at this game. "Incidentally, I've seen no interns here in quite some time, Ms. Scuhl – except, of course, for that young lady who was assisting you. How is your pet project coming along?"

It was Ms. Scuhl's turn to grind her yellowed teeth. "That program was approved by everyone here, yourself included. In fact, it has been the only program so far implemented with concrete results toward expanding both recruitment and retention." Her thin, cracked lips curved almost imperceptibly. "As for that young lady, I'm pleased to announce that Ms. Sickel is showing an aptitude for numbers that I'm confident will one day see her seated at this table."

And there it was. There was utter silence in the boardroom as the executives considered the gauntlet that Ms. Scuhl had thrown down.

Everyone knew that should Ms. Scuhl indeed become CEO, she would have the power to replace Mr. Reiper with one of her own. Mr. Reiper had no retort – there was nothing he could say, and he knew it. Mr. Dullaird paused in his feasting, the brains from his fourth half-skull inserted halfway into his mouth, his eyes going from Ms. Scuhl to Mr. Reiper and back again. Mr. Nekro studied the players carefully, scanning for an advantage he could use.

Only Mr. Corpus seemed nonplussed. "Reminds me of my first intern," he said. "Of course, we called them apprentices back then. A promising young zombie, he was, with a real head for business."

"Mow mimfrefing," Mr. Dullaird managed as he sucked the rest of the brains into his mouth, clearly relieved.

"Yes, young Mr. Jaksten seemed destined for greatness," Mr. Corpus went on, warming to the topic. "At first he blended in quite well with the living, which was a great advantage, I can tell you. His fame was worldwide, and his cover of being a great pop musician gave him unprecedented access to living humans of all ages, sizes, and flavors. As his features began to decompose, he needed plastic surgery to keep himself looking alive. Eventually, something went wrong in his head – very wrong. He lost perspective of how he was supposed to look, and underwent further surgeries until he looked more like a zombie than most zombies! Then he began to hunger after inappropriate parts of living bodies – and that hunger concerned carnal, rather than digestive, needs. A true perversion of the zombie creed. I confronted him many times, encouraging him to change his ways and return to respectability. Sad to say, it was all for naught. He broke off all contact with DedCo and isolated himself at his ranch, where...where..." Mr. Corpus' voice trailed off, his hollow eyes staring into the past.

"An astute cautionary tale, sir," said Mr. Dullaird, wiping his mouth. "You've certainly experienced it all."

"Yes, quite," Ms. Scuhl hissed from her seat, which she had taken when it became clear Mr. Corpus's tale was going to meander completely off-topic. "But perhaps we should move on to the issue of recruitment."

Mr. Corpus, still staring, did not seem to hear her.

"Sir," Mr. Nekro said, "shall we move on to recruitment, or did you have something further...?"

"Hmm–? Oh yes, quite. I mean, no. Can we see the latest figures on recruitment, Mr. Nekro?"

The young executive stood and addressed the group. "Fellow board members, recruitment figures have hit an all-time low." He bent down to tap a key on his laptop computer and a chart – the first image of his PowerPoint presentation – sprang up on the flat-screen monitor. "In the last fiscal year, we were down 8.6 percent from LY, and 10.3 percent from the 10YA."

Mr. Dullaird cocked his head to one side. "'LY'?"

"Last year," Mr. Nekro explained with a small sigh.

"Right..." Mr. Dullaird then cocked his head to the other side.

Mr. Nekro was waiting for it. "Ten Year Average, Mr. Dullaird. Here, I've brought you another glossary of commonly used business terms so you can follow along. Just like the one I gave you at our last meeting."

Mr. Dullaird took the document without any sign of embarrassment.

"This trend is all the more alarming given the general malaise present among the zombie population at-large," Mr. Nekro said. "We're facing the biggest crisis of our post-existence, and yet the mood among most of us is one of ennui."

Mr. Dullaird looked up again.

"Boredom," Ms. Scuhl explained. "Listless weariness."

Mr. Dullaird nodded and took up a pen. "That's a good word. I like it. Aahn-weee... Yes, very good."

Mr. Nekro rolled his eyes and continued. "If we are to successfully tackle this problem, we need to engage our target demographic." The next image in his presentation depicted a busy downtown street. "We need to be more than just the undead to people. People aren't interested in the Hollywood zombie anymore. Sure, they like to see blood and guts—who doesn't?—but they also know a good swing with a baseball bat will be every bit as effective as a chainsaw at

161

removing a zombie's head from its body, thus ending its post-existence."

Mr. Reiper squirmed slightly at the graphic depictions that popped up on the screen, all taken from Hollywood movies. Mr. Nekro saw this, smiled, then continued with his presentation. "While feeding on the living is glamorous enough to entice just about anyone, scenes of mere kids taking out hordes of zombies makes potentially willing subjects hesitant to enter such an easily-ended state of post-existence. This hesitation often results in a zealous defense that, as we saw from Ms. Scuhl's presentation, has an extremely adverse effect on retention as well. As a result, our numbers are decreasing at a multiplicative rate."

"Let me get this straight. You want us to try *convincing* the living to become zombies?" Mr. Reiper asked incredulously.

"Exactly," Mr. Nekro said, walking around the table as he warmed to his well-prepared speech. "With a well-targeted multimedia campaign leveraging best-practice paradigms in a seamless content solution, we can proactively create value-added synergies that will result in low-risk, high-yield enterprise-wide returns." He paused, his arms spread wide, his eyes blazing. "We shall revolutionize our industry!"

"It'll never work," Mr. Reiper said into his glass.

Ms. Scuhl's moue was sufficient to convey her opinion.

Mr. Dullaird simply blinked.

Mr. Corpus watched Mr. Nekro closely, with occasional furtive glances at Ms. Scuhl. He knew a power play when he saw it. Mr. Nekro wasn't ready to go head-to-head with Ms. Scuhl just yet, but he was certainly laying the groundwork. If the young executive could position himself as the wave of the future, Ms. Scuhl might have a challenger after all. Mr. Corpus found this new turn of events interesting. He leaned back in his chair, placed his fingertips together, and watched the play unfold.

"What...? How...?" Mr. Dullaird asked, predictably.

"We'll show people the other side of zombie post-existence," Mr. Nekro said. "After all, we're more than just a horde of mindless, ravenous cadavers stumbling through the night. The living need to know what makes being a zombie so exciting – so rewarding! We can achieve this objective in a variety of ways. I'm thinking, maybe an indie film at Sundance showing the lighter side of post-existence, sort of a 'lively side of death' motif. Also, a History Channel special on zombies through the ages, featuring interviews with such successful

162

undead movers and shakers as – well, certainly you, sir!" He gestured toward Mr. Corpus. "We'll donate to National Public Radio! Imagine, an insightful piece on eschatology, 'brought to you by DedCo, reminding you: you're not really living until you're dead.' We'll raise the profile of zombies – not by flooding the market with images of shambling hordes, but by selectively introducing upscale, successful power-zombies. Zombies with style ... flair ... panache! Z.W.A.!"

"What does–" Mr. Dullaird began.

"Zombies with attitude!" Mr. Nekro cried.

"I can't believe I'm hearing this," Ms. Scuhl said. "With our finances in the shape they're in, you have the gall to suggest spending money on an image campaign? To convince the living they'd be better off undead? Mr. Reiper, kindly tell young Mr. Nekro how ridiculous he sounds."

Mr. Reiper, in turn, opened his mouth–

–and paused.

He sensed an opportunity. A small one, but few opportunities were large, and of late he'd experienced precious few of any size at all. If there was a chance someone other than Ms. Scuhl might succeed Mr. Corpus, then his tenure at this august table might continue beyond his current expectations.

Mr. Reiper looked at Ms. Scuhl ... then at his second helping of spinach-ganglion dip ... then at Mr. Nekro.

Ms. Scuhl's eyes were as cold and demanding as ever.

Mr. Nekro's were almost pleading.

Mr. Reiper made up his mind, and words began to issue from his open mouth. "Actually, one must spend money to make money. If we can resolve our recruitment and retention problems, then our financial problem will resolve itself!"

Mr. Nekro grinned hugely.

Ms. Scuhl gasped in disbelief. "How can you say that? Have you even been listening to Mr. Nekro's absurd rant? He doesn't have a plan – he has buzzwords and corporate double-talk! Where would we get the resources for such a ludicrous misadventure?"

"They could be diverted from under-performing programs in a general restructuring... Say, from the internship program."

Ms. Scuhl's eyes flashed. "I can't be the only sane zombie at this table. Mr. Dullaird, you don't buy this tripe, do you?"

Mr. Dullaird felt trapped, and his dead eyes flicked from Ms. Scuhl to Mr. Corpus, who had not given any indication which of his executives he would favor. Mr. Dullaird hadn't understood a single syllable of Mr. Nekro's presentation – but then, Mr. Dullaird found revolving doors challenging.

In the past, it had always been clear that the best choice was to side with Ms. Scuhl, because she always got what she wanted. But now there was open dissent, and Mr. Nekro seemed rather confident in his ideas, enough so that Mr. Reiper had sided with him instead of Ms. Scuhl. If energetic, ambitious Mr. Nekro became the next chairman, then disagreeing with him at this point would be the beginning of the end for a certain Mr. Dullaird... His sinewy tongue flicked across his dry lips.

"Before you answer, Mr. Dullaird, watch this..." Mr. Nekro advanced the PowerPoint presentation. "Here's a pilot advertisement, targeting the 18-to-34 demographic, that illustrates the kind of image makeover I have in mind."

On the monitor, a stylized yin-yang appeared, a neon-green D separating the curved black-and-white halves. Around the perimeter, in a stylish serif font the same color as the D, ran the words IN EXTREMIS, VITALIS.

"Our new logo," Mr. Nekro said proudly. "At DedCo, there's new life in death! Latin — a dead language, you'll note — makes everything sound more sophisticated." The logo began to fade, and the first few notes of an aggressive guitar riff started, then abruptly stopped as the monitor flickered and turned blue.

"Damn!" Mr. Nekro said, frantically hitting keys on the laptop.

"Maybe your computer has one of those virus thingies," Mr. Dullaird said.

Ms. Scuhl smirked.

Mr. Reiper gloomily opened the second bottle of wine.

Mr. Corpus said, "You know, I remember when I was talking to some Hollywood executives back when we were first considering using zombie actors in movies. Back then, nobody had computers but the big universities and corporations, because the damned things were each as big as a room. Nowadays, there's more computing power in most wristwatches than there ever was in one of those massive old computers. In fact, the watch I'm wearing right now has several highly complex functions that I know I'll never use. For example, it'll give me my exact location on Earth using satellites. Satellites! True, I don't know how to interpret the numbers it gives me, but still, I'm wearing satellite technology. Who'd have thought? My first watch I got for a nickel. It told time just fine, as long as I remembered to wind it. And I did! I wound it every morning, like clockwork, right after I dressed.

You know, if you make something part of your routine, you'll never forget it."

"Yes, sir, that's sage advice," Mr. Dullaird nodded, happy to be back in familiar territory. "I do the same thing before I go to bed, checking to make sure I haven't lost any body parts during the day."

"Z.W.A.," Mr. Corpus mused. "Zombies with attitude. Somebody said that earlier. Young Mr. Nekro, I believe. Yes, I rather like that. That logo was pretty, too. You seem to be having some computer trouble there, Mr. Nekro."

"Yes, sir," the young cadaver said. "It'll be just a–"

"Oh, never mind that," Mr. Corpus said with a dry chuckle. "I'm sure whatever you'd cooked up for your presentation was perfectly fine. Forget about all that techno-gobbledygook. Let's just talk."

Mr. Nekro nodded, sat down and pushed his laptop away from him. "I'd like that, sir."

Ms. Scuhl leaned toward Mr. Corpus. "Sir, I would like to point out that–"

"Oh, shush!" Mr. Corpus said.

All of the other executives gasped. No one had ever shushed Ms. Scuhl before.

"I remember, back when I was alive," Mr. Corpus said, gazing with his mind's eye into years past, "if a store-owner wanted me to buy an apple, he'd tell me the apple was sweet. Juicy. Delicious. If a car salesman wanted me to buy a sporty Camaro, he'd tell me it went fast, attracted chicks, and would make all the other guys jealous. If you want somebody to buy something, you have to spell out the *benefits!* Back when I was courting the fair sex on a regular basis – I used to be quite the ladies' man! – I would tell those fine darlings, 'Come with me and I'll buy you champagne and a lobster dinner! Stick around and I'll give you a diamond ring and a fur coat!' Oh, I wined and dined them, that's for sure. So maybe young Mr. Nekro is right. In fact, there's no 'maybe' about it. He <u>is</u> right, completely right! We need to wine and dine the living! We need to show them that being a zombie can be an incredible, fulfilling adventure! What an exciting new direction for us! In fact, all this excitement is giving me an appetite. Mr. Dullaird, fetch me a plate of those brains on the half-skull!"

"With pleasure, sir!" The deceased flunky hurried to the food cart.

Mr. Corpus turned to Ms. Scuhl and flashed a gap-toothed grin. "Ms. Scuhl, would you pour me a glass of blush?" It wasn't a question.

"I beg your pardon? I'll–" Ms. Scuhl was about to say more in a decidedly angry vein, but then she spotted a fire in Mr. Corpus' eyes she'd never seen before. Was the old coot actually feeling a bit ... frisky? She found this unprecedented development altogether intriguing. "I'll get you that blush right now, sir."

Mr. Corpus turned his attention back to Mr. Nekro. "Remember what I was saying about computers a few minutes ago? You and I are like that. You're like a compact, highly advanced wristwatch and I'm like one of those old computers as big as a whole room. You're the future, Mr. Nekro."

"Yeah, the future!" said Mr. Dullaird as he set a plate of brains on the half-skull before Mr. Corpus.

"Indeed," said Mr. Reiper, who also had been loading up a plate at the food cart – for Mr. Nekro. "The future."

Ms. Scuhl prided herself on her ability to handle any situation, any twist of fate that the zombie death-style might throw at her. She filled two glasses – one for Mr. Corpus and one for Mr. Nekro. "I must admit, Mr. Corpus' enlightening insight has put Mr. Nekro's vision in an entirely new context. Perhaps my earlier role as devil's advocate can safely be dropped." She gave the young executive a wink as she gave him his drink, and did the same for Mr. Corpus. "When dealing with the living, one must never underestimate the power of suggestion. Yes, this new concept certainly has possibilities. Why, by the time we're done with them, the living will be dying to join our ranks!"

"Atta girl!" Mr. Corpus cried.

"That's the spirit!" gushed Mr. Dullaird.

"I'll have Paolo bring us some more wine," Mr. Reiper said, gazing at the two empty bottles on the cart.

"Better yet, tell him to bring us a magnum of champagne! The best we have!" crowed Mr. Corpus.

The board members continued to chat and make plans for the new campaign. They decided that perhaps the slogan IN EXTREMIS, VITALIS was a bit too academic for the living, and that they should really just stick with the Z.W.A. concept. Zombies With Attitude: certainly that said it all.

Paolo entered the room with the champagne.

"Ah, the bubbly! Give the bottle to Mr. Nekro," said Mr. Corpus. "He's a strong boy, let's see if he can pop it open. I'm afraid I might lose a finger, wrestling with the cork."

"I'd be delighted," Mr. Nekro said. He seized the bottle with one

166

hand and began to twist at the cork with the other. "It's certainly stuck tight!"

"Put some muscle in it!" Mr. Corpus said.

"Yessss, here we go," Mr. Nekro said. "I think it's starting to give..."

And sure enough: give, it did.

With a mighty pop!, the cork shot out of the bottle, hitting Mr. Corpus right between the eyes.

The old man's bones were so exceedingly fragile, the projectile cracked his skull like an egg. A chunk of brow fell right off his head and his rotted brain slid out of his skull. The greenish-gray mass hit the floor and the whole body soon followed suit, tumbling out of the big chair at the head of the table.

Mr. Corpus was dead.

Once-and-for-all dead.

Really-most-sincerely dead.

Ms. Scuhl, Mr. Reiper, Mr. Dullaird, and Mr. Nekro all stared at Mr. Corpus' empty chair. For a full twelve seconds, nobody said a word.

Then chaos erupted.

"It's mine!" Ms. Scuhl screamed.

"Me! Me! Me!" blubbered Mr. Dullaird.

"In your dreams!" shouted Mr. Reiper.

"Out of my way!" cried Mr. Nekro, swinging the heavy champagne bottle like a war-club.

The bottle hit Mr. Dullaird at the base of the noggin and the old glutton's head fell right off. Mr. Reiper got the same treatment. His head popped free, bounced off Mr. Dullaird's thick skull and rolled into a far corner of the boardroom.

Mr. Nekro flipped the mighty bottle around, grabbed it by its base and thrust the neck right into Ms. Scuhl's right eye. The bubbling beverage rushed into her brainpan, sending chunks of gray matter gushing in a carbonated flow out of her nose and ears. Her left eye shot out of its socket, along with the rest of the champagne and her brain.

Mr. Nekro sank into Mr. Corpus' seat with a satisfied sigh. The chair's leather was soft, so very soft.

He then noticed Paolo, still standing by the door after delivering the champagne, looking at him with wide eyes.

"Ah, Paolo!" Mr. Nekro said. "Just the man I wanted to see. A bottle of pinot noir, please!"

# Arlene Schabowski Of The Undead
## (with Kyra M. Schon)

Really? Right now?

Okay.

Let me tell you about a nice lady, who lives not too far from here. She was in the movie. And still is, in a way.

Her name is Lorraine Tyler – and also Arlene Schabowski. Lorraine is in her early forties, though you couldn't tell by looking at her. She has long, wavy blonde hair. Arlene is nine years old, and she has long, wavy blonde hair, too. Most people would agree that she looks quite dead.

Lorraine played Arlene, all those years ago. Lorraine stopped, but Arlene kept right on playing.

After the zombies swarmed the building, Arlene devoured most of her parents – they were hers, so she certainly deserved the best parts – and then simply wandered off into the night. And the night was filled with shambling, ravenous corpses, feasting upon the flesh of the living. But the undead knew she was one of them, so she was safe from their hunger. Her body held no warmth, no nourishing spark of life to entice the other zombies. That was the last the viewers ever saw of her.

But she needed food, for she was – and still is – always hungry. Deliriously hungry. For there is a deep black coldness within her that constantly needs filling. Sometimes, right after she has eaten, she actually feels alive again. Perhaps even better than alive. She felt that way after she ate her parents, and she wanted to feel it again. So she wandered through the woods, through the darkness, until she came to another farmhouse.

Now at this point, One might ask, "They never showed what happened to the little girl after she wandered off. Didn't the police get her when they came and shot all the zombies' brains out?"

Obviously not.

One might also wonder, "'Fear-Farm of the Undead' was only a movie, wasn't it?"

Well, yes and no.

Lorraine Tyler's father was one of the producers and stars of the movie, which was made on a shoe-string budget. The money her family put into that movie back then wouldn't even buy a decent new car these days. Her father, mother and some of their friends wanted to make a movie, so they pooled their resources, found a few more investors and did it. And Lorraine got to play a little girl who gets bitten, turns into a zombie and eats her parents.

Lorraine went on to become a school teacher with a cool website selling "Fear-Farm" memorabilia. Teachers get time off during the summer, so she started going to conventions, meeting fans, doing a lot more to promote her memorabilia sideline. She did that for years. Made good money, too. Last year she made enough to buy a nice little vacation in Mexico.

People still watch that movie all the time. Still think about it. "Fear-Farm of the Undead" has spawned hundreds of knock-off versions, most of them released direct-to-video. And Lorraine has watched every one of them. Because she is also Arlene Schabowski, and wants to know what other zombies are doing.

Somewhere out there, it is always night, and a little dead girl who is also a living school teacher is always hungry.

Anyway. Back to that other farmhouse.

Arlene could hear cows mooing in the distance. The sound made her hungry. She crept up to the house and looked in the window, into a quaint, tidy living room, with knick-knacks on little cherrywood tables and furniture draped with lace doilies. An old woman was sitting at her desk, reading some papers. She had long white hair and wore a dark-gray housecoat. Of course, everything in that world is black and white or shades of gray, just like in the movie. The old woman must not have turned on the radio or the TV that day or night – she looked so peaceful, it was clear she had no idea what was going on.

The little dead girl went to the front door and knocked. The old woman called out, as cheery as can be, "Who is it?"

Now, none of the other zombies in that movie were able to talk. All they ever did was grunt and roar and squeal. But Arlene was able to think really hard and call upon the abilities of her other self, Lorraine. And she managed to rasp out the three-word phrase from the movie for which she is best known. She also says a four-word phrase early in the movie, but most folks don't remember that. No, they only remember what she says just before she turns into a zombie: "Help me, Mommy."

"Mommy? I'm nobody's Mommy!" the old woman cried. "Who's out there? Is this some kind of a joke?" So saying, she threw open the door. "My God! Little girl, are you hurt? There's blood all over you!"

Arlene held out her arms, just like she did before she killed her movie-Mommy, who was played by her real-life mother. Again, she said, "Help me, Mommy."

"Of course I'll help you, you poor thing." The old woman knelt before her. She must have had something wrong with her knees, because she winced with pain. "So tell me, who did this to you? Who–"

Her next few words were lost in a thick gurgle of black blood, because by then Arlene had her little teeth embedded in the old woman's throat. And even though the dear old thing was past her prime, she was still full of warm, delicious, intoxicating life.

Arlene ate her fill and by the time she was done, that sweet old woman looked like a car-wreck victim, sans safety belt. Arlene turned and strayed into the night. She didn't wait around to watch the old woman's gnawed carcass scramble back to hungry life.

Mind you, while all that was going on, poor, confused Lorraine was hiding in some bushes in the school playground, screaming and wondering why all these bad things were going on in her head. The other kids thought she had gone nuts. Her parents and the teachers talked about it later, and based on what she'd told them, they decided she had an over-active imagination. They told her not to let the bad images scare her – they were make-believe, so they couldn't hurt her. It was all in her head, they said, and in a way it was. Hers was a sort of Reality Surplus Disorder. It's hard to concentrate when you've got another personality playing in your mind.

My best guess is all the movie's fans created that personality, that black-and-white world of death – all those watchers in the dark, thinking about that movie, those zombies, and of course, poor little Arlene Schabowski. All that feverish brain energy. What is reality, anyway? A mental collective, that's all. The result of multiple minds, mulling over enthralling stories. I'm sure that somewhere, out there, Moby Dick is still swimming and the House of Usher is still falling. I'm sure Dorothy is still wandering down the Yellow Brick Road, having new adventures, fighting more witches and flying monkeys. And I'm sure she's still a tiny young thing, just as Arlene Schabowski is still a tiny dead thing.

But let us return to Arlene. She walked down a gravel lane until she came to the highway. Car lights were heading toward her. She held out her bloodstained, skinny arms and waited. The driver would stop. Of course they would. She was just a little girl.

So she waited. And the driver stopped – a fat, middle-aged man with a bulbous nose and horn-rimmed glasses.

"Was there an accident?" He ran up to her, crouched and thrust his fat face near hers.

"Help me, Mommy," she said.

"You poor thing," he said in a low, sad voice. "What the Hell happened to you?"

Another one who thought she was simply a poor thing. She smiled, leaned forward and bit off his nose – it was too large and juicy a target to resist.

He screamed, so she bit off his lower lip, which made him scream that much louder.

She gnawed and gnawed until he was too cold for her to stomach. Then she began shambling down the road. And because that entire movie took place at night, the daylight never came. She wandered an eternal night of fields and rural backroads and farmhouses, feasting on innocent country folks who only wanted to help her.

And Lorraine ... She endured Arlene's adventures in her head, and finally even got used to them. A person can get used to anything, really. Folks who live near airports soon learn to ignore the roar of planes coming and going. Lorraine grew into a tall, willowy lady. Always slender. Having a zombie in your head is enough to spoil anyone's appetite. There were plenty of times when she would sit down to dinner, and Arlene would suddenly go on a rampage in her mind. Little zombie-girl would rip apart a couple farmers, tear out their guts and gobble them down, and suddenly that plate of lasagna would seem like a hideous, visceral thing. But Lorraine wouldn't scream over it – wouldn't even bat an eyelash. She'd just push the plate away.

As I mentioned, Lorraine eventually became a school teacher. Because a part of her was still a little girl, she liked being around children. She lived in a big nice apartment building, surrounded by families – all the kids her thought she was great. Some of the people in her building had seen her movie, and they were always telling their friends that their neighbor was a movie star. Sometimes folks who had seen the movie would call her Arlene. She'd smiled to be polite, but she didn't like it. "Hey, Arlene – 'Help me, Mommy!'" was the favorite greeting of the fat guy who lived six doors down. She'd always try to take a different route to avoid him if she saw him coming.

Eventually she started dating the school's janitor, and all of her friends made fun of her for that, joking that the lovers were probably always sneaking off to the boiler room or some such place. The janitor, whose name was Kurt, was a good-looking man, only in his

171

mid-thirties and in fine physical shape. And truth to tell, the two did sneak off together sometimes. To Kurt's office. His door had a fancy title – environmental control specialist – but it still meant janitor.

Once while she was in his office, Lorraine saw a key hanging from a little nail on the wall behind his desk. The key had a scrap of paper taped to it. The word ATTIC was written on that scrap in blue ballpoint ink. She waited until Kurt's back was turned, and she took that key.

Even while she was reaching for it, she wasn't sure why she was taking it. She just knew she had to have it. After school, she stayed behind, waited until everyone was gone and then went up to the attic. It was all storage up there, and the things that had been packed away up there so long ago were now all but forgotten.

Remember where little Arlene ate her parents? In the attic. That's where the movie-family went to hide from the zombies. The movie-attic had a bed in it, where Arlene used to sleep. She says her four-word line while she's in that bed. The school attic had a broken cot among its various odds and ends. Obsolete schoolbooks, tennis shoes, sacks of that pinkish, pulpy stuff to sprinkle on barf to soak it up and make the smell go away. Lorraine strolled among rows of dusty boxes and stayed up there for about an hour, looking at spiderwebs and old papers and outdated globes. She realized then that this was the first time she'd been in an attic – any attic at all – since the filming of that movie. Her parents had always lived in apartments. Her dorm room in college had been on the ground floor. A life without attics. She now felt oddly at home – but was it a good home?

When she came down from the attic, left the building and went to her car, the world around her seemed different somehow.

A little less – colorful.

A moment later, Arlene Schabowski saw red in her night-world for the first time. Usually the blood of her victims was shiny black. But she looked down at the hitchhiker she had just torn to bits and saw red, red everywhere. Then she saw that her dress was stained not merely with various splotches of gray, but horrible gouts of rotted filth and gore – red, yellow, brown, green, a veritable rainbow of decay. It made her smile.

A few days later, Kurt was completely confused by Lorraine's birthday gift to him. "Rainy," he said, for that is what he called her, "this tie – don't get me wrong, I think it's great. And silk, it must have cost plenty. But purple? I don't know if I'm the purple type..."

"Oh," she said quite softly. "Is it purple? I thought it was some

172

kind of dark silver. Are you sure it's purple?"

Lorraine sometimes would bring a book to school to read in the attic, after hours. In the days to come, her students became more and more confused by some of the things she said – especially during art class. Whenever one of them did a drawing, she would ask things like, "What color is that horse?" Or, "That's a very pretty mermaid – which crayon did you use for the hair?"

Arlene began to notice green leaves among the gray, when car headlights hit them just right, and some of the towns she meandered through were bigger than the little country burgs she usually came across. One even had a supermarket. She would hide in the bushes bordering the parking lot and watch the front of the supermarket. Watch all the people rushing in and out. It made her hungry. Sometimes one of the shoppers would hear something rustling in the bushes and go see what it was, worrying that it might be a lost child. They were right to worry.

Lorraine found that the drive back to her house seemed a little shorter every week. And there were fewer cars on the road. Not as many buildings behind the sidewalks. Less kids in the school, but more birds in the light-blue sky. There was still a bit of color in her world, but not much. The changes were all huge yet gradual. Kurt usually wore a nice polo shirt and some jeans to work. It didn't even surprise her when he started wearing coveralls, or when his voice started to take on a rural twang. He even took to calling her 'Honey.'

Arlene just kept on wandering – she was so good at it. Wandering and eating, eating and wandering, always keeping to the shadows, which was getting harder, since there were so many streetlights around. But she was finding more homeless people, so at least she had been eating more regularly. No more fields – she was in the suburbs now, and the skies were starting to lighten. Night was slowly giving way to a light-blue morning.

You see what was happening, don't you? They were starting to meet in the middle. Why do you suppose that was happening? Maybe it was because Lorraine was spending so much time up in that attic. I suspect attics have strange powers. They come to points at the top, like pyramids. They're rather intriguing, aren't they? And bear in mind, zombie movies were becoming more modern – perhaps the imaginations that had pulled Arlene into existence were pulling her into the present day.

Lorraine was getting pulled, too, but in a different way. Into something – but what? One morning she thought she saw a tractor drive past the school. Later that day, she knew she heard cows mooing in the distance. She broke off her relationship with Kurt. He was becoming more and more rural, like some of the extras in 'Fear-Farm of the Undead.' He was growing too much hair and losing too many teeth. That wasn't the kind of boyfriend she wanted and this certainly wasn't the life she wanted to lead. She didn't like it. No, not one little bit.

Especially when she found herself chewing on what was left of the Algebra teacher, late at night up in the school attic. She couldn't even remember what she had done to get him up there. Not that it mattered. There were shreds of flesh under her nails, and her belly was swollen with food.

She wasn't sure if what she had done would turn the skinny old teacher into a zombie, but better safe than sorry. She went down to Kurt's supply closet, grabbed a hammer, and used it to cave in the old man's gnawed head.

And then she waited.

Pretty soon she heard the tappity-tap, tappity-tap, tappity-tap of little-girl heels coming up the stairs to the attic. And then –

That's when you walked in, Arlene.

You walked in and said the four-word phrase that you said in the first half of that movie, in the scene when your mother was putting you to bed: "Tell me a story." Most people don't remember that you said that. But you did, in that sweet, soft, cheery voice. Though that's not what your voice sounds like now. You sound like a record that's slowly melting as it plays.

So. Did you like my story, Arlene? It was all about you – and me, too. But I said "Lorraine" instead of "I" because... Well, I don't really feel like me any more. But I'm not you.

I don't know who I am, where I am or even what I am.

Hmmm...?

No, I'm not your Mommy, and I'm afraid I can't help you.

But who knows. Maybe pounding your head open with this hammer will help me.

# ABOUT THE AUTHOR

**Mark McLaughlin**'s fiction, nonfiction and poetry have appeared in hundreds of magazines, newspapers, websites, and anthologies, including *Galaxy, Writer's Digest, Horror Garage, Black Gate, Cemetery Dance, Midnight Premiere, Dark Arts, In Laymon's Terms,* and two volumes each of *The Best Of The Rest, The Best Of HorrorFind,* and *The Year's Best Horror Stories* (DAW Books).

Collections of McLaughlin's fiction include *Motivational Shrieker, Slime After Slime,* and *Pickman's Motel* from Delirium Books; *At The Foothills Of Frenzy* (with co-authors Shane Ryan Staley and Brian Knight) from Solitude Publications; and *Twisted Tales For Sick Puppies* from Skullvines Press.

*HorrorGarage.com* features his online column, *Four-Letter Word Beginning With 'F'* (the word in question is Fear). *GravesideTales.com* is the home of his blog, *Time Machine Of Terror!*

Also, he is the co-author, with Rain Graves and David Niall Wilson, of *The Gossamer Eye,* which won a Bram Stoker Award for Superior Achievement in Poetry. His poetry collection, *Phantasmapedia,* was on the final ballot for the 2007 Stoker Award for Poetry.

With regular collaborator Michael McCarty, he has written *Monster Behind The Wheel* (Delirium Books/Corrosion Press), *Attack Of The Two-Headed Poetry Monster* (Skullvines Press), and *All Things Dark And Hideous* (Rainfall Books, England).

McLaughlin is also a successful public relations executive who regularly writes articles for business journals, newspapers, trade publications and websites. He is also an active member of the Horror Writers' Association and writes a marketing column for the association's members.

To find out more about his work, visit **www.myspace.com/monsterbook** and **www.myspace.com/phantasmapedia.**